He Will Stay

Till You Come

The Rise and Fall of Skinny Walker

BURR McCLOSKEY

Moore Publishing Company

Library of Congress Catalog Card Number: 78-59114

ISBN 0-87716-090-2

. . .also by BURR McCLOSKEY

In Futuro

A TRILOGY OF SELF-DISCOVERIES

Volume I
Aspects of the Day
a book of poetic celebrations

Volume II
The Counting House
a collection of loving ways

Volume III
Moments of Home
a poetic album

MOORE PUBLISHING COMPANY

Acknowledgments

With deep gratitude I acknowledge the special contributions made by the following persons which allowed me to see this book to publication—Hugh Brand, Joseph Butler, Ed Ferentz, Dr. Eugene V. Grace, Luis Kutner, Steve and Rose Marlin, Jason and Lyn Phillips, Dick and Kitty Young. *In everything give thanks...*

PREFACE

This is the story of a man and a city, of the women
of this man and of the times of this city.

There is no such city as Akron, Ohio, anywhere
in the world. You will not find it on any map.
A man would have to be a fool to invent anything
like it. But if somewhere, sometime, a man
with workworn hands should read this book and
find familiar things in it, to him this book is
dedicated.

I cannot say with certainty if there is or ever
was a man named "Skinny Walker." If there is,
he will not read this book, nor will he refer it
to his lawyers. If there is not; that is, if
"Skinny Walker" is wholly imaginary, then why am
I so full of knowledge of him?

If there is no "Skinny Walker," of course, it
follows that all these other persons are imaginary
too, which is just as well.

B. Mc.

(From *Hamlet* Act IV, Sc. III)

KING: Where is Polonius?
HAMLET: In Heaven; send thither to see;
        if your messenger find him not
        there, seek him i' the other
        place yourself. But, indeed, if
        you find him not within this
        month, you shall nose him as
        you go up the stairs into the
        lobby.
KING: (to some Attendants) Go seek
        him there.
HAMLET: He will stay till you come.

1

Time Magazine, during the week of June 17, 1957, was saying:

> "Never did an ill wind blow so little good as did the expensive tempest of the Senate Labor investigation—until last week when random senatorial puffs uncovered the General President of the Joint Labor Congress.

> "Hard-minded, sledge-fisted Erskine ("Skinny") Walker, 42, felt the breeze in the form of seven Justice Department indictments (4 on perjury, 3 on a conspiracy rap).

> "Top bullyboy of U. S. labor, Walker of the sharp tongue and the built-in sneer found himself dramatically deserted by the bravoes of his JLC General Board, six of whom had turned state's witness. Their erstwhile leader began to resemble an orphan in the storm.

"After hanging on the Senate Committee's hook for six months like an old boot drug up from the mill pond, one-time tirebuilder, West-Virginia-born Walker began to wriggle. He now faces a grand total of no fewer than sixty years in prison. Kansas liberal, John Hobhouse gloated from the Senate floor, 'It looks like we've got him this time.' It does, indeed.

"Slab-faced Walker (an unskinny 200-pounder) is quondam leader of one million dissident wage hands, core of which is his rambunctious home union, the American Rubberworkers Council (with a scant 190,000 membership). President Walker's fall from grace has been grimly precipitous.

"How precipitous was made plain by his behavior in his Akron (O.) headquarters when the indictment storm broke over his head.

"Walkerian commentary is coarsely trenchant, as a rule. This time the slow-speaking, slit-eyed boss was caught with his prance down. 'I got no Goddamned comment,' said he.

"One thing was sure. Skinny Walker may have stopped frightening America with his rude, IWW-like bellicosities, but America was beginning to frighten Skinny Walker. Observers wondered: if the hard kid from Devil's Own (W. Va.) was inarticulate now when the blade is being sharpened, how would he act when the axe finally fell?"

It was to be regretted that *Time's* fruity photographer with a British accent could not have been with Skinny Walker when the axe did fall. As it happened, he was all alone. He had just left Thymer's office in "Mahogany Row" of the

Goodstone Company Tower. He had closed the door with a smile on his face, which meant he had been humiliated. In fifteen years he had been rarely photographed with a smile, because in fifteen years of being photographed he had been rarely humiliated.

Back in the hills of West Virginia, barefooted and in patched britches, he had smiled at the moon whenever he chanced to stub his toe or he cramped with a lover's knot. Or at any time in any way to have suffered a mischance or a failure. It was a wry sort of grin directed at the moon. It was his wink at fate. Here in the after-hours quiet of the office building he tossed it at the ceiling as he rang for the elevator.

Thymer had acted quite the little man.

"Walker," he had said. "On advice of counsel I'm not responding to any deals. I'm not swapping horses with a horse thief. In fact, sir, I'm not even going to pass the time of day with you. I have it on good authority that you are washed up. So do me the favor, please, of quitting my office?"

Nobody, nobody ever, talked like that to Skinny Walker. Especially not Clyde Thymer, Goodstone's Personnel Director. But tonight he did. And Skinny Walker felt his slab face twist into a crooked smirk of fatalism. Thymer was sixty. He was wide in the hips. He had little pale hands. He also had the power and the glory of the Hobhouse Committee behind him. . .

Skinny almost laughed out loud when he recalled the haste in which Thymer had delivered his last sentence. His ". . .quitting my office?" had ended on an uphill squeak. The gutless little bastard, Skinny thought. I'll quit his office—I'll burn it down!

A light flashed and the elevator door rolled smoothly open. A little red-haired girl operator was at the controls, smiling at him.

"You already, Mr. Walker?"

She was wearing a union button far out on the crest of one breast and she was leaning forward on her operator's

3

stool to arch her back and show how finely she was fashioned. It was pretty fine. "Maintenance classification, 1.90 per hour straight day work," Skinny thought. He patted her little rump just for luck.

"*Mis*-ter *Walk*-er!" she giggled. "Don't you do that—now, of *all* times!"

The Goodstone girls all knew he was single. More than that, they knew he was reputed to be vigorous and usually ready.

"Why not now, Red?" he asked her. "Wrong day?"

"Oh not *that*!" She blushed at the thought of ever menstruating. "It's just that here I am on this graveyard shift, and you, and here—*Mister Walker*!"

He had tested the position of her union button. He had personally designed its artwork (two clenched hands encircled by a rubber tire). Who had a better right to examine the geography of its resting place? She moved to reach the controls and brought the car to a sudden stop between the seventh and eighth floors. Through custom (or sheer instinct) she managed to flick off the switch for the overhead light.

Skinny found her (even in the dark) to be young and smooth-skinned. She had that iron-magnetic readiness of true redheads from the hill country. He lost his smile in the lubricated hospitality of her open mouth. Now his face set itself in the combative earnest expression he wore when addressing a woman in the act of love. He was embracing her against the back of the car when their activity knocked down a framed sign and they heard the tinkle of its broken glass. Both knew, without seeing it, that it was one of thousands posted by the Goodstone management in all its outposts, temples and latrines. It read simply: *Protect our Good Name...*

"I'll do my best," Skinny vowed. Then he remembered his visit to Doc Milliron the day before. He shouldn't have remembered. It made him smile again. The girl felt his smile and she took it to mean that she was pleasing him. She

4

prepared to couple—but he was not prepared.

Doc had shown him test tubes and pictures and had talked, pleasantly enough, about many unpleasant possibilities. The worst of these was that his days as tender to a woman's fires were numbered, if not over. An old infection from a Case Avenue tramp was taking its toll. . .

"As a rooster, Skinny," Doc had warned him, "your barnyard days are all washed up."

Red wriggled in an anguish of disappointment. She wanted him to be ready. He might not ever be ready. Skinny thought: *at a buck-ninety an hour she could have worse work than making me ready.*

The girl was good. He felt her flesh like flame beneath his big skilled hands. This stuff was rich and lush and fierce. This was good the way a hill country woman gets good, part twister and part open fireplace waiting for a new log. Clyde Thymer, for all his mahogany office, would never know how good it was. Skinny knew. His mind knew and his lips knew and his hands knew. He also knew that Doc's verdict was right.

"—*the hell?*" the girl exclaimed in disgust, backing away from him. He heard her pull the cloth of her skirt down; the switch being turned on. He stood stupidly in the light and studied her look of scorn as she moved the lever and the car rose to the eighth floor.

"They said you was a wash-out," she spat at him. "Boy, and *what* a wash-out! Boy, could I tell 'em!"

She opened the door and stepped out of the elevator.

"Thanks for nothing at all!" she said, and strode off to the women's washroom. Not until then did Skinny realize that he was in Goodstone's elevator, with his trousers gaping wide, his shame apparent, and that he was smiling. He knew he should not be discovered in this condition.

With a push of a button he closed the door. With the twist of the throttle he sent the car upward. There were only ten floors.

Somehow the thing passed the tenth and nudged itself tight against the top bumpers. Skinny arranged his clothing and smoked a cigarette before he thought of getting back down. When he set about it, the controls became mysterious and stubborn and unresponsive. They wouldn't do what he wanted. He pushed every button and jerked the throttle back and forth. With no result. It was stuck and he was stuck. Damned if he could make the machinery obey his commands. . .

There was an overhead door for emergency escape. He stretched high to push it open. Then pulled himself up through it. The car's light showed him a maze of cable, wire and unfinished lumber scaffolding. Oily gears, each three feet in diameter, faced him on either side. Skinny Walker crouched on top the elevator car and surveyed his position. When his eyes adjusted to the half-light, he spied a trapdoor and a makeshift ladder to it, beyond one of the gears.

Let *Time* Magazine and Clyde Thymer and Josie Kenshaw (the red-haired girl) figure out what happened then. The trapped man stepped over a gear and felt for the door's opening. It's just a pity it wasn't photographed.

Senator Hobhouse and the Company would possibly have enjoyed the look on Skinny's face when (for some strange reason) the car shifted on its cables and sank below his one foot while the other braced itself upon the gear. He didn't make a noise. He didn't weep and he didn't curse as the cables became engaged and his one leg was almost severed. He wrapped his arms around a two-by-four and held on with great strength. He could hear the fabric of his trousers rip. He heard the blood hiss forth from mangled arteries. He held very firmly with his arms while the unmanned machinery pulled his leg the other way and he smiled in the semi-darkness.

This is how he acted when the axe finally fell.

6

Now, look at the world...

It is the world before turnpikes, the long-ago world of the Depression movies, violet in tone and absurdly precious. This world is not forgotten, not-quite remembered, because it brought us here (without knowing where the here and now may be) and it is always with us, refusing to go away...a stray but affectionate cur of a world, held now in our hands for a down-the-nose examination.

It is the world in 1938 with April fragile in the morning air and there is no dust showing on the unnumbered black-topped county roadway where walks a young man whom you, other than on these pages, will never know. Only he walks this way. There is no other traffic. It is thirty-eight miles to Wheeling, West Virginia, and a millennium to anywhere.

He walks northward and he walks well. He is twenty-some miles en route from the cabin where he was born. His mother's grave he carries with him. Already, this is foreign country, because these are the flatlands, and the people are strangers. He is a hillboy and the level goes easier beneath his feet, although there are no cars and he had hoped, temperately, there would be.

This is backcountry, nonetheless, with now-and-then farmhouses, corn cribs, unpainted barns, privies and the aromatic vibrations of poor land and rich decay. (The flatness of land would seem humped and rolling to a city person.) The trees along the roadway are furred with Spring foliage. The cows by the lonely fences are all bone in the hip and the birds are furtive, for no good reason.

There is an unidentified snake, asleep in the torn asphalt. Our young man ignores it. The snake feels, turgidly, that it is being ignored.

He has ground to cover more than snakes to tease, which is a new manner for him but not unlikely. He is wide in the chest and April is burning him like a violet light. He is walking well in farm shoes that are half-unsoled, and his legs are strong. He wears blue jeans, a grey shirt and carries a sweater. In his pocket, wrapped in a bandanna kerchief, he has exactly four dollars. He will never, he thinks, return to this country nor look upon this land again.

The hills are behind him and the river ahead. He is older than he is. His age is tempered by growing up among men, and without cities. Women soften a boy and cities hold the blood back. His eyes, slitted above high, tawny cheekbones, are blue with April, with the crystalline memory of wood smoke in the clearing and with the luminescence of the abandoned hills, which are behind him.

Sometimes he chews a leaf and stalk to quiet his thirst, and when he breaks water, jealously, on a stump by the road, there is the sound of his splash in the middle of this backcountry quiet, and his thirst returns. He walks because he is thirsty, because he is hungry, because he is lonely. And he walks for none of these, except that he is drawn by the innate knowledge that when he is done with walking, he will not thirst nor hunger nor again be alone.

8

The road lopes ahead of him, twisting and turning to follow its grade. If he does not tarry along the way, he reckons to be in Wheeling by nightfall.

This is the world of then, in that time, beneath his feet, which turn it, not perceptibly, and which alter its course without notice.

He stops. There is a one-pump gasoline station with a frame shed. All-but-obliterated signs advertising Red Man chewing tobacco and Knee High soft drinks offer muted patches of color. There is a heavy sense of quiet here. An old woman is sitting by the door. She is very old in her shawl and with her cruel-white look at the traveler.

"Mother," he says, "I could sure stand me some drinkin' water."

She stares at him with frightening nobility.

"How'd yew know I was your mother?" she cackles.

He stands with a hand on his jeaned hip, the sweater curled in insolence over his arm.

"Just knew, that's all."

Her laughter is old and quiet, yellowed by her breath.

"Then yew know whar the pump be!"

He already knew where the pump be. Taking her ribaldry for consent, he goes to the side of the shed to draw water in his cupped hands. It is very cold, iron-tainted and gravel-stained. It is wet in his throat and on his young flesh.

"I'm much obliged," he speaks, standing before her with his chin wet and the smile dripping.

"It's only water. But it's West Virginny water. You'll not be gettin' any whar yew be going."

"How'd yew know whar I be goin'?"

"Jest knew, that's all!" Her laugh comes again, screeching like the pump handle, echoed by the old mossed well, and unsorry. "I seen you walkin' a long piece off, and you've just begun. You're like to walk your britches off afore you're done."

To the boy, the encounter is clean and meaningless. An

ancient woman and a drink of water and no echo coming from the well. He talks to her without greeting. She is part of the wilderness, that's all, and unrelated.

"I'm goin' a far piece. That's for sure."

She waits with an indecent grin for his confession. She is old and she has learned to wait on men when there is no further reason for waiting. She smells like smoke from smouldering old newspapers.

"I just might be goin' up to A-kron in Ohio," he continues.

"Yew just might be comin' back agin," she retorts, with a snicker squeaking through her disjointed lips. "Ever think of that?"

They are quiet, the young man and the crone, along the grey, forsaken road. His legs want to walk, and her withered shanks to tease, and April marries them for the moment.

"Trot along, sonny. Tell them your granny sent yew. Tell them yew can always come back."

"I'll tell them that for sure."

He takes his first step away, but he falters, uncharacteristically. The thing is unfinished. Something more, a curse or a bleat is due him, and he holds his step, waiting uncertainly. He is an open hand and she is a fist, and they must strike, bone to flesh or he is forever rooted here.

Then the woman asks him accusingly, "D'yew believe in prophesy? Are you of a mind to see your future?"

Time is white and the hour is burning with an incandescent quiet along a backwoods road. It is a stage setting of low-keyed naivete, with a young man, an old woman, a gasoline pump, a soft drink sign, and the mood of April out of context, the magic of witchery and the strange glow of personal histories burning at the stake of inevitability.

On both figures, the young and the old, the clothes are dark and the faces are pale. The crone's face is like ragged lace, etched with discarded smiles, an unused library of frown and approval, the paths of expressiveness where no one now

10

treads. The face of the boy has the cruelty of bland granite. It is the mask of young tissue and arrogance. The eyes are flags of selfhood, combining meanness and a mock patrician cast. The mouth is ready to bite, to sneer and snarl and bleed when called upon.

There is a hatred between the two, and the cartooned incredibility of the roadside setting has been created by this hatred. He wants only to ignore her. He wants to deny her any existence in the arena of his self. He would kill her by leaving her hatred unattended. And she? She would condemn him with the end of the road. She wants to join him and his own shadow. She would lie with him coldly in the grave of the day.

He hangs on the moment. He is held by the leash of their mutual hostility. It is her moment and she sits on it like a hatching hen. They smell foul to each other. He to her because he is wet with the moisture of panic-to-come. She to him because she is cleanly dry and sweats no more.

"I'll tell y' fortune, boy," she whispers seductively. "You can carry it along with m' water you've drunk."

"Don't need no fortune, Mother. Thank y' kindly." He whispers back.

"Thank y' no thanks. Air y' afeared o' your fortune?"

"I fear me no fears. I'll carry it as long as I carry your water."

Giggling, she reaches for his hand, holds it unlooking.

"You're walking high in the dust like you'll never come back. But you'll be back this road."

"I'll never be back."

"You'll be back and be glad. You'll be back and you'll stay. You have nothing in your pack now you're going. You'll leave some of it behind."

"That's a bad fortune, Mother. You're not giving me any fortune to come home with."

"It's your fortune, boy, not mine. You'll meet up with a million men but not one will be coming back with you.

11

You'll lay with women, but none to wife. You'll have your hand on gold, but your hand will be bare."

"But I'm leaving some behind?"

"Part of you will stay behind. And you'll be closer to the dust on your return."

He smiles, and winks at the old woman.

"If that's my fortune, Mother, then I'll go."

"It's hardly worth going after."

"What kind of fortune teller are you? It's not for me to say. It's *my* fortune, whatever it is. Thanks again, most kindly."

She watches him turn from her and she screeches at his arrogant back,

"You'll give a lot more than you git!"

But he walks undeterred, above the dust, into the April incandescence.

12

3

CHAPTER THREE

When Erskine Walker first walked into East Akron he had just left behind him: the downtown bus station; Devil's Own, West Virginia; being twenty-two years old; and a soft feeling of complacency. None of which was ever to be his again. . .

Akron was a tough little city built on hills. On one of these hills he found a factory that made the coal mines and feed mills of Devil's Own seem tiny and provincial (which they were). The heart of this discovered city (for young Walker) was Case Avenue at Market Street. It was the solar plexus of an urban body whose every organ he was soon to know.

Market Street, in Akron, all for its own reasons, runs along an East-West axis from the factory district to the svelte suburb of Fairlawn. If it were an elevator and had a sweet, toothy operator in a wrinkled uniform to call out the stops, her announcements might sound something like this:

"From the slums along the canal," she might chant, "where hard-working women keep their men—to elegant apartments where befurred women are kept by men who do no work at all." At Case Avenue, she might say, "Bargain basement—picked-over trifles. Shopworn merchandise and factory throwouts. Great savings for those with strong stomachs!" Scooting her car Westward and upward, "Next stop for the quality trade. Fancy ladies and rich old men! All luxury items here, with the blood wiped off and the stink of soapstone covered by Chanel Number Five!"

Market Street is like this. Or it was in 1938 when a rangy twenty-three-year-old ridgerunner first saw the Goodstone plant and felt an uncontainable shock of fear at the sight of it.

Above him, on its cupola-topped tower, the Goodstone factory clock chimed three o'clock. He watched the smoke loosen its grip on the factory and rise like a growth above the stacks. He felt himself shudder under the impact of the dark red shadow of the Goodstone plants as they spread around the valley of East Akron and were enthroned on the hill above him.

Just below the plant, a broader avenue called Exchange Street begins a wending journey westward, roughly paralleling Market Street. It bellies over in a rambling sweep until it crosses Main Street (a mile south of Market). This is Downtown for Akron. It is lined with shops and stores in cluttered adjacency. It is sprigged with neon and masked with colored glass. Akron's Downtown can never lose the one-storied primitive look or the bandit's look of a frontier settlement. The stubby spire of the National Bank enhances the bleakness of the skyline.

There had long been a torsion to decide which intersection was going to be the heart of town—Main and Market, or Main and Exchange? Main Street's crossing of Market to the North is discouraged by its sudden transition into a long viaduct over the Hole. The Hole is a gutted valley and its other side is North Hill. On the opposite end, from Exchange Street to the South, Main Street is forced to tunnel through another

14

factory site. To old Akron's indecision, the center of gravity wavered back and forth, without resolution. And then gave up. There was simply nowhere for Main Street to go. *And that is Akron's story...*

Skinny had walked all the way from Downtown out to Goodstone. He had walked fast. It took him thirty minutes to reach Case Avenue from Downtown. It was going to take him three years before he found out what lay in the other direction...

From Main Street West, Market Street plunged up a hill, out of the Downtown sector. It passed Saint Vincent's church, gradually climbing, chained to some ignorant destiny only streets can know. It followed old trails which were deeply trod. Three miles more and can you guess what happens? Exchange Street returns, surrendering to Market's magnetic pull. Surveying the point of their union was the Harley Goodstone manor. And a manor it was—in the grand style. From behind rows of tended hedges, its polished eyes bade Market Street to carry on westward, serving the Buicks and Packards and Cadillacs of Harley's favored clansmen.

Which it did—forgetting the grime, the clatter, the spilled blood and cheap liquor back yonder at Case Avenue so far away.

Forgetting Skinny Walker who was looking at Goodstone's tower and feeling the stomach-shake of fear. Girding himself to walk right in and tell the boss-man that he was here and ready.

In those days Akron was a one-industry town with a shifting population. Depending on the lay-offs, it counted roughly a quarter-million souls. Market and Exchange Streets started together like the marks of a parenthesis (). Main Street crossed them in the middle like the bar on an H. The streets never dared to break their patterns. But Skinny Walker recognized no patterns and he dared to break them. He couldn't bear frustration. The fine homes in Fairlawn knew of his existence a long time before he knew of theirs.

He stared at the walls of Goodstone as a simple country boy would stare at moats and turrets and battlements. In Devil's Own there had been hills and wilderness and company houses and deep mine shafts. But here above Case Avenue was the biggest thing Skinny had ever seen in his life. It had been fashioned not by God but made by men.

If Man, dressed in handmade denim and buckskin could have peeked around Time's corner from an English plain to see industrialism puffing and throbbing and entrenched in blood-red factory walls, he would have seen it somewhat through the eyes of Skinny Walker. It was an enemy. It was a trap. It was a challenge. It was not a Thing, nor a piece of property. It was a mammoth, powerful Presence. It was a dragon squatting there with a gigantic punch press for a tail and a furnace for its guts. Iron spike fences for its fangs, hissing whistles for its eerie cry.

To many city folk, the miner and his pits are a fascinating subject. To outsiders, the lowering of a man into the depths of earth with a little lamp and a pick, with the danger of cave-in and falling shale—this seems the big thing in labor.

The country folk of West Virginia have seen coal mines and so had Skinny Walker. (His daddy was an inspector.) Mines are part of the earth. Mining is a job but not a strange one. It is not unlike the peasant's chore of walking into strange black forests and poaching twigs for the fireplace in his hut.

But the architecture of a factory—floor to floor, six-high, and mile after mile, all walled and guarded—this is something else. Mines are part of nature. Factories like this are unnatural to the stump-jumping people of Skinny Walker's tribe. Every brick is full of threat. What can possibly be going on inside those walls? Terrible machines? Furious fires and gargantuan hammers? Steam and noise, trip hammers, treadmills and thunder?

Skinny walked around all four of Goodstone's plants. He wasn't done until midnight. He watched the shift change. Men and women streaming from every gate. A torrent of buses, cars and trolleys. Clang of machinery, dong of bell, hoot of whistle and screech of things indescribable.

"I'm going in that mill," Skinny resolved. "I'm going in first thing t'morrow and I'm going to find out what makes her tick. . ."

This was the only way he could quiet the shudder of his blood. He made his vow to himself in a bar filled with men who had just come from their machines at midnight. They were men like any other men. He sat and watched them, while drinking rye whiskey and hearing the rich accents of Georgia, the Carolinas, Alabama and old West Vay all around him.

He sat at the bar with his wide shoulders sloped deceptively. His light brown hair fell over his brow. He looked not twenty-three, not new to town, and certainly not "skinny." (Mountaineers save proper given names for strangers. Among themselves they find a soubriquet. *Erskine* becomes Skinny, and it was always this way in Akron, anyhow.)

His head had a Roman Senator's cast to it, a lean high-cheeked distinction with the forehead monumental above eyebrows darker than the hair. There was just a touch of "poor white" to the way Erskine Walker looked, and in later years not even expensive hotel barbers could cover it up.

Here in a Greek bar across from the Willard Street gatehouse he looked very much at home. Between the dark brows and the slanted cheek bones, his squinted eyes seemed aggressive even in meditation. The quiet, Southern-type gentility of his features had a ferocious look, all the same. This distracted you from knowing that you never (or rarely) looked directly into his eyes. Although he was always looking into yours. When he opened his eyes widely it was a very special occasion. This happened in love, in debate and in any sharp physical encounter. It was always surprising to discover that his eyes were very blue. His nose was a long, lean nose and when he came to Akron in 1938 (just turned twenty-three) he

17

wore his sideburns long.

Around him the men talked in terms of baseball, which he understood but had no real interest in. They talked about women, for whom he had great interest but little understanding. They talked in terms of "rates" and "pieces" and "rawhide" and "making out"—an industrial language he wanted badly to know. He heard mention of the "Banbury" in the millroom and of "curing" in a place called "The Pit." He listened carefully to new words like "beads" and "treads" and "plies." He wanted to know which job was which. Which job was the job that counted, and how to ask for it in the morning?

After six shots of rye he knew with confidence that truckers and bandbuilders and pit men were all right—but the job that counted was building tires. He watched the men with great deformed hands, with welts of callous across the heel of their palms. They were the builders. Skinny Walker would be a builder too. He began thinking of himself as a tirebuilder. He looked down at his hands nursing the shot glass. They were young lean hands, well-shaped. The skin of them was pliable and leathery from work in feed mills and in the field.

"They can have my hands," he thought. "But I'm going inside that shop and it belongs to me."

Skinny Walker had spent his first afternoon and evening walking around the great Goodstone factory. He had it surrounded. After sitting for two hours he had observed the men of the factory and heard the sounds of their language. His strategy was set.

He didn't know it and nobody knew it at the time, but his young lean West Virginian hands were reaching for the throat of the entire industrial system.

18

Betty Marshall, sometime during the hot summer of 1956, was sitting in a cool, dark cocktail lounge, talking warmly to a middle-aged girlfriend, thusly:

"It was a rotten thing completely. I was young, y'see? Married to Bennett for just an eternity, of course, but well—like they say, 'untouched.' Where would I meet a man like Skinny Walker? How should I know? Who was going to tell me? Think about that for a moment, will you? I hadn't even seen 'Gone With the Wind'. . .

"He made me feel. . .*nervous*. Yes, nervous. That's the proper word. I didn't tingle, the way a Lamba Chi is supposed to tingle. Fact is, never did tingle. Haven't tingled yet. Y'know? But *he* made me. . .I'll tell you what he did, but if you ever quote me, I'll call you a liar. *He made me itch*! It's hardly couth, I know. I'm talking about long before he ever touched me. Just seeing his picture in the Beacon. Just having Bennett mention his name. It's not fair to call it unpleasant. It's a nervous condition, like everything's too tight. Skin too tight. Hair too tight. Everything. Not tight enough to. . .to explode or anything. Tight enough to be uncomfortable.

"It's been years, obviously. Since parting with Bennett, I've. . .well, naturally I've become more sophisticated. O, stop smiling! You're green with envy, I know. Marrying Cyrus was a Godsend. Who would know that better than you? It gave me a place to go, an image, so to speak. And I very much needed one, let me say. I've had time, on the run, to reminisce, of course. But I never like to think about the Skinny Walker episode. Not that I itch any more, but I know in my conscience that it was rotten, because, well, fundamentally, you see, *he* was rotten.

"I should temper that remark and I probably will. For all I know he's dead and gone, although I doubt it. It's simply silly to think of him as a victim of any kind. He was an animal, I tell you. . .a living *thing*. He'll never die, or if he does, he'll never admit it.

"Of course, he touched me. I insisted on it. Really. In the beginning. It was rather like an affair with a colored chauffeur. I'm only guessing, so get that look off your face! He was practically obsequious. Mrs. Marshall this and Mrs. Marshall that. In all my innocence, it was still up to me to provide the initiative. I didn't actually—you know, not actually take him by the hand and lead him, but you might say it was somewhat that way. You might say that. I really don't think he'd ever made love in a home before. Perhaps a parking lot; perhaps a—a *house*. But not a home. Not with sheets. He was adorable, in our early days, but perfectly rotten inside. I won't go into the gory details. I've forgotten them, really. Don't we all?

"O, again and again. I discouraged him, naturally. What am I saying? I *rebuffed* him. That's what I did. But that type will never admit defeat or rejection. They're simply not like. . .*us*. And so—I got to know him rather well. It was painful. You might as well know that. He was a savage man.

"Rather like a child—a big child, I'll admit. A giant, but a rotten one. Treated me like a china doll. Brute tenderness. I suppose he idolized me, although to be quite frank, you were lucky to get a few oaths out of the creature. No manners at all, y'know? I'm not coming through to you, I can see that. I'm painting a picture of some kind of cave man. He wasn't hairy. Do y'know what I mean? His skin was sleek, very blond really.

"I might as well say it: I loved him, in time. In a *peculiar* way. After all of his pressure, the idolization, I'd have been less than human if I hadn't responded. I wanted so badly to *help* him. Do you understand? It's because I was childless, I know that. He was young. . .and big. . .and his skin was sleek and tawny. . .all over. . .

"Nothing worked. Couldn't work because he was so rotten. Basically. I couldn't *reach* him. Believe me, my ego wasn't hurt by it either. Nobody could reach that monster. I tried to coach him, y'know, in little ways? Straighten his tie; say a word over carefully so he could learn he was grossly mispronouncing it. O, sweetie, I tried so desperately to lift his horizons! I was the only one. He let me understand that. In his rotten way, he tried to be kind.

"Which is probably why it came to a bad end. Had to. No other way. He wanted to be free. . .wild. Uncaptured, in his raw state. And as I remember his raw state. . .well! From his point of view—not *mine*, certainly—it was a sad thing, I suppose. Let's give him that. I was a rare, precious, rather fragile thing in his life. Beneath the rottenness, he saw that. When I think what I meant to him! It was like a dog listening to classical music. Begging to be let in on the secret, do you see? And, really, there's simply no chance of it. None. I was a language Skinny Walker could never learn to speak.

"How? Sign language, I suppose. Braille. I'm not being funny. We communicated on a carnal level. I'm not ashamed of it—it was the only way. And booze. We drank like fishes. For my part, I drank for courage and so he wouldn't hurt me too much. He drank, I should say, to cover his shame, y'know, his humiliation at being locked out of the sophisticated world. He knew, and that's what made him so rotten, that he had no right in *my* world. I could never belong to him. He appreciated my sense of noblesse oblige but it was really salt in his wounds.

"Of course he beat me. Shocks you, doesn't it? Shocked me the first time, you can imagine. I don't mean a slap or a cuff. He almost *killed* me. Relentless, rotten–through and through. I had brain concussion, plastic surgery. Really! O, I can't talk about it! It's another world with a man like that. No lawyers, no police–none of the *civilized* trappings! It's just you and he. Like the end of the world, sweetie. Really. The end of the world.

"He'd have killed me, and if I had resisted him, he would have killed Bennett. No great loss there, really, but the mess. A rotten, violent man. But beautiful. Isn't that sloppy of me? I'm still wearing braces from the brute's beatings, and I can sit here and tell you he was beautiful? Which is how we women are. D'you admit that? We're masochists, after all.

"We want to help. Isn't that our weakness? I so wanted to help that Skinny Walker. Just lift him up. You know? Save him! I never wanted to save Bennett, or save anybody. Skinny's the only one. And he was rotten. Isn't that a gas? He was rotten through and through. I didn't even want to save him from his rottenness. He could have *stayed* rotten. That's how good I was to him. And when I say rotten, I mean rotten. Honey, if I told you. . .

"*This* is one martini I don't need, and I know it, which is the only way I know I'm not going under. How can I be drunk so long as I *know* I'm drunk?

"But I will tell you. Tell somebody. Skinny Walker was a rotten ape to me. He forced his way into my life. . .did I ever tell you? In his own stupid way, Bennett, the dear, set the whole affair up. Had no idea. No! He had *no* idea! There was more difference between Skinny Walker and Bennett Marshall than there is between an ordinary man and an ordinary

22

woman. Can you conceive of that? Believe me, Bennett *never* suspecfed. But in he came. Skinny I mean—all sleek and tawny and rotten. I had everything a young girl needed, you know? I could have had quiet affairs all over the lot. O no! Bam! Bang! In walks this rotten kid and ruins my life. All because he's rotten and won't let me reach him. . .

"Don't worry. I am holding myself together. Probably the strongest, *noblest* act of my whole entire life was breaking off with him. Get out, I told him. . .*out*! Treated him like a rotten stray dog. I hate myself for the way I treated him. What else could I do?

"I know, I know. It's not your fault. Nobody's fault. Except him. Did I tell you? I told him to GET OUT! Take your damn sleek skin with you and GET OUT! I don't intend to yell. It's jus' emphashiz. . .Would you tell the waiter I'm ver' sorry?"

"Er-sky-enn! Err-skienne!"

He'd always been able to judge exactly when it was time to respond when his mother called him. She paid him mind when she needed firewood, or the slop jars wanted emptying, or when he was too high up a tree. She'd call him with a high-pitched nasal cry set at a wave length meant exclusively for her only child. It began with sharp, peremptory sounds, disguising the love-song (which it really was) and he'd wait for it to hit its usual, inevitable progressions. At five years of age, he would freeze like a deer when his mother's voice slit the mountain air. Five hundred feet away, without seeing her form, he knew the nuances of expression on her face. So many times in a given day, the thought would strike her, "My son?", and without a break from her activity (stirring, sweeping, peeling, scrubbing) she'd begin the call. At first covertly, eyes unlooking, face blank and her work noticing no interruption, she would call. Twice, not more than thrice, and then hands would get wiped on the unbleached muslin apron.

24

Crouched in a rotten stump on the edge of the clearing, the lean little boy could visualize her preparation for the second stage of signals. Just the beginning of an impatient grimace on her lips, and the voice deliberately more contralto:
"Er-skinnn! Er-*skinn*!"

It wasn't time yet. But it was getting close. Blue eyes aslit in his Indian-cheeked, anonymous five-year-old face, the subject of her attention held himself from running to her. Of the humans he had come to know, father, uncles, neighbors, passers-by, this voice high in the air was the only one he loved. Her form was the only one dear to him. Her warmth was the only warmth he coveted.

When he was little, before the age of speech, he had stayed as close as he could be to this woman, crawling on the corn-shucked floor of the cabin, clutching to the apron string, begging to be picked up and held. Because the men would laugh, he learned to beg mutely but he could see her armor strengthening day by day. Not because there wasn't time enough, nor because he was too heavy. He saw her resistance to him grow because she thought it was wrong for a boy-son to be too close to his maw. She was training him to live without her.

So this was how he punished her. Now she had to call in series and call many times. It was a game in which he held himself in abeyance, letting her savor the separateness she had enforced. "You drove me away," his silence was telling her. "Now call good and loud before I return. . ."

Depending on her mood, or the press of her chores, she'd call him good and loud. Then the fret of it would overwhelm her and she'd march to the cabin door, so that her demeanor was most formidable, saying with the angry swish of her skirt, "This game is over. . ."

"ER-SKIN" she'd bark, making it a consolidated syllable, the love drained out of it, and he'd know it was time to slowly concede. Which he'd then do, reluctantly admitting his

25

whereabouts or his recognition of her existence. He'd return, but the raggedy-pitiful little boy stance of cunning and defiance was muttering a postscript, "Mought be, some day and I waon't come atall."

It was a question between them, the two of them. Which one would not return?

Goldy Walker was twenty-two when Erskine was five. She had lost three babies before him and two since. It all made her paler and sterner and justified in sleeping alone. Not until J. B. made a fuss about it did she insist the boy sleep on his own, which was when he turned two. She was a big-statured blonde woman, with skin like fine silk, and Erskine never forgot the blue-veined cushion of her white, willing breast. His mind's eye could recall the tart sweetness of her nipple, and how they'd grin at each other over the moon of maternal fulfillment; how he'd choke in a winking chortle and Goldy would coo to him from deep inside the harp of her love.

She was not given to much talk. Her life was taciturn and her man was undemanding. Erskine could remember nothing his mother had ever said to him. He could only remember her calling his name, and the tug o'war they'd played while he slowly responded.

At the supper table, his father would say something on this order. . .

"The mine'll be down come Monday."

His mother would say nothing.

"Me and Doug Lathrop will go to town Saturday. You make me a list of what supplies I should bring."

His mother still said nothing.

"The whole District is going down. We just might be down all Spring."

Then his mother said "Oh?", not because it was an honest query, but to let her husband know she understood.

"It's the operators, not the Union. There's too much coal from Belgium or some such place. The price ain't right."

And his mother was silent. The tiny son would watch her

26

face for reaction and it wouldn't reveal itself. Perhaps she was thinking about the list for supplies, or how the shortage of cash would pinch them. Or how the garden patch would need extending, or how she'd have J. B. around the house and underfoot for a good long time. Who knows what the mother was thinking? She didn't say.

She'd look at *him* now and then, in a wondering but friendly fashion. The boy would look right back. He had no fear of his mother. Quiet she might be and call shrill-ly she must—but her bland, blue eyes were on his side and he knew the meaning of that. He knew the beauty of her, the fineness and the remoteness, and how nothing claimed her. She belonged not to the shack, and not the mine; not to the torn, disordered countryside and not at all to the morose man who called her wife. Her quietness came from the serene temple of her independence. She belonged to no one except the son who answered her look with impudence as he planned some day to never return.

The mines must have been torn down because there were men around more than was right and there was hunting almost every day and poker on many nights. The boy was in his fifth year. It was an important year because his paw had let him pull the trigger on a shotgun for the first time, holding him and bracing him. As the hammer fell the whole world ended. In the violence of the explosion and the shock of the recoil (despite his father's support) little Erskine Walker tried not to cry, and knew that if he ever recovered from this that nothing would ever hurt him again. His shoulder hurt all winter following, but there was one thing that year which damaged him utterly.

She hadn't called. The men were out with the rifles and the sun was past its high point, but the song of his mother's call didn't come. He took it first as a matter of rejoicing and he strayed farther into the woods. At intervals he'd cock an ear and wait. Then, because he was bored and hungry to boot, he worked his casual path closer to the cabin.

Disgusted, he sat on the turf and played with pine cones for a long spell. It was a melancholy wait. He was resentful at the length of her indifference. He sneered to himself, in the manner of his father, that "the woman" should oughta have meals on time. He figured on running away and he decided to give her the time it took for a stray cloud to pass the northern ridge. When that had come to pass, he gave her an extension—as long as it took for him to hear one more hound baying in the distance. Or—as long as it took for him to get all these derned pine cones piled in a pyramid of sulk.

At last, with the shadows longer and edged with tragedy, he decided she had simply won the game. He'd return all right, but the next time she would really learn a lesson! He trudged back to the cabin, smiling at how mean he'd be the next time she called.

When he saw her lying on her bed he knew immediately that she would never call again, and that he'd never forgive her for dying. The blood was stiff on the coverlet and trailed across the floor where her last hemorrhage had stricken her. He put one small hand in a sticky pool. Her face was up and wide-eyed, paying no attention at all to him, so he wiped his hand on his jeans with slow and awful disobedience. Not even this could make her notice.

She was gone without a word. She was claimed by forces other than his own. He'd seen death in the woods when it strikes wild things with the stillness of eternity. He'd seen the deer's limbs that would never run again; the hawk's wings frozen, the throat of the butchered calf. Death was an enemy like a fierce winter or a mountain storm; it came from far away and all you saw, if you survived it, were the traces of its scorn. His mother lay stiffening on her lonely bed like a gracious tree that is down and now will rot, leaving the ground richer and emptier with its memory. He sat crosslegged in the doorway.

He thought, "I'll bury her before the men come back. I'll bring the dirt in here and cover every inch of her. They'll say,

'Where the hell all that dirt come from?' an' I'll just look sharp and not tell 'em. I'll throw the dirt all over her, like they do, and we'll just see how she likes *that*. I'll put so much dirt on her she just up and disappears, is what I'll do. When they scrape it all away, she'll be in heaven."

It took him a long time, in his fancy, dragging in enough grave's soil to hide his mother's beloved form. He shed tears, without crying, and at last he slept—an inconspicuous form, huddled in the doorway, representing a mourner too young to mourn, a lover grieved with no love really to remember.

He took pains not to cry at the funeral. He never visited her burial place on the slope to the east of the clearing. For a while, he listened for the cry of "Er-sky-enn!" and he thought, "If ever I hear her, I'll go sit by the grave." She, of course, never called.

Pauline Danver Morrison washed the breakfast dishes on the morning of December 2, 1953, and drank two cups of coffee by herself, while thinking:

The thing I always had was lots of trouble. With Burke I took it as it came, because it was my due, for better or for worse. But it was always worse, right up to his dying. A woman has to think, somewhere along the way, "What is all the trouble for?" When I looked at Skinny Walker, all I ever saw was trouble.

He was a kid, just twenty-three, when I first came across him. He did a lot, for a kid. Nobody can take that away from him. But it was a dead end ahead for him, with trouble along every mile of it. I could read trouble in the way he walked. The way he did anything. I don't blame him for anything that happened after. It was the trouble that got to him. Like it was bound to.

He liked me and he made no bones about it. Except for one time, he minded his P's and Q's and treated me right. I liked him as far as that goes, and Burke liked him too. But Burke liked him for the Union, because the Union was a religion to Burke. I don't mean this Local or that Local, but the Union—in principle. That's how it was to Burke. He ruined his life and mine too, just for the principle. As long as he had a breath in him, I was for whatever he was for. If it had killed me, I'd have gone along and asked no special favors. I did it because Burke was my man, not because the Union was my Union.

Long before Skinny Walker came out of the hills I knew that nothing good would come out of the Union. Nothing great, the way Burke wanted it. A lot of people don't know it, but he picked the kid up and made him President. I think he did it out of desperation. He'd been treated so badly, and the cause was a lost cause unless it had some spark and thunder. Skinny had that, all right. And you saw what came out of it. . .

A woman can't afford any principle of her own. You stick to your own man, and hope he has a winner. If he doesn't, then you're going to go down when he goes down. Which is the way it should be, although it's always sad when it happens. It happened to me. But the difference between Burke and Skinny was plain to see. Burke was like a man bewitched. Skinny was always his own man. Burke didn't have any self whereas Skinny was all self. Skinny didn't have any room left for principles or theories. I loved Burke and I love his memory. But I have no love for the other one.

He didn't have any room left for love. He was filled with himself. Not like a blow-hard, but there was no mistake about it. We tried to help him in more ways than one. You'd never guess how many speeches I worked over for him. He took all the help and I guess he used it to good advantage. It didn't do Burke or me any good, and when all is said and done, it didn't do anybody any good. Skinny rode high and mighty when it was happening, and I don't think he looked for any good in it, especially not for himself. He just didn't need anything.

That's why he wasn't lovable. I blame his mother for it. If he had one. He never said. But he always acted to me like a kid that was looking for a mother. He'd stare at me over the dining-room table and he'd have stars in his eyes, and I'd hear his voice calling me when he wouldn't be talking at all. I could pity him. If he hadn't been so strong, but I could never love him.

The difference in age is not so important, really, between a man and a woman. After Burke had gone, he'd call me and to tell the truth, I would consider answering him. A widow has her own problems. Then I'd think better of it. He was a loving man, all right, or so I believe, but he had no lovability in him. I suspect he loved his mother and she abandoned him, in one way or the other. He shut that kind of love off inside himself. It made him cold as far as I was concerned. But I was never moved to play the part of mother for him.

It's all trouble, anyway you look at it. Charlie Morrison is no trouble at all. He's not the greatest man that ever was, but I feel no regret for that. A woman's entitled to one good man in her life, and I had that one. But Charlie's goodhearted. And he's steady. And he is no trouble at all. At my age, after what I've been through, you need a husband to keep your feet warm at nights, and for help with the house payments, and to keep yourself busy. But I'm through with trouble. Trouble breaks your heart and your back too.

A mother might have given Skinny Walker some Christianity. It was too late for me to do it. Burke never went to church but he had Christ in his heart. A lot of people, especially Goodstone management, thought Skinny was possessed of the devil, and I don't think he really was. Except that a Godless man is like a boy without a mother. It's a kind of emptiness. You could never talk to Skinny. I had a reporter from New York here not long ago, wanting to know what it was like in those days—when Skinny and Burke were running the Union. Well, I don't think I ever said two conversational words to Skinny in the years I knew him. He didn't pass the time of day in, well—in *idle* talk. You'd have a point and Skinny'd have a point. It was like a supper table, "Please pass the potatoes," or "Anybody want more bread?" You can't call that conversation. He was just an *empty* man, from a sociable point of view. Never went to movies or ball games. He played some poker during the caucus days, but that was just to organize, not because he was a card player of any sort. It wasn't in him.

I don't think the devil had him. Nobody had him. He was somewhere out in left field, between the Lord and the devil. His mother was the only one who could have changed that.

Burke, you know, was ruined by the Union. I mean his Union business had him hospitalized and he was *ruined*. He and I were the only ones that knew it. He's gone now, and there's no shame to it. . .no personal shame I mean. He couldn't be a husband. But he was a man, all right, even without his manhood. He gave himself up for a Union that never cared for him. He gave me up, in a wifing sense, at the same time. You can live without it. Charlie fools around, but honestly! I'd never miss anything if Charlie got himself ruined, although I don't wish it on any man.

We had a good marriage, Burke and me, in that way—when we were young and sassy enough to enjoy it. What if a man should go blind and lose his eyesight all the way? You'd still read to him, wouldn't you? He was good to me, as good as he could be right till he died.

I was closest to Skinny when he got himself beat up down at the Mayflower Hotel. We all thought Goodstone had done it. He was a mess, all right, if you recall. It just tore my heart out when I thought he was ruined too, like Burke was. Then I found out it was all over a floozie and no Union business at all. I found out too that he wasn't ruined either. Poor Helen MacDougal told me. God, wasn't it awful the way she went?

Don't you believe it! No man can ever ruin a woman. Helen asked for everything she ever got from Skinny Walker, or anybody else, for that matter. May she sleep in peace. She had no mother either. She took what she wanted just like Skinny did and she was shameless about it at the time. I felt bad about her, and I still do, but I don't lay it at Skinny's door. His doorstep has got enough piled up as it is. I'm not here to sit in judgment on Skinny Walker or Helen or anybody.

Burke Danver, yes. I'll vote with the good Lord on Burke. Burke *believed* in things. It leads to trouble, belief does, but it's no sin. I'd look at Skinny when he was radio broadcasting, down at the station, and I'd study his face when he was whooping it up for a general strike or some affair. He never *believed* a word of it. This is not to call him a liar. He just didn't care. What he cared about was making *you* believe it. That was his object. I could read his face and believe me, it was empty—as far as believing went.

In my heart I know that Burke and I will be restored in Heaven. I'm not nearly qualified, as far as Heaven goes, but the Lord will give me back to Burke when my time comes. A man that had so little on earth and never got mean about it is surely entitled. But dead or alive I know I'll never cross paths with Skinny Walker again.

When he was seventeen, on a trip to Parkersburg, two unusual things happened to Skinny. Mostly because of his Uncle Daren's kindness, but also because his father and grandfather didn't want him underfoot at the saloon, Skinny was sent to a moviehouse. If it wasn't the first movie in his life, it was the very first he could remember. The house was *The Strand*, and it was a very splendid theater with a twinkling marquee, ushers in high regalia, and a curtain which told of the commercial wonders of Johnson's Eatery, Buster Brown Shoes, Tommy's Auto Repair, Camay Soap and Courtesy of Mayor Ronnie Lenton, Parkersburg's Friend.

Going to the movie had been a very special event. At the same time, Skinny experienced a transcendant emotional impact, part of but above the film itself. He fell in love. He fell in love utterly and irrevocably, surrendering his heart in a swift, secret pact that was never disclosed. It was never consummated, either.

He fell in love with Myrna Loy.

It was a Saturday night crowd, with many dates throughout the audience. Many were "dressed up"; that is, with ties on the boys and flowered prints on the girls. Skinny sat in the third row, unadorned in any way, with his rough backwoods clothes, unshorn hair, no date, no Cracker Jack, no premonition of what was about to happen to him.

When the titles told him the feature film was "The Thin Man," he kept waiting for an emaciated figure, perhaps on the order of Bones Watson who had the T.B. He had no prior knowledge of New York City, or sophisticated crime, or the suave city-ability of William Powell. He knew there were "talkin' pitchers," and he took the techniques of cinematography for granted. If he had any preconception, it was that all movies should be "Westruns," but it wasn't strong enough to cause any disappointment with the fare of the evening.

He was dazzled with the music and the city noises emanating from the screen. Taxi-cabs fascinated him, and headwaiters, and the elevators of swank apartment buildings as they were revealed. For the hero he had only an impatient sort of recognition—that he was a "nice guy," but he'd better keep on his toes. With his big nose and greased hair and his cocky way of talking like gentry, William Powell was only a necessary evil.

But the lady! Myrna Loy stepped forth from the screen in bas-relief. Richly befurred and sculpted in indecent gowns, she walked into Skinny's libidinal orbit as if she were Lady Eve. She was iridescent while all the rest was black-and-white. There had never been a female like her (and there was never to be hence). To the boy's pubescent vision it was as if she paraded through the film in her naked pelt. Deep-breasted, strong-thighed, dimpled shoulders. . ."I betcha anything that's all she's got on!" he told himself, as her silver gown rustled over the sleek-lioness contours of her rear end.

In time, he had eyes only for her. The dialog, like the subordinate characters, became muted and obscure, except when *she* was talking. He studied her body as if he were an

36

anatomy student, an artist, or a beast about to devour it. Which is about how it is with a seventeen-year-old boy fresh from the hills. . .

He forced himself to look from her sloe-eyes to her lips. From her lips to her soft white arms; from her arms to her breasts; breasts to belly; belly to arse and back again. He'd wrench his eyes from inventory-taking for fear some afore-mentioned item might disappear and never be seen again. He tasted her. But never in violation, never crudely. She was the Grande Dame and he was the peasant lad. She was womanhood as he had never imagined it was packaged. From the third row, she was a giantess who swayed and moved and stretched and glistened in a panorama of strange, unbelievable delights.

Myrna Loy, in her time, has been taken by millions of eyes and (at least in The Thin Man) by a herd of William Powells. But never so thoroughly and so sweetly as by young Erskine Walker in *The Strand* on that exceptional night.

Since his mother's death, no woman had existed for him in any kind of personal attachment. Aunts and schoolmarms, store clerks and neighbor ladies—the womenfolk of his world were plain, scratchy-voiced and out-of-focus. "Girls," the female peers of his age group, were inept specimens and unworthy of special regard. He had never, until this night, felt the murmur of interest in women, let alone the clamor of love.

Now his chest cramped with the asphyxiation of love for the new lady. His whole person (he was five foot-nine and weighed 148 pounds according to his Fortune Card, "You have great determination and the will to win out over great odds.") thrilled and pulsated in her Presence. The yearning to serve her was so great he clutched the armrests with both hands to keep from floating.

It was all unfocussed and de-genitalized. He had no mind to project himself to the screen and place himself in Powell's stead, as the lady's partner. He simply could not see himself in the settings portrayed; nor could he believe they existed. To him, the glamorous city and the multitude of players who populated it were as contrived as the sounds and the shadows—all conjured up by the movie-makers. The only reality was Myrna Loy and she came out of the light and shadow and enveloped her boyish lover as if she were a solidified cloud of incense, ethereal and aphrodisiac. He submitted. If she wanted him, he was hers. He was slave and subject, son and husband, chief and owner of all the treasures she represented. They were all his because he yielded to them—the flesh and the lips, the gowns and the jewelled fingers, the limpid eyes and the voice-tones which told him, "I am the Lady, your creation for loving."

They drove back home in a Ford pick-up truck with Skinny in the back, his legs dangling over the tailgate and his eyes to the stars. He was bruised and tender from the agony of falling in love. He heard nothing that was happening, not the gear-grind nor the rattle, nor the racket of tires climbing into the mountain country. He watched Orion in the heavens and winked at the moon in his pain. Every cell in every fiber jammed to escape the prison of his form. He wanted to dissolve into the night.

He was jammed with a lust too great for lusting. He wanted to fell trees and spit down mine shafts, fight with men and shout into the blackness of the road behind him.

By the time they were in the cabin, he was angry. His bed was too empty and his life was too barren. He reckoned that behind that silvered image of city life there was *some* reality. Take away the hokus-pokus, whatever fraud they'd pulled on him, and there was still a life with ladies *something* like that. And the shivering reality of it, however debased, was so removed from this cabin and these hills and the aching solar plexus of himself that a crime was sure enough being committed.

He lay on his tick and held himself. With eyes closed he could remember Myrna Loy; could breathe the heady stuff of

38

her being. She towered over him and over his life, exquisite, monumental, untouchable. He writhed in his subjection. He cursed as well as he could. He tried to strip her of her glories, tear away the bandages of illusion. "Hell almighty," he told himself, "She craps, same as a mule. She eats, by God—I seen her eat—and if she eats, she's got to crap!"

It didn't help. Try as he would, her image would re-establish itself, part Mother and part Goddess, pure and radiant beyond spoliation.

From beneath his bed he lifted a cigar box with corn silk cigarettes, his private hoard. He wasn't allowed to smoke in the house, but this night he struck a match noisily and blew out the draught of smoke with an aggressive puff.

After a while J.B. called angrily.

"You smokin' in there, boy?"

Defiant pause before answering, then the answer with just enough snarl to get even with the world of lights and shimmering shadows.

"Yeah. I'm smokin' in here."

A deferent pause from the other room, just enough to know the crown was being doffed.

"See you don't set the place on fire. . ."

Skinny smoked his corn silk, remembering the cigarette holder *she* had used (with no idea of what such a holder was for). He felt himself growing, inflated with his longings and his angers. Set the whole damned place on fire, he vowed. Get out of here and get me a job in a big town. Go up to Akron and hire out to one of them rubber shops. . .

He had a swift vision of men in "them rubber shops" working in tuxedos, dining on white linen, being wooed by waitresses of the Myrna Loy quality. There were swarthy men with small mustaches and hand-pistols (both items were unknown in Devil's Own) and Skinny Walker walked big and heavy-loined among them all.

The cigarette was crunched out on the wooden floor. The new pain of being in love was no less but it was ready to sleep for that night, if never to leave him. His eyes closed reluctantly and he wondered how old the lady was?

He had no way of estimating. She was ageless by any frame of reference he could fix. But she was older by far than *he* was. So he pictured her many, many years from now (unspecified), her big body just the same as at *The Strand*, but her hair white and her face sunken and pinched like old Granny Hanks. There was a blizzard or a bad fire or maybe a flood. She was alone, abandoned by her fancy courtiers, mostly because she had become old, of course. Quite by chance, Skinny stumbles on her, in an alley or a back street. She looks at him from out of her wrinkles, and those beautiful eyes are just as they were, but no longer saucy. Their comic mystery has turned to appealing helplessness. He reaches down to rescue her and she is already smiling in brave gratitude.

"Just leave be," he tells her. "I'll take care of you. I'll always take care of you. . .M's Charles."

Because that was all he could call his first real love. Star billings and "Cast of Characters" notwithstanding, he didn't know that the Lady's name was Myrna Loy.

If you'd tell him now, what difference would it make?

40

Ruthie Rastek was talking to a co-worker one night in 1956, in the corner of a Case Avenue cafe:

"I've had me a pimp or two but none for very long. Long enough, I guess, to know why a hooker needs just one guy—a guy a little crummier than she is, but strong. You can drink your dreams in Dago Red, or hit the needle if you can afford it. All you want to—but sooner or later you got to come home. Take your medicine and pay the bill. You need a pimp for the same reason they have churches, and I'm not rapping churches, either.

"They can bumrap Skinny Walker all they want but he's the strongest son of a bitch I ever laid. I oughta know. Which is not to say he's a pimp by any means. I'da give him every quarter I ever hustled if he'da taken it. He never asked for nothing from me.

"All he ever asked was a little lovin' from time to time and I tell you something—he gave as good as he got. Maybe better. I'm not the lay I used to be.

"What I liked about him, he was educated. He could talk-talk-talk, but I don't mean that. I mean he had finesse. He was a sweet daddy and carried a lead pipe but he never split your belly wide open like some of them damned gum miners. You'd think they was sailors coming in from sea. I mean Skinny took it easy and he took it—nice.

"When he laid a hand on you, it wasn't some kind of punishment. He was so strong he didn't ever have to prove how strong he was. You been there? It was never some wild scene where he said You dirty crow, now I'm going to let you have it. Not like that. You get with Skinny and he'd talk sweet and hold you nice and you'd talk back. You know? Like a conversation? First thing you know he's in you and you're hotter than hell but it didn't start bang! It was always going on. It's hard to explain.

"With him, just knowing him was the main event, not just when you got screwed. I been selling coozey since I first flew the rag. I've had me queers and crazy coots and some fine gentlemen too. But Skinny was the only real gentleman. He wasn't out to hurt me. He wasn't out to help me, or write my life story like some college jerk. The thing about it was that I didn't make much difference one way or the other with Skinny Walker, and *still* he treated me right.

"I hustled him. He was a big shot, but just a kid when I first seen him. I went after him like he was a big red rooster at a ten cent dance. I needed him. He didn't need me in any way. I could smell how strong he was. How sweet he was. It was on him like a kind of perfume. When I was close to him I knew nobody was going to hurt me—cop or pimp or jazzed-up trick.

"He had a touch. He made you know he was the man about the house, all right. But you liked it. At least I did. Between you and me, there's not much I like. I hear most of these dirty Greeks panting and snorting on top of me or behind me or wherever the hell they like it, and I think You Bastard, I hope you make out and die in the process.

"Skinny was straight. I never even copped him until he was dead drunk and it was all I could do and he didn't know what I was up to until he got the message. He wasn't square but he was straight. I'da taken him in the armpit or the ear but when he was strong he was really strong and there usually wasn't any point in fooling around. It wasn't the size, no. I been with niggers twice his size. It was the feel of him and the timing. I could smell him a block off and he smelled like all man and clean whiskey.

"He liked me. He told me he liked me. Even if he hadn't told me, I'da known. Just the finesse he had. Skinny never fooled around with people he didn't like. He didn't have to. No matter what you hear, he wasn't no politician. A politician will feed you lies and steal you blind. Not Skinny Walker. Oh, no!

"When he made out, it was a good thing, not some slimy blast-off he had to get out of his system. I never made it in my life, as far as I know, but the closest thing I ever came to was just holding onto Skinny while he made it. I felt proud to be there. O, it was a very good thing when it hit him.

"I never knew about his personal life. He wasn't married. Never was. Fooled around with some shop girl and as far as I know laid every hotpants that came near him—if he liked her. Lots of squares claim he hung one on them, but I know better. He was like a real expensive whore—he could pick and choose. Never when he didn't like 'em.

"He liked me, but he never made me rich. I didn't ask him and it wouldn't have helped anyway. Always a fin. Just a fin. And I've gone through his wallet when he had three hundred dollars cash but he never gave me more and I never asked for more. He pegged my rate. It was top scale for me at that. My rate was five bucks and he would never go over the rate. I respected him for that. I really did.

"He claims I dosed him a long time ago, which maybe I did. Who knows? If I did, it means some Greek dosed me and who could I yell to? But Skinny wasn't mad. He was a gentleman. A fink would've clobbered me. Clip-clap, like the fellow says, if you don't like the heat, stay out of the kitchen.

"Last I ever heard from him, I was in jail. He owed me absolutely nothing. Understand? And if it had just been a streetwalking charge, I'da never rapped to him. I had this dead Greek on my collar and I think they were fixing to put me away. No lawyer, no pimp, no family. Nobody to blackmail even. If you ever seen a bloody outcast, kid, you're looking at one right now. I get me a hundred regular tricks a month and not one phone number to call when they throw a murder charge on me.

"Which is why I called Skinny. And he answered me. How does that grab you?

"Christ, I don't think *I* would have answered me, if I'd a called myself up on that kind of a fix. But Skinny answered. He got the mouthpiece and the bondsman, and he sent money. He never asked. Sure he must've figured I shot the Greek, which I did. Everybody knew that. But he saved the day and it must've cost him a bundle. It was good enough to spring me from Lima inside a year. I never heard from him again.

"I probably never will. What it means, I guess, is that I better not kill me no more Greeks because with Skinny gone, I got me nobody to call."

For the first time in his life, in the Spring of 1938, Erskine Walker was a number.

He was in fact a collection of many numbers. He had a payroll number, a clockcard number, a department number and a machine number. On the first night (he started at midnight) he discovered they wanted more than just his hands. They wanted his back, his arms, his legs, his groin—and his mind.

It might have been different if the buildings had been brand-new. But they were older than sin, Skinny figured, with certain of the brick walls (by the railroad tracks) covered with ivy. The stone floors and wooden stairs were grooved with the shadow of a million foot treads. Generations of rubberworkers had been here before him.

And there was so damned much of it. . .so many operations. Such a maze of floors and departments. So much all-around involvement and paperwork to keep track of it. Those first few weeks, his head hurt as much as his back—trying to keep from being dizzy and afraid or getting lost within the Goodstone plant.

Where he worked had a weird and hateful appeal for Skinny Walker. It was a long room on the fifth floor with its lines of machines and glare of unshaded bulbs, the ripe stink of fresh tread being trucked in to the tirebuilders. Above all there were the swift, swift motions of hundreds of men engaged in the business of "making out." The noise of the tire room entered him through every pore, like a multi-voiced scream. The grinding racket of old machines as they complained against being switched on at the start of the shift. The whir of many belts revolving many drums. The steady relentless drone of the conveyor scooting over his head dangling empty hooks. Every hook hungry and menacing, demanding more tires, more tires, more tires, more tires, more tires, more tires. . .

He fancied he could hear the individual gruntings of the builders as they would knead the rubber plies and pull the resisting stuff. Mostly it was the smell he detested. In the richness of the room's stench he smelled the sweat of colonized black men on rubber plantations. He smelled the suffocating holds of cargo ships. He breathed the exotic exudation of nature's material as it was given shape by human labor. Skinny suspected the rubber was amused (in a wicked way) by what they were doing to it. The rubber could know that the agony of its being changed was changing men too. Changing men as much or more than its own reformation. . .

This fifth floor was just high enough so that the switch engines bringing in more crude rubber at ground level could send up enveloping fumes from their smokestacks. They made the soapstone smell sweet by comparison. Whenever this happened, somebody was sure to yell, "There's 'at ol' Boogerhole Express!" Then the builders would laugh as they coughed. Nobody thought of asking for better ventilation. (It wouldn't be long until Skinny Walker thought of it. His lungs were still used to the green fresh air of the piney hills.)

46

Although he wasn't pleased at the idea of the Union. He (at the time) thought of the "Union" as some kind of business run by strangers. It somehow threatened his independence and his manhood. He resented anything that came between him and his machine. It was hard to understand why the best of the men (the strongest and most manly) all seemed to swear by the Union.

In the meantime he went through his labor-training and was soon on his own. He needed to build so many tires to "make out," or earn a desirable daily wage. Each tire was made up of "pieces." Every operation in the building of a tire was called a "piece." He had to get so many pieces in a shift or he was behind. Unlike coal digging or tree chopping or potato picking (the work Skinny knew something about) this tirebuilding business appeared to be more art than skill. The science of working the body and the hands together had to be dexterous and precise. The plycutters made them "bands" of rubberized cloth. These were slipped over a revolving drum (the diameter of a tire, but much thicker). When a skilled man did it, it was child's play.

When Skinny did it, trouble happened. You pulled the one edge of the band over the drum like a sock, and then started your machine. With a rounded stick or an air hose you then applied pressure inside the band so that it tended to whirl on the drum all the way. At sixty miles an hour, the revolving core could tear the stick from your hand in a vicious way. On big bands the fabric could thrash about and knock you down—or worse than that.

Once your band (or ply) was on the drum all the way, you "heeled" it down on each side like a pie crust. This was done in rhythmic, staccato motions. It took power from the shoulder running through the wrists to do this right. "Heeling" was the action that deformed the tirebuilder's hands, more than anything else. After this, you started up the drum and "stitched" the sides tight with a revolving disk. At certain intervals a "bead" was inserted (the wire-strengthened inside diameter of every tire).

Finally, Skinny was learning how to throw a heavy tread over his shoulder and to inch it onto the top band, cementing it along the sides. He was doing this one night when he felt a sharp *thump* on his shoulder. He thought it was a supervisor tapping him to correct some error in his work. He turned his head but there was no one there. In the aisle, some six feet away, he spied a human hand. All by itself. Tirebuilding was not all child's play. Somewhere over the whine and roar of a hundred machines, he heard a man screaming. . .

Before his first month was over, he saw many signs that rubber was dangerous because it could be worked so swiftly. He understood fully why the rubberworks were famous for their pace. He saw how the tirebuilder was a certain kind of man—strong, with a great capacity for speed. And how some men didn't make the grade.

While using a flammable solvent to soften his bands one night, a builder (down the line from Skinny) was caught in the thrashing violence and the solvent ignited. Like a wild snake, his air hose pulled him into the revolving core and his machine became a tower of fire.

Helpless in the few critical minutes, Skinny watched the poor fellow burn up.

On another occasion, a neighboring builder came over to lie down on Skinny's tread rack. Skinny smiled at him in a friendly way. He thought the man was sick with a hangover. He thought this until black blood came spurting from his mouth like a fountain. Then it was obvious that an internal hemorrhage was at work. Skinny helped wheel the lifeless body to the dispensary, but his mate told him, "Don't you worry. He won't die here. He'll die on the way to the hospital."

"Man, he's *already* dead, I'm telling you," Skinny argued.

"Nobody ever dies on Goodstone property, insurance pays double if you do. Y'understand? They *all* die outside on the streets."

It took a few weeks, but Skinny understood.

He would come in early to walk around the many floors in different buildings. Studying the fast-moving workers on their machines still rawhiding to "make out" on the evening shift. From the sidings to the offices he began to assimilate the pattern of the factory. He was cataloging its many processes.

When you finished building a tire it looked like anything but a tire. Its shape was cylindrical and its tread was smooth. He saw them cure the tires in the watchcase molds in the hot, subterranean chamber called "The Pit." Here, high heat and high pressure vulcanized the tire. It shaped it to fit on wheels, and left the tread with its waffled markings.

It was a while before he found out exactly what kind of tire he was making. (It was a truck tire.) He noted that while he weighed one hundred and ninety pounds, he was still the lightest man on the floor.

As he worked he felt his forearms strengthening. His hands swelled and cramped and ached as they deformed themselves. But he also heard cells exploding in his brain. They signaled new, comprehending connections as he strove to make sense of the factory. This was Skinny Walker's school. He had never studied anything so big, so complex and so exciting as this damned old "gum mine" (as they called it).

He asked questions. His mates answered him. Their answers almost always included the word "Union." It surprised him to find an older man, Henry MacDougal, was his shift's committeeman. MacDougal was oak-grey and carried a deliberate authority with him. He was very much a part of the tire room. Skinny was thinking that the Union was somehow alien to the shop, and this was why MacDougal's position as an official representative surprised him.

MacDougal insisted on talking to him as if he were already a member. His attitude was plain. He was confident that Skinny would sign up in a matter of time.

"The women are having trouble," he told Skinny at lunch time.

49

"What do they have the women doing?"

"Making up bands in the band room, beads in the bead room and cutting plies. Things like that."

"What's the big trouble?"

"The thing is this benny, y'know? The benzine you wash your treads with? It stops the women from bleeding."

Skinny Walker was mystified by two things. First, that a little solvent should interfere with a woman's monthly period. And secondly, that the news of this should be broadcast among the men of the Union.

"How do you know?" he asked MacDougal.

"They tell us. They got their own doctor reports. Some of them got husbands in the Local. This benny is ruining their female works. None of them gets pregnant any more."

Skinny tried not to grin sheepishly during such a discussion. (I bet, by God, I could get 'em pregnant—he thought.) Then as MacDougal continued to growl about the Company's indifference, Skinny was struck with the meaning of it all.

It all added up. No ventilation, losing hands. Burning up. Dying "on the way to the hospital." Now, women who stop bleeding. Through it all, a hard-nosed Company that doesn't care. It's like a blight, he thought. A boy from Devil's Own can understand a blight.

"You mean it's like a blight?" he asked Henry MacDougal.

MacDougal told him yes that it was like a blight. With that, Skinny Walker was able to see the Union in its place within the plant. He was just about ready to ask for an application blank. He was getting ready to join the first organization he had ever joined.

He was a part of it now. He was joined with it because he was against the blight. And because he was overcoming his fear of the factory's immensity. He was getting ready to conquer.

50

Shirley Faber typed these comments in 1957 and after reading them, as she said she might, she destroyed them. . .

It was always a source, not of pride, but of reassurance (a feeling I very much needed) that I invariably knew what I was and what I was not. For example—although I've traveled several times around the world, I know I'm a poor traveler. I react badly to poor water, or no water, and this is the main reason I elected to be a "domestic" reporter and surrendered the field of foreign correspondence to the other girls, particularly the bitch at the Herald Tribune. In the same way, because I recognized other various, specific limitations in myself, I stayed away from Sylvia Porter's financial field, away from the Broadway circuit, and away from lovelorn advice, beauty tips and sports.

Everything else belonged to me. I found out early in my free lance days that I could sit through a Committee hearing, read the pending bill all the way through, and—if I tried hard enough—I could understand what was under discussion. Not only that, I could write down all that I understood as clearly as if I were writing a letter to my Aunt Maude, and write it in time to file, that is, to make my deadline.

From this kind of self-guidance, I've built a creditable career. Actually, it's a bit more than simply creditable. Not only do I have several very nice bank accounts and an investment portfolio of blue chip securities, I'm listed in the right editions of "Who's Who." Which is pretty damn good for a gal from Des Moines who has no Aunt Maude to write to anyway.

What I am (or was) and what I am not (or was not)—these were the questions I spent a good lifetime answering. The decisions of self-definition always came easy for me. I call it honesty—but it may very well be based on masochism (how do you really know the distinction?). Some decisions are thrust upon you—such as Montezuma's Revenge. They hit you right in the duff and you'd better recognize them. For example—I was never a pretty girl. Now, I didn't *decide* not to be a pretty girl.

For a time, probably par for the course, I went through the throes of adolescent self-analysis. Is it because my nose is too thick at the base? The ungainly way my head sits on my shoulders? Or what? A healthy girl can't spend too much time in this kind of negative reverie. The *fact* was, I wasn't pretty. So, I accepted it.

I accepted it in the manner of a career decision. Why fight City Hall? If I was *not* a pretty girl, and if I was interested ·in boys—given these two acceptances, what was I going to do about it? I believed then as I believe now in the assertive power of the mind—my mind, your mind, anybody's mind. Your mind exists to make up for the special deficiencies of your general system. I've been called "strong-minded," and it's true, but only because I've used my mind to good advantage, and if you use anything, naturally it gets stronger.

It wasn't until I was in my thirties that I discovered the source of my lack of the prettiness quality, and by that time it no longer mattered. I wasn't pretty, I discovered, because I wasn't *feminine*. (I wasn't masculine, either. I was in No Man's Land.) I had a strong mind, a ready tongue, good grooming and the beginning of a reputation. My name was Shirley, but I didn't belong to it, and at the same time, I wasn't ready to have people call me "Mac."

This isn't a True Confessions piece because that, too, is one of the things I am *not*—a True Confessions type. If anything, I'd like to be a female John Gunther, and so far at least his writing hasn't been in the purple tradition of intimate journalism. I have only one point to make, and when I write it, just as plainly and clearly as I can, I'll probably destroy it. That's a girlish-enough act, isn't it? Would dear Aunt Maude understand?

My one point (about time to make it) is that a meeting with an ignorant, probably corrupt, young hillbilly changed my entire life. This Enfante Terrible called Skinny Walker made me understand what being feminine is all about. I don't know how he did it. It isn't as simple as it may sound. He is no Rubirosa and I'm certainly no Gabor. Meeting him just changed my life. It's too early to say, but it may very possibly have *saved* my life. Aunt Maude, why do I feel this way?

Violence and energy and unmannered lust are all disruptive parts of it. I can report them without blushing, but they don't tell the story. To begin with, he ignored my strongest part—my mind. Ignored it. He paid no attention to my reputation if he was even aware of it. He didn't inquire about my being pretty or not being pretty. He had none of the Square-John attitude which meets you at a bar and asks, "Now is this one pretty enough for me to brag about?" Instead, he reached through the veil of all my pretenses and he said, "Here you are, you Girl you!" And he was right. I was there.

I feel just what a girl can and should feel. It's gratitude, sheer and simple. I'm grateful for the impact of the discovery, the unveiling. I'm grateful for getting out of No Man's Land. I know what I am. (Until then I was an expert on what I was *not*.) He didn't create me. He *found* me. I really don't know why he bothered.

With the men I have known (what an *awful* lead line that is!) it is always a matter of ego. Every sexual encounter is an effort to prove to their own ego's satisfaction that each of them is a man among men. To some of them, it is a desperate campaign to prove they are *not* women. Skinny Walker, bless him, wasn't proving anything. It just never occurred to him to ask a question. I was about to say they don't make many men like this anymore, when the truth is, they don't make many *people* like this, period.

However, I do have the notion that Skinny Walker belongs to an older time, before doubts and uncertainties and confusion about identities took over. He's so unsubtle that it convinces you that subtlety is just another form of confusion. He wandered in here, direct to Stage Center, from the hills or somewhere, and didn't even bother to learn the lines. Now they're booing him and stoning him, and telling him to get off.

He'll get off, just like Douglas MacArthur or Joe McCarthy got off. And he'll disappear. My Aunt Maude will never ask where he went. She'll be so happy that the "stranger" is gone from our midst. I'll tell Aunt Maude, "Don't worry. I don't know where he came from, but now he's gone."

I won't remember him in time. He didn't leave me any funny valentines or engraved lockets. He didn't even make me pregnant, although—honestly there were times when I wished it, and other times when I *expected* it. His secret is that he doesn't suspect that he has a secret. His power, at least for me, came from not being conscious of power in any case. I'm trying to tell you, Aunt Maude, that Skinny Walker was a man because it never occurred to him that he could be anything less. . .

It was a shock to know him. He wasn't brutal, it wasn't

that. He wasn't even drunk (which was a switch, as far as I'm concerned). But he was strong indeed. Not like the circus strong man or the high school show-off, but like a workman who knows exactly what he's doing, and (thank the Gods) wants very much to do it.

So, that's my point. He delivered a note to me, like a Message from Garcia. If you can visualize it, I was standing in the stag line at the school dance, where nobody wanted to dance with me, and I knew why they didn't. I knew why so well that I wasn't bitter or aggrieved. I opened Skinny's note and in a stupid hillbilly scrawl he'd written, *You are a girl.*

Aunt Maude, if you ever get such a note, hide it and treasure it, because if you're like me, it's the only one you'll ever get, and its author has already forgotten you. . .

Asleep by day in his roominghouse bed, "the hard kid from Devil's Own" was visited by ghosts. Authentic spectral visitors, day after day. He didn't know it was happening (just as you won't believe it) but the ghosts knew—and they were the important ones.

His cubicle (during his first year at Goodstone) was a second-floor rear, almost eight by nine feet in size, with the noisy bathroom down the hall. There was a bedroom window with a fretted yellowed curtain and dark green blind. The blind was torn and through the tear could be seen the unpainted clapboard siding of a neighboring roominghouse six feet away. Skinny never raised that blind, never peeked through the rip, never questioned his quarters. He came here only to sleep between shifts—and to be had by his ghosts.

To prepare for bed he would throw his outerclothes over the foot of the bed. There was no wardrobe, no clothes tree, no hangers. He dropped his underclothes to the floor and fell face down on the ancient slab of knots and lumps and jutting

56

coils which had once been sold as a mattress.

To sleep, then, he'd stretch his arms forward, gripping the brass posts at the head of the bed. The old metal cooled the hot calluses of his hands and as his fingers relaxed his grip would loosen. The rawhide bonds of Goodstone's piece work system slackened, and when Skinny Walker's young hands—puffed and stiffened and grotesque—fell inertly between the bed and the peeling wallpaper, he would be asleep.

It is useless to speculate on his pre-sleep reverie. There was none. Simply none. He didn't toss and turn and think of home (wherever that was) or strive to recollect his mother's face, so longtime dead. None of these things. He lay prone on his ugly pallet with his big sore hands around the cold brass posts—and he went to sleep.

This was not for any lack of depth to "the hard kid"; no proof of his spiritual bankruptcy. It signified, rather, one undeniable condition: he was drained dry, played out, exhausted. Skinny was tired. Which was why he had gone to bed.

And that's why the ghosts of Akron (who may visit you some day) delighted in crowding his small room in order to work their curious spells—with rancor and vigor and magic too.

Ghosts are like that. They like the husks of fleshly clay, all milked free of mundane juices, all cleared of worrisome mental irritations. They like to visit the very young, the untainted, the ill and the dying. They also like ripe vessels momentarily stunned with fatigue, and these they visit for their own reasons. Their reasons, in the main, are common enough—they want to fertilize the present with the seeds of the past. Mealy-mouthed observers often call such ghosts "historical influences."

Who were the specters in Skinny Walker's room? They formed a freakish assembly, dancing in the dusty morning's sunlight as it speared through the rip in the morbid window shade. A chain of spirits, mismated and misbegotten, they made a smoky carousel around and around the prostrate boy, weaving their spells and accents and carving on the maiden statuary of his intuition.

For example, General Lucius Beirce was there. He had been commander-in-chief of the Patriot Army, headquartered in Akron, one hundred years before Skinny Walker came to town. The General had been a man of spirit, and his spirit now was a thing of considerable power.

There were no medals on his ghostly uniform. Akron's General Beirce had led outrageous campaigns to free Canada from British rule, and what medals have been struck for such as these? His first attempt was launched from upper New York State and only one man escaped from it. Shortly thereafter, the General in person led one hundred and thirty-seven men in an effort to seize Windsor. Seize Windsor he did, only to be surrounded by forces of the Crown in a counterattack so vicious that only thirty of his men survived to escape, the General among them.

This was his military record, and what honors can there be for the leader of an annihilated army? Trial in the courts of his own country for violating its neutrality laws? Scorn for having been defeated, and shame for having survived? Akron, Ohio, did what it could. It made him its Mayor (after he escaped federal imprisonment) and kept him on for six full terms. . .

This is what makes a man turn ghost and look for strong recruits while they sleep among the roominghouses which stand in Akron like a tented encampment overlooking a military plain. And General Beirce leaned low over Skinny Walker's ear and breathed the command, "*Attack again!*"

Jim Brown came too, from Akron in the 1820's—"a man of rare talents and wonderful energies," the archives say. Six-foot two in height, of commanding presence with the eye of an eagle—Rubber City's first famous outlaw, this Jim Brown (no relative to John Brown, the abolitionist, who set up shop in Akron a little later). Jim set up "the Money Shop" on Akron's outskirts, surviving lightning bolts, riotous sprees and numerous arrests, all in order to turn out counterfeit money, both coins and bank notes, so authentic only the experts could detect it. And turning out millions and millions of dollars' worth of the spurious stuff.

Legally dead, at last (in 1865) from a fractured skull in a canal boat scuffle, Jim Brown went into ghosthood to walk the earth too big and too rich for any grave. Not, of course, before little Akron, Ohio, did all it could to honor him by making him Justice of the Peace the better to run his gang's enterprises.

Jim Brown with the ghostly glint of his once-eagled-eye, sparks the green gloom of Skinny's bedroom and barks his gangster imprecation, "Screw 'em all, laddie. Go do it, y'self!"

Now and then the company of shades would include "Father" William Miller whose tabernacle on Akron's High Street had been blown heaven-high before he joined the netherworld to preach his injunctions without flesh or voice or earthly weight.

Father Miller's army, like General Beirce's, had met with total disaster—in preparing for the cataclysmic end of the world on the 4th of April, 1843. Or was it March 22, 1844? April 23? *Perhaps August 13*? At any rate, Akron's Millerites had sold their possessions, paid off their debts, suspended their businesses and dressed themselves in snow-white "Ascension Robes" for April 4th. Or April 23? Some even mutilated themselves ahead of time. . .

All of which is quite enough to make any man reject the grave for a while and travel, wraithlike, through the ashes of his old campfires. And to touch the slumbering form of Skinny Walker, saying softly, "The world *did* end, my son, and *they didn't know it at the time*!"

This is what happened to Skinny Walker, as he slept midst the daytime of his newfound city, inhaling its odors, suffering its vibrations, being inhabited by its ghosts. And these are some of the ghosts who had a hand in the shaping of Skinny Walker. Jim Brown, Father Miller, General Beirce, and a trackless assortment of bodiless legends and vaporous heritage. Some forlorn and vengeful; some charged with purpose; others buoyant. . .

Newton Chisnell came. Once he had been a young actor in Akron, playing the Second Grave Digger to the great Booth's Hamlet. As such he had stolen the show from America's greatest Shakesperean performer. To accomplish this he had used his own local claque of bully-boys to stomp and whistle whenever Newton could be seen. His message to Skinny was an obvious one, "Don't let any bastard upstage you. . ."

Others of the host were fairly fierce. George Brodt, among them, had been an Akron City councilman in 1900 when he led a lynch mob to City Hall. Fired with indignation, his followers dynamited City Hall. They set fire to adjacent buildings. They razed all traces of the city administration to the very ground. Brodt's riot was a thorough example for civic reform, inasmuch as the morning after had left a great hole in the center of Akron, marked only by smoking ruins. He was later exonerated of any mischief, as all Akron felons, sooner or later, are always exonerated. But he was consigned to limbo and his "influence" works too in Skinny's room, with a banner that reads, "Give 'em hell!" and means every word of it.

Later on, when the biddies and the old maids (of all sexes) wondered whatever it was that made a man act as Skinny Walker acted, it would have made sense to call these witnesses to his character, being formed in a despicable little room on Willard Street. No man is an island, in time as well as space, and Skinny's mainland was the antic, robust, explosive roguery of a bastardized town named Akron, which means "the highest."

These were true ghosts of a true history. They need mention in the chronicle of Skinny Walker if that chronicle is to be understood at all. Very real events were currently

60

happening and about to happen but the ghostly non-reality of a riotous city and its spectral traditions was also at work.

Skinny Walker slept soundly. His only dreams were vague, incoherent and far beyond his ken. Giants, generals, clowns, and clerics pervaded his sleep and counseled him with commands and curses from a troubled past.

But mostly curses—because curses are the wind of violence. . .

12

Helen MacDougal sat thinking in a Thursday twilight in 1952, preparing to end her life. . .

"It was all my own fault. I knew he was a red apple first time I ever laid eyes on him. There was something about him. . .like a wild animal or a stray. He never made me any promises. I was a kid, but he was a kid, too. So what does that mean? I was ready for what happened. He didn't make me ready. I can't blame everything on him. He jumped me and I let him jump me. I had no mother to tell me, 'Cross your legs, kid. There's a Skinny Walker coming.'

"A wild creature, he was in fact. I don't mean a bear or a lion, not roaring or tearing you to pieces. He was like a dog that has no master. Or mistress either. That's a laugh. . .

"He came into our house out of nowhere. A greenhorn from the hills. He was handsomer then than now, with his skin glowing and his blue eyes colder than glass. And he sure was quick. I let him know I didn't trust him any farther than I could throw him. And you know something? I couldn't

62

throw him at all. He got me on the porch that first time. If my mother could hear me, I'd tell her right now, fourteen years later, it was beyond right or wrong, that time on the porch. No young girl, in her health and all, could have turned him away. That's how quick he was. And strong. . .Lordie, he was strong.

"It was wrong. Of course, it was wrong. . .the whole thing. But the time on the porch wasn't wrong. I had no life of my own. I loved the kids but I'd be lying not to admit I got tired of scrubbing and cooking and playing little Mama. I never had good things. I had no small pleasures. Not even the movies. No sweethearts, no pretty dresses. All I had was a big emptiness ready for filling. That's how come he jumped me so fast. He moved in like a wild thing if you leave the door open.

"I was never anything to him and he didn't make a pretense out of it. It was me that put a claim on him. He never recognized it. He never gave me anything. No I.O.U. and no I-Love-You's either. He took what he wanted and I was glad, at the time, to let him take it. It was my own fault. Being so close to him and never being that close to any other human being, I began to think maybe he was human too. That maybe he'd feel what I was feeling, and that after all he'd give me something back. I couldn't believe that I could feel all that he meant to me, without him feeling some of the same for me.

"Not for long. It's a lie to say that I thought that for long. He never gave me any hope. He was always on a take-it-or-leave-it basis. Why should I lie about it?

"My ace in the hole was always to have a baby. I figured he'd have to recognize that. Every time we made love, I'd hope for a baby. Many's the night I felt like this was it. I knew for certain we had made it. I could feel full and enduring, and I'd look at him asleep and I'd think, 'Skinny Walker, let's see you walk away from this one. . .' Then my monthly would roll around and off he'd walk. It was my fault. It just wasn't meant to be.

"Even if he hadn't married me, a baby would've given me something. I would've got over him, or given him up, or been occupied. The old man would've killed him for sure, but I'd have ended up with something all my own. I could have left Akron, as far as that goes, and raised my baby. No matter what Skinny did. Or my dad. . .

"He thinks it was his fault. Ever since he suspected we were sinning, I lost him as a father. It was months before he did. He's just a good, dumb man. But when he figured it out, and got over the shock, the shame of it was too much for him. The trouble is, he's that kind of man, the shame was his. Not mine. He took all the shame. I could see it in his face, his eyes, the way he looked at me and talked. Never said a word—not to me and not to Skinny. For him, it was his fault that Mom was dead and that I didn't have proper advice, and that he invited Skinny into our house in the first place. All his own fault.

"So the shame of it made him treat me like a different person. As if he had done wrong. As if he had committed a shame so big it could never be undone.

"Everybody has to pay his own way. The shame wasn't what bothered *me*. I know very well you're supposed to be married. I *wanted* to get married. I had no way to bring it about. I wanted to have a baby, if only to make Skinny walk right. What I didn't want was ever to let Skinny get away. And that was my fault. Because I never really had him. He was never mine. He was a stranger slipped in and took what he wanted, and never gave me a by-your-leave. So I had nothing to hold onto, nothing to keep. So what was I hanging onto?

"I had nothing but the shame of being private with him. Of making love like an animal and liking it so much, because it was all I had. I'm not really that low. I could like lots of things if I only had them. But if I hadn't been jumped by Skinny in the first place, I might not have even had what I had.

"When I say that, I'm lying again. Because there would have come fellows. I'll bet you I would have had fellows. When they finally came, they knew I'd been had by Skinny, and the thing was I shouldn't keep from them what Skinny had got so easy. So I was ruined for fellows. For any one of them that might have married me. That might have made me a mother. . .

"It was that first night on the porch that screwed me up. Of any nice memory I have that's the one I don't want to give up. On my mother's grave, I can't put it down. That was my fault. All the other wrongs come from it, and there's no denying them.

"Why couldn't he have loved me? I was lovable enough. Why couldn't he give me a baby? That was my fault too, I suppose. They say it's mostly the woman. I always figured if he was a father, he'd have to claim the child. That's a laugh, thinking of Skinny Walker as a father. But I did, year after year, and I wasn't laughing. Even when I knew he was sleeping around. Even after I slept around myself. Why couldn't God have been good to me, even if I was a sinner?

"I'm not very lovable now. I let myself go. You can't stay a kid forever; not working in the shop, keeping your old man's house and belonging to nobody. If I went to a beauty parlor the girls in Hollywood would pee their pants.

"The whole thing's a laugh. I lost my father just as sure as I lost my mother. I lost my chance to be a decent mother in my own right. I lost respect. It all happened on the front porch.

"To him it was just another load of ashes. I knew that. God Almighty, I knew it! No preacher had to tell me that! So here I am, and the only good thing that ever happened to me was that night and I'm supposed to be sorry for it! To hell with all of them. . .

"I don't blame anybody. It was my fault and I'm not sorry. My whole damned life is ruined and I'm supposed to let go of that one night. After that first night, I thought

Skinny Walker was a god. I thought he'd see the light. I felt powerful, like a beautiful woman in love, and the world would come to me. It was all my fault. I would have died to have him touch me again. It was the most innocent thing I ever did. I don't call it sin and I'm not ashamed. So I'm ruined. I might have been ruined anyway. I might have got drunk on Market Street and a truck run over me. How many ways can you get ruined?

"There's no way going I can touch Skinny Walker. He's riding high and never thinks of me, even when I reach him. He's a wild creature without a conscience. I couldn't even give him a son to bring him to bay. My dad is another story. He's got my shame on his conscience. He's taken my shame away from me and himself with it. My shame belongs to me. It's my fault, and not Pop's. Who the hell does he think he is? Doing nothing and then taking the rap for it. . .

"I *did* something! I gave myself willingly to Skinny Walker and he has no use for me. But it was *my* doing. I've got to get my shame back. It belongs to me.

"If I cut my rotten throat, they could all stand there in the morgue and know that I belonged to me. Ruined as I am, it would be *my* doing. They could see me cold and still and know, 'Well, she finally got *hers*. . .' A razor blade and one quick slit will let that night on the front porch run out for good.

"I can't do it here. It'll be a mess, no matter how you look at it. Oh, I could do it here. Somebody else can clean the bathroom up. They'll know, the bastards, that Helen finally claimed her own, but it will be some woman that'll clean up after me. You can bet on that."

When he saw the first woman's scalp flopping he thought it was a loosened bonnet.

Goodstone's main entrance on Market Street faces the Boulevard. The brick-faced factory is a dark, moribund mass on one side. Across from it are stores, cafes, repair shops, a cemetery, and (of course) a theater. The Rialto was a little neighborhood picture house and Skinny could see its marquee still blinking gaily.

Coming toward him were many of the Rialto's recent patrons. Mostly women, mostly hysterical, many of them bleeding. When he saw the blood, of course, Skinny understood about the scalps. Far in the background, the blue coats of Akron's police advertised the fact that a riot was in progress. The badly injured women were like so many cats in a fit. They ran with their knees high. They let out high-pitched, keening noises. He could see at least a dozen women whose scalps had been laid open neatly by some nicely-wielded nightsticks.

The street was thick with the crowd. There was no room for litter-bearing. There was little question of applying first aid. The crowd was a moving, disordered mass on foot. It had all the signs of a great migration in miniature. It was moving toward hazard, toward struggle. . .

A shopworker hailed Skinny Walker. It was Henry MacDougal with a frozen mask of bewilderment on his face. He had been born and raised in Akron. He was very excited.

"Skinny! My God, Skinny!" he cried.

(He didn't know that his hoarse cry of "Skinny!" would be like a shout in an echo chamber. Skinny. . .Skinny. . . *Skinny*. . .SKINNY. . .*SKINNY*!! That it was only beginning now and would later boom in a throat so tremendous it would require a million men to form it.)

At that moment it could hardly be heard. But Erskine Walker, a tirebuilder just through his learning period, heard it. He knew that much was happening and that he was part of it. He gripped MacDougal by the arm and led him forward, toward something. They made way for some of the women who were screaming and running in the other direction. They knew these were housewives, otherwise undistinguished, who had left greasy dishes in their sinks to "take in" Bank Nite and a double feature at the Rialto. Coming out of the movie house at midnight, they had run smack into a riot. Or a riot had run smack into them. Zealous cops had given them new hair-do's.

The two men found themselves at the arena's edge. There was a gaping of bodies through which could be seen the sight of violence in progress. A uniformed figure (one of many) was lashing his club at all and sundry. It was fairly efficient because so many people jammed the street and because Akron's brave boys in blue (at that time) knew how to use their billies. Especially against women. . .

Then someone sounded a warning cry.

"Gas! *They're using gas*!"

A rasp-throated man crouched next to Skinny and

MacDougal. He was wrapping a wet handkerchief about his lower face.

"Where'd you get water?" Skinny asked him.

"Smell it, buddy. Just smell it!"

Nobody thought of laughing at a urine-soaked rag. The air was gaspingly acrid now from the tear gas bombs and it was hard to breathe. The two men (without knowing why) pushed their way toward Case Avenue. At Willard Street they saw the second-story headquarters of the Union being pillaged. Smoke curled out of its broken windows. Chairs were flung through, falling on the squirming traffic below.

About this time the shameless crowd-scurry began to hesitate. The convulsive movement to escape was dying down. Only those who have seen it (in riots across the world) can believe that bare hands with angry fingers can pull up paving bricks from the street. Skinny found himself heaving bricks at the cops., And dodging the heavy porcelain-cased gas shells that were flying into their midst.

For a while, the assault of the police was answered with sticks and stones. The mood of the crowd was changing. The police were regrouping now, getting ready for a main charge to clear the streets. But among the wounded, asphyxiated, stupefied crowd there was rising a sense of resistance. Skinny felt the transformation like an electric shock.

The two men huddled in the shallow doorway of a corner store to think about strategy. According to the legend on the window, this was "Shorty's Swap Shop and Gun Repair."

"I can't believe it!" MacDougal kept saying. "This is America!"

"It's Akron, anyhow," Skinny admitted.

"It can't happen! Christ love us, it *can't* be!" MacDougal's plaint was almost drunken gibberish.

"It's sure hard to figure," Skinny Walker agreed. His young mountaineer's face was set in a mask of watchfulness, not anxiety. His eyes were slitted like a hawk's as he surveyed the streets and marked where was the enemy. In the years to come he would be labeled as "ruthless." This night of the famous Goodstone riot he learned what ruthless meant.

In the shelter of Shorty's doorway they had a brief time to piece together fragments of reports about the strike's beginning and how the riot came. About a chain picket line which had been forbidden and how the order was defied. . .

"Every cop and would-be cop in Akron is here tonight—."

Then it began again. The billy clubs were swinging and the gas shells were lobbing in. (The force of a shell was enough to knock a man down even before its discharge blinded the area.) For years, Mac and Skinny would relive this night. They hacked and spat and wept. They ran and they hobbled. Market Street down to the bridge at Case Avenue was an impassable swampland of men. There was much coughing in collective spasms, as if the crowd were a giant hound dog having nightmares.

For the moment, all that these hundreds upon hundreds could do was to fall back. This was what they deserved for daring to resist forces without leadership, without strategy, with no arms. It was their punishment, too, for believing that this was America, by God, and it just can't happen here!

This was Akron, in May of 1938 and it was happening now.

At the foot of the hill at the little bridge, Skinny held up and looked it over. The police had darkened all the street lamps. Only the Case Avenue traffic light shuttled from green to red to amber neutrality, with a thousand faceless men cluttering the street below it. Far up above, the Goodstone clock tower was also dark. Except for the irregular flashes of the tear gas guns being fired from the ramparts. Mixed through the mob were many, many bandaged heads, white turbans among the welter of forms. A siren was whining unceasingly.

It took a while before Skinny figured out that the special mission of the fire engine (periodically clanging down Market Street) was to serve the enemy. The crowd was politely

70

cleaving itself to allow them passage.

"They're bringing up more gas!" Skinny yelled. "Those bastards are hauling ammunition for the cops!"

Before tonight's industrial war, construction had been started on a replacement for this rickety bridge. There were stacks of piling, lumber and material in the shadows of Case Avenue. With these, Skinny and MacDougal (assisted by eager volunteers) formed a barricade. The next fire engine roared imperially up. It was balked by the barricade and awkwardly withdrew. The crowd cheered. It was a sorry triumph, Skinny knew. But it was the first blow struck for our side all night...

A plain man in a plain cap came up to address Skinny Walker. When he talked it was clear that he was slightly drunk.

"You in charge here?"

"Why, I reckon I am—," Skinny answered him.

"All right, then! Do your damned duty! Get these men together and let's get up and burn that damned plant right down to the ground!" He waved toward the hill and the black monstrosity of Goodstone in the night.

"You get on back to the bar, buddy. We ain't fixing to burn nothing down," Skinny said.

"Did they crack our skulls or didn't they? Did they wreck our hall or didn't they? Hey? Are you a yellow-bellied red apple or not?"

"Red apple" was the dirtiest word in the gum mines. After a month on his new job, Skinny Walker knew that well. He did not hit the man. (Later, certain union politicians falsely claimed that Walker had injured one of his own men during the riot.) He did pick him up and carry him like an armload of lumber to the edge of the barricade where he threw him to the ground.

"Stay out of my way, Slim," he told the man. "I got things to do."

The murmur of the street caught itself up into a dead

silence shortly after that. The steps of a man on the bridge became audible. It was a policeman with shiny puttees, shiny buttons and a shiny badge. His holster was empty.

"Hold up, copper!"

But he was already there. An ordinary fat-faced specimen, his skin beaded with sweat and his eyes popped in terror. He pleaded for a hearing, but a deep scornful muttering answered him.

"Honest fellows! I'm only a traffic squad man. Gee—I ain't mad at nobody. But I left my motorcycle down here, and the Chief says—"

"Tell the Chief your bike's in the canal—"

"Where you belong!"

Several determined figures wormed their way toward the cop.

"We'll take care of the rat. He won't club any more women! Let me at 'im! You oughta see my old lady's head!"

Skinny Walker stopped them.

"One lousy cop won't make us feel any better!" he shouted. (It takes something special to be heard in such a situation.) "Send him back without his scooter!"

His motorcycle was, actually in the canal, along with a police cruiser upside down and the body of a young striker named Leonard Allen with a bullet from a Police Special through his head. He was one of four who died that night but it was never proven who killed him.

Probably a thousand had been badly injured (not counting the gas). Two hundred hospital arrests had been made. The cemetery fence had been hung with a long row of bloody caps, which would have made a dramatic news photo if some paper had chosen to print it. The whole town was shaken by the news of the riot that night. Nobody was asleep within a five-mile radius. More men were pouring into the area, and perhaps twenty thousand of them were now in the shadows where Skinny Walker was. A quarter-million people were learning of this event, being touched by its sparks. Tales were spreading through the night—about rivers of blood, mountains of dead. Hundreds will have bad stomachs for the rest of their lives from the gas they took. Scalp-scars will itch and ache for long to come.

Now the men knew that the City of Akron had laid by a special store of ammunition. That special deputies had been sworn in ahead of time—just for this occasion. They knew that the riot had been planned-for and arranged on a split-second timetable. The only ones who hadn't known were the rioters themselves. . .

"You know?" Skinny whispered to MacDougal. "They'd better call it a night right now. It's been time enough for some of these hillbillies to get home and get their squirrel guns. . ."

To confirm his thought, a fusillade of shots flashed from the parking lot.

"Down we go, Mac!" Skinny hissed. "It's really going to come now!"

It really did. It came in the unpunctuated fury of many bullets. It made a dreadful din. Case Avenue at Market was a valley filled with the racket of gunfire. It only required one such night in Akron for Skinny Walker to decide he was a union man.

They sat in the gatehouse and smoked. The tire room saying was that "You may give out, but you never give up." When the whirring, thumping pace had them ready to "give out," they came down to the gatehouse.

After Skinny had broken the barrier and was making out, he'd grab his cigarettes from his shirt (hanging on the corner of his machine) and hail his neighbor.

"Take a break, Alabam! You trying to break the rate tonight?"

The tirebuilder was (in his way) like a truck driver. If he could make his destination by shift's end, he could pace himself along the way. Stop for a breather or a smoke or even a cup of coffee across the street—if his energy was up to it.

The danger was that company men clocked such "holidays." Once their notebooks showed evidence of too much free time, the stopwatch appeared. The tire was re-timed. The new time study would bring lower piece work rates and the builder was pushed that much harder to make out.

On the other hand, if he didn't stop for smokes along the way, and if he were young and hard like Skinny Walker, he might "run over," make too many pieces. . .The piece work system punished the slow man and penalized the fast one. The big thing (Skinny figured) was to take that stop watch away from management.

Skinny liked the gatehouse—the worn benches, the plain concrete floors. There stood the time clocks, row on row, waiting for the whistle. Tired hands punch out; fresh hands ring in. The massive wrought-iron gate to Willard Street was drawn closed. The guards smoked in their stupid way in an office behind the time clocks.

There were women too. Because of their lower rates, the women did not come so often to the gatehouse. (They smoked in the toilets mostly.) But the bolder ones did, out of defiance and for other reasons. Skinny liked the women. He knew a little, at twenty-three, of hill women and their solitary passions. Of broad-thighed farm women and their warm earthiness. Of women in river towns with their hard-tongued strutting lust. Since coming to Akron, the bachelor Erskine Walker had visited a whorehouse three times at a total cost of two dollars and seventy-five cents. (One girl had offered him a discount and he had taken it.)

But he didn't yet know factory women. Now a pair of them noticed him on the gatehouse bench. One of them whistled a wolf-call in his direction. He looked up at them as they passed. They were wide-hipped in slacks and their eyes were hot and muscular.

"Eatin' stuff," one said, pointing to Skinny.

The other threw back her bandannaed head and laughed like a man. Skinny thought: My God, there's only one way you could shut these women up. . .He ground his cigarette out on the floor and was about to stand when a girl came over to him. She was surprisingly short and surprisingly young compared to the women who had taunted him.

"You're Skinny Walker, ain't you?" She was daring him to deny it.

"I reckon I am," he replied, looking her up and down.

"I'm Helen MacDougal," she said. They stood staring at one another. "I work in 141." Each of her remarks was a belligerent announcement. "Henry MacDougal's my old man."

"Oh?" Skinny grunted to recognize her father's authority.

"He said he signed you up."

"Is that what he said?"

"That's what he said." She was waiting for him to call her father a liar. To prove he was a red apple and not a union man at all.

"That's what he did then," Skinny laughed at her.

She turned to leave, hesitated and turned back to face him. Her face was heart-shaped, with auburn hair drawn strictly into a bun above her pink neck. Her eyes were narrow and dark, her mouth large above a delicate pointed chin. Skinny couldn't make out the details of her figure. The jeans and the jacket revealed only that it was sturdy and small.

"You think you'll ever make a union man?" she inquired.

"Hard to say," he responded. Her hostile attitude baffled him. If she'd been a man, he would have hit her. . .

"I doubt it," she announced.

"Is that a fact?" He laughed openly at her.

"Yeah. I doubt you'll ever make a pimple on a union man's butt."

Skinny just wasn't accustomed to a woman like this. She was challenging him in an area where he felt uncertain. And she did it in a ridiculous, disconcerting manner. Now she turned again to leave.

"MacDougal?" Skinny's voice recovered in time to catch her attention. She wheeled to look at him blankly.

"You a union woman?"

"You're damn right I'm a union woman."

"Tell you what, MacDougal. I might make me a union woman before too long."

Her narrow eyes opened for an instant. Her wide mouth with its dark full lips pursed as if to spit. She decided instead to shrug and slapped her hand against the taut rump of her jeans.

"Kiss my kiester," she told him and walked away.

Helen MacDougal was nineteen years old, with two years of continuous service at Goodstone. She served as secretary for her father's union caucus meetings, just as she had served him before coming into the shop. All through high school (when meetings were more secret than now) she had kept the minutes and made the phone calls to alert key men to one gathering or another.

Her mother had died of pneumonia at the pit of the depression. (There were four other kids, all younger.) Helen had carried coffee and tin bottles of soup to her Dad's picket shanty during the great strike of '36. (His shanty bore the name "Jenny" which had been her mother's name.) She hated cops. She loathed the Goodstone management. She adored her father. She mothered the younger MacDougals.

And she had never been kissed. Which was why she couldn't understand why Skinny Walker aroused her animosity so. In his presence she became inflamed with a will to hurt, to criticize, to belittle. Her father had been rather proud of recruiting the young hillbilly. Helen (for reasons beyond her understanding) treated him as if he were a company spy.

When he came to their old frame house off Arlington Hill for a meeting of the MacDougal caucus, she opened the door.

"My God," she greeted him bitterly. "The Squadron's here."

Goodstone's Flying Squadron was an apprentice system for foremen. The likeliest, most ambitious, best-looking red apples qualified for its ranks. Which may betray the source of her reaction to Skinny. He was too good looking for her. His sideburns were too long. His eyes were too blue.

The men sat around her mother's old dining room table.

There was a large, melancholy, glass-beaded chandelier over their heads. The floor was bare and a lithograph of Franklin Roosevelt hung on the wall in the most honored position. Some men were on chairs in the living room. Others stood in the kitchen doorway and in the archway to the living room. There were fifteen in all. Big men, little men, old men and some not so old. Skinny was the youngest and he was standing.

Henry MacDougal presided. It was his house and his caucus. He knew how to speak to his men.

"The riot set us back five years," he was saying. "It was their riot and they knew what they were doing. The last dues collection gave us a membership of only eight hundred. Paid up, that is."

"Aw, Mac," a man complained. "We had us eleven thousand just last January. . .?"

"So now you know what the riot was for. These figures is secret. They get out to management and we're all done in."

The air was thick with a feeling of defeat. It made the meeting inarticulate. The agenda bogged down in expressions of irate despair.

"That damned Mayor and his tear-gassin' deputies. . .!"

"Mahogany Row is out to kill us, one by one. . ."

"This is worse than thirty-six. . ."

Helen sat a little behind her father with a note pad on her lap and a pencil poised. She was waiting to record any motions of positive intent. None came. Skinny watched their faces and felt the troubled lack of purpose. He signaled the chairman.

"Skinny?"

"These eight hundred we got. . .The ones still on the roster?"

Every man looked at him. He was new but his voice was familiar. Kentucky, Alabama, Tennessee—they all recognized the coal-marked drawl of West Virginia. . .

"Way I figure, Mac," Skinny said. "These are good men.

78

This storm's kinda thinned us out some, but that's all hickory that's still standin'."

They watched him closely. MacDougal especially frowned, waiting for the point. These were men on the gaunt side, used to hard lives and hard times. They were not given to fat, emotional, self-lauding speeches.

"It's still only eight hundred outa 'leven thousand," Jess Slaughter put in with a dry rasp. He was a big, solid pit man with soapstone on his collar. Helen gripped her pencil. Her breath was bunched in her breast like a sob, waiting to see Skinny proved right or wrong. Why did she care? What if they threw him out for a snot-nosed whelp? But she knew she cared. . .

"Christamighty!" Skinny Walker put one hand on the drapery rod which divided the dining room from the living room (although no drapes had decked it since Jenny MacDougal had died). "Don't give me no more of that eleven thousand bull! You let me talk about that eight hundred, y'hear? Pay me no mind 'bout how good it used to be—and how bad things are now! You give me eight hundred good men, all hickory like I say, and I can tear you down that Goodstone mill and put it back together again—brick by brick!"

These were combat men and they knew a rallying cry when they heard it. This was Skinny Walker's one speech. In the years to come (after this meeting in Jenny MacDougal's parlor) he will give that speech over and over again. It will always work because he means it. Helen knew he meant it. And the Union reversed its trend toward extinction on that night because he said what he said. Big Alabama Gibbs, who was there, always recounted the event by saying, "And that's when the lightnin' struck the outhouse. . ."

It was quite a speech for a lad from Devil's Own who didn't have the faintest idea how many bricks there were in all of Goodstone's walls. The entry Helen made in the minutes read like this, "*Moved and 2nd to throw out local officers responsible for riot*."

This was a nineteen-year-old girl's diary. It was not complete. When the men left, her father went up to bed and she checked the kids. Her next job was to lay out the breakfast dishes. As she was latching the front screen door she saw the shadow on the step. She knew it was Skinny Walker.

She slipped through the door to join him in the dark.

"What are you after?" she demanded in a husky whisper.

"I'm here to kiss your kiester," he said. The only way she could make him be quiet was to place one hand over his mouth and throw the other arm desperately around his neck.

The moon was up over East Akron and its limed light sifted through the porch railings. It was May and the meeting had been a good one. Skinny was tired of mating with a tirebuilding machine or discounted whores and Helen MacDougal had never been kissed.

They lay on the rough boarding, with Skinny's strength skewering her to the floor and his answer to her taunts was hard between her legs and heavy in the fresh wild cave of her belly. The first hurt left her after a while and she lay as if she were crucified. She felt him pulsate within her. His head and shoulders were silhouetted against the smoky moonlight.

She thought: *if the old man comes down now he'll kill him right*. Skinny lowered his face to her and she could see his eyes. They were livid scars across the white mask of his face. They were intense and fearless and alive with what he was doing to her.

He don't care if the old man hears or not—she told herself. She raised her lips to meet his and she thought: *I don't neither, neither, neither. . .*

80

Following is the text of a Confidential Memo from John J. Hobhouse to Harley Goodstone, transmitted sometime in May, 1953:

It has been suggested to me that the attention of my Committee be directed to the activities thought to be illegal, at least in part, of a personal faction within the jurisdiction of your management concern. In support of this suggestion many pertinent files have been forwarded to my office, and these I have personally reviewed.

Such material at hand, reinforced by general information already at my disposal, indicates that the labor authority within your collective bargaining area has been seized and is now successfully held by a small clique headed by a young unlettered workman bearing the name of Erskine Walker.

In my early assessment of this situation which is causing you alarm I am moved to submit some preliminary observations, both as a courtesy to you and as a partial explanation for my reluctance to devote my Committee's energy to this case, at this time.

It appears to me that the bargaining units within the great rubber industry have been placed in the general dominion of a clique which can only be characterized as ruthless and irresponsible. My lifelong crusade for personal liberty in behalf of our industrial citizen has brought me to grips with more than one such "colony of tyranny" in the industrial complex. Please believe me, Harley, I have heretofore found none so savage, none more violent and none quite so detestable as this represented in the Walker regime. Rest assured that I do, indeed, share your attitude toward this "Robespierre-in-rags."

The documented record plainly shows that Walker seized and has entrenched his power through an energetic assault on every principle held dear to the hearts of decent American workmen. He has repeatedly rebuffed mediation, nullified arbitration, and made a standing mockery of the spirit of negotiation. Not only has he encouraged "wildcat" strikes, he has, as shown in our film file, led them in person. He has run roughshod over the sanctity of a signed contract. The record gives ample demonstration that he has incited violent attacks on property as well as persons. He has abused management in public and in private sessions in an intolerable manner. Moreover, he has engaged in an extravagant circus of immorality since his very first hour in office.

Knowing that I believe all the foregoing, Harley, you will find it passing strange, after such a recitation, to now stand informed that the range of my Committee's inquiry does not, in my opinion at this time, strike within the orbit of those offenses.

For five years we have been concerned with excesses within the American labor movement flowing from two broad points of origination:

a. The Communist conspiracy
b. The Mafia

These focal points of our committed interest are, and have been, well defined. We have widened our range, perforce, to

82

include all varieties of leftist radicalism, as well as organized gangsterism. I have felt secure in this wider range, with the Committee's concurrence, and we have fortunately found good support both from the White House and the Hill. To depart entirely from these tracks would threaten our legislative existence and generate resentment from many sides.

I must tell you that no scrap of evidence has come before me to suggest that Walker is a product either of the Communists or the Mafia, or any combination of such forces, and my present machinery does not afford me any direct application to his case.

Having told you this, I must hasten to add a postscript which may help you to be of good heart. I cannot abandon an old friend in his distress simply because of procedural difficulties. Walker, I am convinced, is an episode in the long and generally beneficent continuity of your industrial empire. He represents an expensive, an irksome, nay a noxious episode, but only an episode nonetheless. However, ways and means do exist that may bring this episode to a quicker end than to let it run its worrisome course.

My many years as a friendly inquisitor of the true American labor movement have taught me the wisdom of an old, albeit cynical-sounding, adage, "There's more than one way to kill a cat."

For reasons given above, I do not feel free to move my official inquiry into the Akron cauldron at this time. I am prepared, dear friend, to engage myself in a quasi-official mission which offers me greater promise of halting Walker than any other means now available. My own knowledge of the situation, buttressed by thousands of secret informants, carries me to the conviction that Walker can be most expeditiously removed from the scene via some form of *purchase*. This news won't shock a sturdy businessman like yourself who knows that a market price can be set wherever a market can be found. You know, too, that my own passion for liberty makes me prefer the open tactic of riding the rascal out of town on a rail.

Since this is impractical at the moment due to larger considerations, I am willing to pay Walker the price for his departure. I say "pay him," meaning that I am willing out of sympathy for your predicament to serve as intermediary in such a payment.

It is a complicated course, to be served best with no publicity at all and with few, if any, accounting principles to honor. Many, many factors are involved, too numerous to itemize, and each of them is costly, per se. It will require the deposit of *eight hundred thousand dollars* in a third party account. From your point of view, this money must be a good-will investment, much as your advertising appropriation represents. For this sum, once deposited, I can make you a personal guarantee that Erskine Walker will see fit to remove himself, or will be removed from any opportunity to cause you further damage.

In the unlikely event that he does not respond to direct appeal at the level of "purchase," you then have my pledge of my Committee's unqualified pursuit of the same objective. Please have the above-named figure deposited in the Kansas City National Bank, credited to the account of Sylvia Hobhouse.

We send our cordial best wishes to you and Henrietta and all the family.

Jack.

Two 'factors made Goodstone stand out in the complex of Akron's tire factories. The first was its recruiting system which was based on a cliche and was unabashed about it. Goodstone wanted them fresh and strong, straight from the hills, if possible, and ready to mate their brute energies with machinery. Goodstone recruiters had a talent for finding them big and wild and fast on their feet. The other shops did likewise, but not so well, not so thoroughly. This was one thing that made Goodstone what it was.

The other thing was Goodstone's philosophy of "no ceiling" in earnings. This second factor flowed from the first, of course—since the fresh and the strong like to respond to incentive without any limit. The incentive system of the rubber industry's piece work scale was like a powerful motor, pulling a hundred thousand workers, faster and faster and faster.

At National Rubber and the smaller competitors, management knew the capacity of such a motor. They knew it needed to be governed. Overpowered motors burn up their components and accessories, which, in this case, were the human laborers lashed to the rawhide tempo. The others knew this, and established maximums or "limits" to individual productivity per shift. But Goodstone didn't. . .

When a good factory wage was $1.08 per hour, a strong, well-coordinated tirebuilder at Goodstone could make $4.00 an hour, almost four times the mean wage. It was a wondrous sight to behold, when the right man was at the right machine and there was no limit to inhibit him. Great arms flailing the plies, rippled shoulders in hard rhythm, neck swollen with the effort and sweat like oil covering the mighty torso.

To a young bucko such as Skinny the all-out magnificence of piece work production with no holds barred had a great appeal. It became an athletic event, not from any kind of desperation but from challenge and the thrill of doing what no builder had yet done. The bigger pay envelope was only an added sweetener to the event.

Against this release of productivity, the Goodstone Union pelted its own philosophy of the *"limit."* Departmental meetings of union men set their own limits for various tires on various occasions. This kind of unionism is difficult to enforce. In one sense, the voluntary establishment of a reasonable "pace" meant that the stronger, faster men were asked to hold down their effort for the slower, weaker men. This was not much of a sense. . .

In the Goodstone tire room there were no weak men. No slow men. They were all strong and fast men. So it required good logic to set a limit and better discipline to abide by it. Skinny knew all the rationale about Goodstone's breaking the rate, and how the company would "retime" a job at intervals, basing a new lower rate on the production history of the men who "ran over."

This wasn't enough to hold the limit. The fast men were very fast. When Goodstone's time study engineers considered the thousands of motions necessary for the fabrication of a single tire, and the foot pounds of energy expended in its making, it seemed utterly incredible to them that such workers could over-produce their quotas. Still, they did. It required an exorbitant devotion to principle to restrain them from excessive production.

In building his own concept of a union philosophy, Skinny Walker was forced to decide what his personal attitude felt about this issue. Skinny himself could whip out truck tires now with cunning speed. His machine was close to the stairs, and he always had time to talk or joke with his mates. Always had time to smoke. Always time for a long lunch. Yet he always "made out"—hit his limit on time, and was washed up and dressed in street clothes long before the shift ended.

Skinny Walker was one of the fresh and the strong. He belonged naturally to that group of the giants who would set the limit, hold the limit, enforce the limit—or break it all to smithereens.

Bull Wheeler and Rudy Haddon were of the same elite. Each was highly intelligent, superbly formed. They towered over Skinny and outweighed him individually by twenty-five pounds. They agreed at one point to go whole hog and break the limit.

"Forget it, Skinny," Bull advised him. "It's for the kids. Goodstone won't retime our tires—they'll be happy for the extra production."

"Won't they be using your records against all the others?" Skinny inquired.

"Someday, maybe. So what? We're here to work, not to sit on our butt. The money's *now*, not someday. Rudy and I can make two hundred dollars a week on the ticket we're running now. You could too."

"That's right," Rudy said. "Goodstone's got to run on averages. They can't retime just for the three of us. They got to keep the whole department in business."

Skinny pondered their argument.

"You'll bust your butt this year and for a while. What

happens when your G-string busts? Ten years from now you're petered out and the money you're making now will come back to haunt y'."

"Ten years from now?" Rudy laughed. "You'll be in a trench somewhere or deader'n a mackerel, courtesy of A-dolf Hitler and Bennett Marshall!"

"You're working us out of a job," Skinny asserted. "There's only so many tires to build. The thing over all of us is whatever Goodstone has on order. Once we fill the order, we're done. Isn't it better to spread the work?"

"Crap!" Bull exploded. "So many tires, so many dollars! An order's an order—fill it in a week or in a month, and then you're done anyway and there's only so much for wages any way you cut it! I'm building a house out in Tallmadge, kid, and I'd sooner work a week and be laid off for two than to work three damned weeks straight at a pace fit for an old lady!"

It was a hard issue for Skinny to resolve in his own mind.

Industrial citizenship is made up of such contentions. Skinny felt a strong kinship with Bull Wheeler and Rudy Haddon. He had identified with the Union, but so had they. He was emotionally opposed to management—but so were they. And the force of momentum was on their side. It was much easier to speed men up, even sluggish men, than it was to hold strong men back. In Soviet Russia, at this particular time, a version of Akron's rawhide system was working very well and on the same principle. The Bulls and Rudys there were called "Stakhanovites" after a coal miner who allegedly tripled his quota.

The two pacesetters proceeded to break the limit, while Skinny held to his discipline. In three days, a third of the department was inching over the agreed-on level of production, a dollar's worth here, two dollars there. Henry MacDougal and his stalwarts came to Skinny, ready for showdown. . .

"This whole place is going to go up in smoke," Mac told

Skinny in heavy warning tones. "It's getting like it used to be when the company union was running things."

"Maybe they're right, Mac? Maybe this isn't a union thing at all. Look at all that experimental machinery they're putting in upstairs. In six months, we'll all be out on our tail. Why don't we grab a few good pays before then?" Skinny wasn't arguing the case; he was stating the terms of his confusion. MacDougal was ready to answer him.

"A union's a union, boy! We just started getting some solidarity in this place. Your few good pays are splitting us all to hell. . .The Union decided on the limit—right? The Union is up for grabs the minute the limit goes by the boards. Forget all the legal talk, Skinny. There's just one question: *which side are you on?*"

It was a good question.

Which side *are* you on? Skinny went back to Rudy and Bull Wheeler to elucidate his answer.

"Sure, we're union, for Christ's sake! But there ain't no strike going on! Where the hell is MacDougal's picket line?"

And this is how Skinny Walker resolved his basic convictions. A union *was* a picket line, permanently working in the shop on a regular trick, just as much as standing shoulder-to-shoulder in front of the gate. A union-originated decision *was* a strike in itself, holding firm against all contrary decisions. The limit was a strike, and right or wrong (as far as legalistic details went) it had to be maintained. This was Skinny's side. He told the recalcitrants so.

"OK, Skinny," Rudy responded slowly. "You hold to the limit. We ain't asking anybody to keep up with us. But leave *us* alone. We'll put out what we feel like putting out. OK?"

No, it wasn't OK, and the next question was: how do you enforce the limit, once all arguments are exhausted?

Civilized society has no alternative to what happened.

The fight between Bull Wheeler and Skinny Walker took place in the locker room, and even the company cops watched it enthusiastically (no report was ever made). Bull's size and strength worried him; Bull was ten years older and had built a lot more tires. Bull was probably meaner, if such a trait could be measured in any particular way.

He hurt Skinny more than a little. At one point he almost choked the younger man into black-faced unconsciousness. At another, he held Skinny's head firmly and banged it like a gavel on the cruel corner of a wooden bench. Later in the conflict, Skinny slipped on a wet patch of cement which allowed Bull the opportunity of hitting him a solid blow before he could pull himself up.

It lasted well into the morning shift, a full hour of battle and the locker room was massed with men, on top of lockers, benches, shoulders, and standing on the wash basins. They were self-contained onlookers at the beginning, but they cheered raucously for Skinny long before it was over.

Bull Wheeler was a hard man to conquer. His weakness was vanity and he didn't really crumble until Skinny had worn him down, braced him with the back of a forearm against a steel-green locker and sledged him well in the mouth with a fierce right hand, three or four times. A vain man loses his spirit when he hears teeth cracking like sugar candy inside his own head...

Not that he yielded immediately, but he thought about it. Skinny sensed his equivocation and grew correspondingly more ferocious. In time, his head red and shaggy, Bull slid to his knees and slumped forward. The fight was all out of him.

"Hold it, Skinny," he mumbled. "I've just made out."

Skinny leaned over him, puffed and torn, ready to pull him to his feet, ready to carry on with the assault.

"Whose side you on, Bull?"

Neither man could talk plainly.

"Yours," Bull breathed. The silent crowd heard him. "I'm on your side, Skinny."

And so was the mass of Goodstone workers. The fight had wrapped the issue of the "limit" around Skinny Walker's shoulder like a gladiatorial toga. In making up his own mind,

90

and the minds of Wheeler and Haddon as well, Skinny had made up the minds of at least ten thousand other men.

Including the "dummies". . .These were the deaf mutes who worked in the shop. They were mute only because they couldn't hear a human voice, their own or anyone's. They called themselves "The Silents" but they were "dummies" to the rubberworkers. To Goodstone recruiters they were also fresh and strong. Their exclusion from audible society gave them a mad kind of concentrating ability. The loss of sense, both sensory and social, made them hard workers and hard fighters too.

Because they communicated with handsigns and notes only, it is likely that Goodstone believed the dummies would remain a clan of their own, aloof from the Union. There was good reason to assume this, until the famous locker room fight.

In sign language, there were no proper names. A mute would identify a third person to another mute with a gesture typifying the person to be identified. A squint-eyed ply-builder, for example, might have been called "Squint" by his talkative fellows. In the silent world it required a quick flicker of muscles around the eyes in order to designate "Squint," the man.

Some of them had watched Skinny lean over Bull, and they had read his lips as he asked the fallen man, "Which side are you on?" Shortly afterward the mutes joined the Union en masse. Their sign for Skinny was a hand movement rolling outward from the lips. It normally signified "speaking."

Now it identified Skinny Walker, "The Voice." Not that he was so voluble. Not that he was so articulate. But he was the Voice, the one the dummies recognized along with many others. His voice was learning to carry far. . .

Alabama Gibbs was puzzled about Skinny's personal life. Changing clothes in the locker room he had a pass at finding out. . .

"Fixed up tonight?"

"Who knows?"

It's hard to get information from a cat. The two men were side by side, stripping their work clothes from bodies still wet with sweat. On the same bench, they unlaced shoes and banged them respectively into the lockers.

"Ain't often you go without. . ."

Skinny laughed and stretched his nude torso.

"A broad's a broad," he said and threw a towel over his shoulder. His partner followed him to the shower room. Taller than Skinny and bulkier, he could still admire the shoulders, the good arms and the flat belly on the kid from West Virginia. He knew as a man (although his own wife had confirmed it for him) that Skinny Walker was a sweet man and could call his own tune with the girls. But it bothered

92

you to see a fellow so genuinely unattached. It was none of his business, really, but if a man can't make a deal with a woman, then maybe his deals just don't hold water? Alabama figured that Skinny would be a steadier cohort if he wore some woman's harness. (This was 1939 and Walker had been a tirebuilder for over a year.)

"How come you don't settle down?" he yelled through the hiss and froth of the shower.

"Wha-at?" Skinny called back.

"I said, you ever fixing to settle down?"

"Well, I *am* settled down! Look how long I been at Goodstone. . ."

"That ain't what I mean."

"What is it you *mean*?"

Briskly rubbing coarse towels over their bodies, nodding to shopmates, laughing at a fellow who got himself goosed just as the hot water went on, Alabama and Skinny didn't resume their conversation until back at their lockers.

"What I mean is, I got three kids. . .".

"You bragging or complaining?"

"They all look like me. That's not the point. I'm older than you, but not that much older. For Christ sake, don't you ever *want* a family?"

"I had a family. I could have done without."

"What kind of family you come from?"

"What the hell you doing—writing a book?"

"I got nose trouble, that's all. If I'm going to keep you out of trouble around here, I ought to know a little about you."

"I'll give you nose trouble, you dumb cracker. You sound like the FBI."

But Skinny smiled as he said it. They tugged up their neckties in unison, and walked together to the gatehouse where they punched their clocks and walked free of Goodstone's shadow.

"Drink?"

"Why not?" Alabama answered. "I'm going to catch hell

when I go home anyway."

"You see why I'm not settling down, don't you?"

They maneuvered the shift-change traffic on Market Street and entered the Lenox Cafe. At a corner booth, each man had a beer and a shot.

"What about your family?"

"I was putting you on. There's only my old man. My maw died a long time ago."

"You never had—?"

"No. No brothers. No sisters. A granddaddy for a while, then just me and the old man. He's a mine inspector near Devil's Own. Still lives in the cabin where I was raised. Where I was jerked up—is more like it."

The foam of the beer chased the bolt of whiskey and sought to comfort it. Alabama studied his friend. He *was* a good-looking man, for a young one. Face cut out of sandstone, eyes narrow and straight; sure of himself, but friendly—a ridge runner just getting civilized.

"What about a family of your own? Skinny, it ain't real good to be a loner for too long. I know that a woman is a pack of trouble but it sure keeps a house from getting lonely."

"It'll come. Maybe it'll come. I been a long time with no woman around the house. I tell you, Alabama. A broad's a broad. . ."

He'd met Florabella Gibbs. There was no way he could tell the man how sorry he felt for him, tied up with such a miserable creature and three kids to boot. She was a dumpy, redheaded, dough-faced broad who knew how to cook grits and not one damned thing more than that.

On the third round of drinks, Alabama said sorrowfully, "I'm not talking broads, Skinny. I'm talking *family*. Every man's got to have a family."

"Goodstone pass some new law?"

"Goodstone be damned! It's just the way it is. Have you ever really been sweet on a gal? I mean all the way—just

94

paralyzed?"

Skinny took a long time answering. He never thought of his mother as a girl, although he was as old now, just about, as she was when she passed away. And the vision of Mrs. Nick Charles passed through his mind, but it was no business of Alabama Gibbs at all.

"I like 'em all when Christmas hits me. If there was a parson built into the mattress, I'd be married every time."

It's hard to get information from a cat, but Gibbs kept on trying.

"There's *good* gals, Skinny! You know what I mean? I mean there's gals who you should lay and gals you should wife. I know Floss ain't going to take first prize anywhere, but I was here a year before I sent for her. She was fresh and ready and home-folks type. She was *all mine.* I jumped all over town, before Floss got here—just like you. You don't know what it means to open the bedroom door and see a big woman under the sheets and know: *that's my wife.* She's for *me.* And no matter where you are or what you're doing, you know she's back there waiting for you. *Just for you.* You been here quite a spell now. Don't you hanker none for apple pie, real home-baked, and your necktie don't get in the way?"

"I don't wear a necktie much."

After four beers and four shots, Skinny Walker was bored with his buddy's preachments. Marriage, as Alabama so vigorously stated, had to be built on a need. He just didn't need it, that was all. He forged his own illusion of permanency by never being without love. The faces were different but the act was the same. The succession of episodes was so rapid, the blur of his beloved's image was a constant portrait. He knew without asking that he was in a woman's flesh more often than this stalwart husband hoped to be, bedded down securely with his grits and apple pie.

"A gal wants me," he confided, getting ready to terminate the conversation, "and I want a gal, then I don't care where she's been before. If she's reasonably clean, I mean. With me, she's all mine while I'm having her. Somebody else can pay the rent after that. Somebody else can pick up the pieces. You marry 'em, Alabama. I'll just take my chances in between."

"I ain't never messed with any of your gals, Skinny."

Skinny laughed, and the contempt was all there, showing. "No? Well, I ain't messed with any of *your* wives either."

They parted at the door. Alabama turned to head for his Chevy in the parking lot and Skinny stood on the curb wondering who would wife him this evening? He couldn't resist calling after Gibbs. . .

"Where you preaching tomorrow night?"

Alabama's answer, if he answered at all, was lost in the noise of the traffic.

Much later, at the Cork N' Bottle, a shoeshine boy accosted Skinny Walker, who was still without a family. The boy was sandy-haired, freckled, mean-mouthed. Perhaps he was ten years old.

"Shine, Mister?"

"What time is it?"

"Midnight. Thereabouts."

"What the hell you doin' out so late?"

"What the hell's it to y'?"

Skinny's hand was around the boy's neck instantly. From a comatose drunk, he was suddenly a stern patriarch, and faster to move than the boy could have guessed.

"Ain't you got no maw and paw to keep you in at night?"

"Sure I have, Mister. They know what I'm doing."

He wasn't plaintive in his responses, but he was being carefully polite. He wriggled to test the grip and he knew the man was strong; he cast an uneasy eye around to see what help could rescue him, if need be.

"Honest, Mister. I live on Case Avenue."

"They know what you're doing? What kind of a family you got?"

"There's six kids—counting me. I'm next to the oldest. My

paw used to work at Goodstone but he was laid off."

"Name? What's his name? You got a name or not?"

"My name's Gene. Eugene Willoughby. My paw's name is Willoughby."

"Your whole damned family's named Willoughby?"

"What's you expect? *Smith*?"

Skinny closed his grip, enough to punish the kid for impudence.

"I expect you to get home. S'too late for a kid out like this. You go home where y' belong. You got a home?"

"Thirty-seven South Case Avenue. I *tol'* you that."

Skinny let him loose. The boy watched him warily while he fumbled in his pocket for money. He placed a fifty-cent piece in the boy's hand.

"Go home, Snotty. Go home and look at all those brothers and sisters. Go home to your family where you belong. Let your maw tuck you in and kiss you goodnight. . ."

The boy nodded that he would and bolted for the door. He hovered there tentatively, and then he screeched,

"*My old lady's drunk and won't be home till morning!*"

Then he scudded out the door and down the street.

His benefactor signaled the bartender.

"Another shot." He stared at his glass and looked at the doorway, with the strident, lost, triumphant cry of the shinie echoing in his ears. "That's all I need," he mumbled to himself. "A family like that would really fix me up."

J. B. Walker patiently tried in June of 1959 to explain things to the Wheeling physician.

"He ain't right, Doc, and he ain't been right. I figured I ought to see a medical man such as yourself and if the cost ain't excessive, you might come on out and take a look at him direct. . .

"Man and boy he ain't had a sick day in his life. The good Lord took care of that department and of course he comes from hardy stock. The best way I could put it is that he seems dimwitted, retarded, like they say. He's my own child and his maw's been gone since he was knee-high. He ain't had a lot of schooling but he was always bright. Matter of fact, he was sharp-tongued for folks like us, and he sure made his way up there in Akron with the unions and all.

"You recollect that? It's been a spell now. Him and me's been grubbing along together at the old place. I don't mind. It was company at first. He wouldn't take no relief, just some whiskey that I gave him. Like you always figure, I figured he'd pull out of it. I figured, just laying around and nursing his wounds would do it...

"The leg is healed, as far as that goes. Bothers him in certain weathers. It ain't his health. *It's his disposition.* What good is a man who won't talk and won't hunt, even if he ain't right for working? It's not that I mind. Between the retirement fund and fill-in work, we got all the cash we require. He gives me trouble mainly because he ain't no trouble.

"He never was a trouble to me—except in the papers. Me and his uncles, we always treated him like a man. His own granddaddy knew him better than me. O, some capers in his teens, on a tear now and then—but he never brought me nothing you could call *grief*. He took off from here back in nineteen and thirty-eight. About twenty-three, he was. No hard feelings, just going out for work, which was proper at the time, the mines being slow and getting slower.

"Never wrote. Never saw no Army service, probably due to that Union business he was in. I'da felt better if he'd gone in, but it wasn't for me to say. I wouldn't hear nought from him for the longest spells, five years at a time, and then I'd read about him in the paper or hear about him on television when I was in town. He owed me nothing except respect which he always gave me. He's my boy, Doc, old as he is, and a man takes care of his own.

"No, he never married, far as I know. We get boys like that. I got me three nephews about his age and they never married neither. One in Pittsburgh, name of Ewell Walker, is a second helper in the mill and making very good wages. At least there's no one making claim on him. No help either. I just can't understand that Union of his. Since they broke away from the Mineworkers they don't seem to take care of their members. He's got no insurance, no pension, nothing. Don't hardly seem right.

"Don't you worry about payment. I'll stand good for whatever it takes to make him right.

"How does he act? It ain't that so much. He don't act much at all. He yells in his sleep sometimes, but that's to be expected, ain't it? Him a cripple and all? And if I left him, which ain't often, he'll get a snootful of whiskey, which any man will do, given a chance. Mostly, he won't talk. Nothing to say. He's too quiet. I don't mean he's brooding. I don't even mean he *minds* much. Mind what? O, mind not doing *nothing*. Mind being such a stick-in-the-mud as he is. He was one time used to lots of excitement, let me tell you.

"Depressed? You mean—let down? Well sir, that's what I'm trying to tell you. What would you call it when a man is so depressed he don't even care about being depressed no more? He's got no spunk in him. Nossir! He'd no more lift a hand to kill hisself than he'd shave hisself, if I didn't pressure him to keep clean, at least as far as two men living together goes. He ain't pretty, but he's not *wild* either. I just wouldn't put up with that. . .

"It's not that he feels bad, and it's not that he's in pain, so to speak. He just ain't *there*. It ain't natural for a man to sit around and lay around and go to pieces the way he has. Nossir! I would not institutionalize him for a million dollars. He's my kin and you wouldn't get anybody in twenty miles to sign a complaint! He harms nobody. And nobody cares. He stays with me, and I'm the one that cares. That's the long and short of it.

"What would I be doing, anyway? His maw is resting up there on my land. He's got any number of stillborn brothers and sisters buried there too. I belong up there, not in some dern boardinghouse where you have to wait to go to the bathroom. And he is welcome there with me. He belongs there as long as I do, which is as long as I can keep my taxes paid.

"I proposed to ask you just to take a look at him, that's all. I didn't call for no X-rays or institutions or charity neither. I figured you'd come out and I would pay you a reasonable sum for the trip. Just you take a look and give me some assurances. That's what I need.

"No! It ain't trouble to me that I'm concerned about. It's just that—well, what if he needed something, y'know? Maybe a tooth pulled or a pill or something? And maybe that would make him right again?

"I'll tell you this—I'll never get him willingly to come into town. He's done with towns, that's for certain. I'd have to hogtie him and carry him, which I'm not about to do. *He* don't know there's anything wrong.

"You know your job. I'm not denying that. If it ain't practical for you to see him, then we'll leave it be. As for me, it ain't practical for me to commit him to no institution neither. Him and me will live our days right in that old cabin with no harm to anyone. I been in that county for sixty-three years and it's good enough for my boy as well. I keep him dry and I keep him fed, which is more than I can say for all your city doings.

Not long after the fight with Bull Wheeler, Skinny became a Committeeman and the Company put his name on the list of men to reckon with. As a representative for his department he learned the complicated arithmetic of piece work rates and the elaborate diplomacy of classifications. By now he was acquainted with the geography of the plant and all its subdivisions. He was becoming fluent with the rubber-making process, and he made it his business to understand the conveyors, the mills, the molds and every important machine.

It was an intense (but not difficult) education for him. If you understand the men who run them, the machines come easy. . .Skinny had to know his own men and this was simple enough. He had to figure out the psychological workings of management too—from the Squadron boys through the foremen, all the way to the plant superintendent and top management itself. The white collar breed bothered him for a spell. He studied them and pondered them and tested them in violent arguments.

Mostly he talked. To the older men, the ones who had grown up in the shop. And he learned. Skinny Walker learned so fast that he could have replaced Bennett Marshall as Vice President in charge of Goodstone Operations. If he had known how to wear French cuffs and drink a Martini. And if Goodstone had known how fast he was learning. . .

The Labor Department had an interesting file (and probably still has). The first notation, in November 1939, on Walker, Erskine reads: "single, rmghse, no educ., commtmn 152 A-102X." Clyde Thymer, Personnel Director, knew what "102X" codified. It meant *"to be laid off first opportunity."*

But—no education? This was false on two counts. First, Skinny's six years in a country schoolhouse were worth more than a contemptuous "no educ." Secondly, Thymer underrated his own environment. Skinny was like a Chinese peasant who has come from a remote village to stumble unknowingly upon the Great Wall. He has felt its stones and mortar, traced its clever joinings. He has slept beside it and huddled in its shadows. Now he stands and looks it over with a measure of contempt. He knows its secret. Inside the factory, *Walker, Erskine* had pitched his intelligence to learn the mammoth meaning of it all. No education? We shall see. . .

For a year and a half he was a dedicated student. His enthusiasm came from his never-ending capacity to be surprised. Surprise is a muted form of astonishment and astonishment is a version of fear. It is an attribute of animals, in the sense that a dog is surprised by a new smell. Just remember that dogs don't run away from smells.

The factories of Akron had surprised Skinny Walker and frightened him—at first. Others had made the factories and they were alien to him. A source of danger and possibly destruction. But he nosed into their innards aiming to find the core of the thing and quiet the fear that moved him.

He had to conquer the unsettling feeling of strangeness and inferiority. He knew (without thinking of it) that he could conquer his fear only through conquering the source of that fear.

The builders of factories are not afraid of them because they have fathered them. The owners have their deeds in their lock boxes so they are not frightened. They have the easy knowledge that they need only turn a key and the noise of the factory would be instantly silenced. Since Skinny Walker was neither an engineer nor a financier, he had only one path for his conquest. He had to lead the brutes who made the factory go. Through a living union of their human capacity he might bring the factory system to heel.

The union hall was part of this. Since the riot, it had been moved to Case Avenue, in the second story of a squatting frame structure which had one time housed the Royal Casino. During the first world war the Casino had been a ribald theater where shimmy queens tied strips of tinsel to their nipples and rolled their bellies at the grinning lust of gum miners too tired from double shifts to go to bed.

Skinny attended many meetings here. He went down almost every morning (at shift's end) to write up grievances and make reports to Burke Danver who was chairman of the shop grievance committee. He learned more from Burke Danver than from any one man.

Danver was Canadian-born—a strong, laconic man. He had a massive forehead, inset eyes and a muscle-clamping jawbone. Skinny had the idea that Danver should run for president of the local union and this idea caused many things to happen. Among them, it caused Burke Danver to talk. . .

"No use to bully me, Walker," Danver said one morning. "I won't run. But I'll tell you why. . ."

Skinny had heard some talk about Burke Danver; he wanted to hear the story firsthand. This was his seminar in labor history.

"I'll say first off that I know *you*, Walker. I spotted you the first time I heard you speak on the floor. Your voice rings out, know what I mean? I said to myself, *they'll eat him too*. And they will. They'll crucify you, boy."

104

This didn't bother Skinny Walker. He wanted to hear the story.

"I was building passenger tires (Burke went on) when Roosevelt's Section 7-A came along. There wasn't anything like a union at Goodstone except the Assembly. I happened to be friends, after a fashion, with Herman Boettinger who was nothing but an out-and-out criminal lawyer at the time."

Skinny knew Boettinger by reputation. He was now a prominent star in John L. Lewis's corps of lawyers.

"So I went to him. I said: Herm, tell me what this 7-A means? He studies it a day or two and then he tells me: *You can organize.* He says the government *wants* us to organize. So we proceeded to organize. I rented a basement hall on Goodstone Boulevard and we put out the call. We hit the jackpot, Walker. Two hundred tirebuilders signed up that first meeting. I had Herman there to tell them what he told me. Man, we were organizing a mile a minute."

"The Company left you well enough alone?" Skinny asked.

"Hell no. They fired me once and hired me back. But how could I go on working? The way we were growing? So the boys voted me into a full-time job with the new Union. I gave up ten years' seniority to take it. Remember we didn't have recognition or a contract or a tiddley-toot. But they voted it and I took it. Before long, by God, we were filling East High School's auditorium."

This was how Skinny Walker learned his history, listening to Burke Danver tell it in a union hall. Burke was a different cut than the bush country boys and Skinny liked him especially.

"A few months of this and we were ready for our own International. As long as we didn't have our own International, old Granny Green was milking us dry. We paid all of our per capita tax direct to Bill Green. We were too big for that and we knew it. Bill Green didn't know it. He said: *No, you can't have your own International.* He loved all that dues money coming in from thousands of

105

rubberworkers. . ."

"What's all the talk about craft unions against industrial unions?" Skinny never had understood that point.

"That's talk. I'm telling you how it happened. You can give that craft versus industrial crap to the birds. We had a meeting to start our own International Federation down in Indianapolis. I went representing Goodstone Local. It was supposed to be a secret but all the wire services were there and when I got back to Akron it had hit the fan."

"You were out?"

"Out? I was out like Grogan's goat! I read about my expulsion in the newspaper. Green's hatchetman said: Burke Danver is as far out of the American Federation of Labor as a Chinaman walking the streets of Hong Kong."

Skinny felt anger rising in him like a sword.

"Didn't it have to come up before the membership?"

"Yes indeedy—it came before the membership. What a damned joke it was! Men I had worked with for ten years—side by side. The same men who had stomped and hollered when they made me full-time Secretary. The membership decided, all right. That's why I'm warning *you*. They packed the high school just to hear Green's motion to expel me. They sat there and listened to a high-priced goon call me names and accuse me of crimes that would make your blood run cold. He ranted and raved for almost two hours on how I had to be railroaded out of the Union. Instead of coldcalking him, I waited for my chance to speak. I'd stayed up all night planning my speech in self-defense. My old lady helped me. She went to high school herself. . ."

"I bet that was a sonofabitchin' speech," Skinny grinned.

"I bet it was. Only thing was—I never made it. They ruled I couldn't say a word. *Not one damned word*! They took a vote, with none dissenting and there I was—*out*."

Skinny mulled it over in his mind. He was never in his life to read a history text (on American labor or any other subject). But he got the essence of the story from Burke

Danver all in one sitting. And Skinny Walker was going to form an International of his own in the not-too-distant future. Without shape, seeds of conviction were stirring in his mind. . .

"I heard something about the waterworks, Burke. What about you and the waterworks?"

"The waterworks? That came later. I sold insurance until '37 when I was recalled to Goodstone when things picked up. In the time I'd been gone the CIO had come in, and your *industrial unionism* was in full sway. I was working with the graveyard shift—no seniority or anything. My second night on the job I heard there was a big strike on the city waterworks. A CIO committeeman comes down the line and he says to me: *All union men at the waterworks first thing in the morning.* . .He don't know me from Adam, but he's telling everybody that."

Skinny waited for Danver to relive the morning at the waterworks, with his big jaws working in a meditative convulsion.

"I hadn't been signed up yet in the CIO but I consider myself a union man, with or without a card. So I head up to the waterworks. It was still dark, but I could see a mass of men already there. I didn't know it at the time but it was a mass of cops and special deputies. I parked down the way and ran into a guy from National Rubber. We walk over to this body of men, kind of feeling our way. They yell: *CIO?* We holler: *Yes!* Want me to tell you right now just how many union men were *actually* there that morning?"

Skinny nodded.

"*Two.* Me and that National man. That's how many. We hollered 'Yes' and we never said no more. They broke my nose, four of my ribs, shattered my collarbone, gave me a rupture and concussion of the brain. When they got me downtown to the station I demanded medical treatment. They said *Sure.* So two cops ran me up and down the three story steps of the jailhouse until I blacked out. Boy, those waterworks just about did to me what Bill Green couldn't do."

Skinny looked at the man, not a big man. A strong fellow with a harsh-angled face and a quiet, meaningful voice.

"First thing my wife did was to call Herm Boettinger. He was the CIO's legal counsel then. He came down in a hurry—*but not for me*. He bailed out the National man, paid his fine and his hospital bills. He had a card in the CIO, y'see? And I didn't."

"I still think you'd make one hell of a president," Skinny argued.

"Thanks, Skinny. But don't forget what I'm telling you. I can see my own shadow on you. Watch out they don't crucify you. . ."

"Me? What the hell can they do to *me*?"

"I don't know," Danver laughed softly. "But we'll find out. I'm going to nominate *you* for President of this Union."

Three weeks later he did.

You've probably seen Skinny in the newsreels since then, during a strike vote or a big union election. He learned to move like a field marshal—campaigning at every factory gate, winning support with a hillbilly mixture of charm and guts and cunning strategy. He wasn't like that at his first election. He worked his job and he drank his drinks, more on the quiet side than usual, as the balloting was going on. Burke Danver built his cross for him. Skinny felt a wave of fear as the crowd assembled to cheer the crucifixion. . .

It was a bigger event than anyone expected. Skinny Walker: 4,560 votes for President of Goodstone Local 2. All other nominees (four nameless fellows) garnered 820.

Something bigger than the factory was rising. It carried Skinny Walker on its shoulders. He was scared by it. He didn't let anyone see his fear. But he looked around for whips and instruments of security. You might have done the same.

108

It is one tremendous feeling. Lindbergh had it when he rode down Manhattan and the ticker tape fell all around him. Babe Ruth had it in Yankee Stadium. A man named Roosevelt was having it at the time. It began with recognition. . .

Skinny walked on the street and they hailed him. He came out of the factory superintendent's office and the truckers signaled in warm fraternity. He went into the chambers of the City Council and the newspapermen clapped him on the shoulders.

Storekeepers, housewives, children—most of Akron came to know the sign of Skinny Walker. There were other Union presidents around, of course. None of them had the identifying distinction that he had. None was so young, so glamorous, or so gutty. He was Ted Williams, Billy Graham and John Dillinger all rolled into one. Before his twenty-sixth birthday the newspaper had printed a cartoon of him. (It showed a callow youth playing marbles and the marbles were

109

tagged "Akron's workers." The caption said, "Hey, Skinny!
No fair cheating!")

Recognition for many was a form of hate and antagonism.
But for many more it grew into love. It was the kind of love
a parish priest receives on Saturday afternoon. A platoon
commander feels it from his men just before the jump-off.
Every college coach knows the feeling (especially if his team
is winning). Kings are born and trained to handle such a
general adulation.

Skinny Walker was a kind of king. But he had no training
for the job. He had his First Minister's warning (from old
Burke Danver) and he hailed his legions on the street. He also
kept his eyes squinted narrowly to watch for daggers. . .

He was a warm, human fellow with strong impulses for
brotherhood and camaraderie and lovingness. This is true of
all soldiers in combat. He was paternalistic (in the clan sense)
and an injury to one, for him, was truly an injury to all.
Industrial accidents appalled him. He therefore made
management suffer with statistics and the expense of reducing
the toll. Injustice angered him. As President, he fought for
solidarity in the rubber shops with a jealous dynamism. He
had a loyalty which never forgot that "*who is not with me is
against me.*"

Say all this and then say (along with many observers at the
time) that Skinny Walker was cruel and savage, merciless and
predatory, ignorant and power-minded. He was, indeed.

A good wife might have tempered him. If he'd had
children of his own, he might have eased up in his
stewardship of the ridgerunners, the Swedes and the Dagoes
and the thousands of plain knotty men who filled the
factories.

When he was twenty-six, Burke Danver's wife was
forty-two. You can't make a marriage out of that. Besides,
Burke Danver wouldn't like it. . .

Pauline Danver was a tall woman with jet-black hair,
stained with gray above her cool white forehead. She had

110

aquiline features and a cameo-pure profile. Her eyes were large and gray with silver flecks. She wrote speeches for Skinny Walker as she had done for her husband long ago. As they conferred over such a speech, she would study him—her big eyes drowning him with their clarity and depth. He had taken to radio for his talks to the union membership and this caused him to confer with Pauline several times a week.

"Tell them I'm sick of this crap about rates that don't hold water," he'd advise her as she'd translate his idiom.

"You can't talk like that on the air," she'd laugh indulgently. "Do you mean they fluctuate the rates from shift to shift and man to man?"

He would lean forward and stare fixedly at the pulse of her throat above her full bosom.

"That's exactly what I mean, little mother. I'm just plain sick of all that horse man-ewer..."

And his radio message would be broadcast later with his robust almost-tenor voice saying: *Management knows I won't put up with rate discrimination! Management knows that arbitrary fluctuation of rates has got to stop! Management knows...*

For his audience they were damned effective speeches. Pauline kept the original flavor (as she cleaned the phrasing up) and Skinny departed from his script just enough to give them the sound of an extemporaneous rendering.

His handsome editor watched him closely. He was reaping all the harvest her Burke had been denied. His nose wasn't broken, nor his collar bone, nor his ribs, nor his militant spirit...Her two children were grown and had homes of their own. The chief difference between Burke and Skinny (now that Skinny was President) was that Burke was still building tires. Skinny, not bound to any shift, had his own erratic schedule. He came to the Danver house one night twenty minutes after Burke had gone to the shop.

Pauline was just settling herself in the tub, ready to soak herself into a ready-for-sleep languor. The bell rang and she

wrapped a terrycloth robe around her. It was Skinny at the
door—unsteady, ashamed, not very sober. . .

"Li'l mother—."

"What do you want, Skinny Walker?"

"You know damn well what I want."

He threw himself on the sofa.

"Start me with a bottle of beer," he commanded.

She brought him a bottle of beer and sat watching him as
he drank.

"You're up to no good, aren't you, Skinny Walker?"

"I'm up to real good, Pauly. Best I ever been. I been
carrying this around for a coon's age and I'm here to unload
it. . ."

"Unload what?"

"*This.*"

He rose toward her and (before she could protest) he had
the robe off her. He embraced her in a giant, irreverent but
irresistible manner. She stood shivering in his arms and
allowed him to kiss her. He looked down at her still-wet hair,
with his hands flat on her bare, damp shoulders.

"Pauly! I got to have you. That's what I'm here for."

She unwound from his embrace. Retrieved her robe from
the floor, donned it and sat down. She needed to rewrite this
speech as quickly as possible. . .

"What would you like, Skinny? A quick lay? Or a long
engagement until the divorce is over?"

He sat himself down and held the half-emptied beer bottle
in his big hands, solemnly.

"You tell me, li'l mother. Just as long as I get you."

"There's no quick lay in this house, Skinny. I've been Mrs.
Danver for twenty-three years. Do you have any idea of how
many nights that is?"

" 'Bout as many as I've been alive, I reckon. . ."

"You try to make a quick lay out of me and I'll cut your
horn off! I'm a professional wife. That's what I mean to be."

He couldn't force himself to look at her. The memory of

her cool skin was in his fingers. The fleeting vision of her succulent body filled him with longing.

"Would you be wife to *me*, Pauly?"

"*Do I look like Helen MacDougal to you?*"

He had to smile at that. The old gal had eyes in the back of her head. He had fancied that the MacDougal affair was less obvious.

She stood and walked briskly to the door.

"I'll tell you something, boy. *You don't look like Burke Danver to me!* Now go do your cattin' someplace else. . ."

(A good wife might have tempered him. . .) He stood with a wry smile on his face, knowing he was defeated. As he passed her, he placed a slight kiss on her brow.

"I'm goin', Pauly. No need to put the leather to me."

As he pulled open the door, by some magic of motion so fast it was timeless she dropped the robe to her feet. She stood there with her breasts up and her legs like marble columns. She allowed him to cover her with his eyes, slowly and tragically. He could never understand why she gave him that last view. Or if he should have gone back. . .

He didn't go back. Instead he hired a girl college student to make sense out of his speech-writing. Her name was Vicky. Her grammar was better than Pauline's and she was happy to oblige Skinny in every endeavor. She was only nineteen and enthusiastically athletic. Her body, however, was no match for the one he had seen (and had not taken) that night at Burke Danver's house.

So you must not think his road to power was without its rough spots. . .As the crowd cheered along the way, there were voices here and there which were not cheering. And if you have heard that cheer (as Lindbergh and Babe Ruth and Skinny Walker have heard it) you know that it is awesome and beastlike—with bloodcurdling echoes.

With Henry MacDougal as Vice President and Burke Danver as Chairman of the Grievance Committee, Goodstone Local Two (with the Walker slate in office) had the strongest leadership it was ever to have. They still had no contract. Fourteen thousand members, of whom over half signed up during the Walker regime, but the company steadfastly refused to sign. Its signature to a contract would mean official recognition. It would establish certain rights—the exclusive bargaining agent's position, a check-off system for union dues, the easing of friction in processing grievances.

Without a contract, the Union held its de facto authority through unauthorized "wildcat" strikes. Skinny was an expert at coordinating wildcat work stoppages. When he passed the word to his cohorts: *Pull the switch*—the switch was pulled. Whole floors would darken. A thousand men mysteriously decided to shut down for the shift. No debate, no vote, no palaver. Just the working of Skinny Walker's will in the effort to force Goodstone to sign a contract. Not a day passed in all the year of 1941 that such a strike did not occur—in some department, by some means.

When *would* the Company sign?

The main switch available to Skinny was the one he was reluctant to pull. He could shut down all plants in the Goodstone system. Shut 'em down hard—simultaneously. The flaw was that other rubber firms had already signed contracts and with no strike at all. By this time Skinny was looking beyond the orbit of Local Two. He was thinking in terms of power wider and deeper than Goodstone by itself. He badly needed a bloodless victory. . .

In his sessions with Mahogany Row he put his case well—to Clyde Thymer, Bennett Marshall and their aides-de-camp.

"I know production is hurtin', boys," he commiserated with them. "I get reports the same as you do."

"Don't kid me, Walker," Marshall barked. "You get reports *before* these stoppages occur!"

Skinny was unruffled by the charge.

"As I say, it looks like feeling is building up in the worst way. It appears to me that just maybe you are all wanting a plant-wide strike. I can't read your minds. You know we

114

represent 90% of your work force. . ."

"Nothing of the kind! We have had wild claims like that for the last twenty years," Thymer complained. "We can't recognize *your* claims, Walker—and then have the A.F. of L. or I.W.W. come barging in, claiming a majority all their own. We can't do it!"

"That 90% is a wild claim in itself," Marshall added.

"Boys," Skinny replied. "You talk about wild and I can *be* wild. I said 90%. *I meant 90%.* That's a nice, easy-going ninety percent, let me tell you. That's ninety percent of Goodstone workers who got every reason in the world to think their management will act white and decent about their petition. I got that ninety percent right here. . ."

Skinny stood and patted one pocket. They were assembled in a conference room, facing each other across a long plain table. MacDougal, Danver, Red Cameron and Alabama Gibbs waited for the signal to leave. It sure didn't look as if the company was ready to sign. . .

"You don't know what I got in this other pocket, do you?" Skinny stared at Thymer deliberately. "*I got 100% in that one. That hundred percent is a mean hundred percent.* Christ — but it's mean. That's every department, every plant, every elevator operator and every office worker you got on your payroll, Mr. Thymer. It's so damned *total* that I even got you and Mr. Marshall in it."

Thymer and Marshall looked at each other. Skinny scratched himself in the crotch with careful insolence.

"Yep. This other pocket o' mine can keep you out of your own offices. You can't take my word, so I may have to rub your noses in it. I may have to take all my men and line 'em up on the street so as you all can recognize them. I may just have to do that. . .C'mon boys." Skinny's men rose to leave with him.

"You do that, Walker, and your strike will have your men so broke and hungry they'll eat *you* before it's over," Thymer cried.

"I'm a hard man to digest, Mr. Thymer," Skinny drawled. "I forgot to tell you something. I got another pocket I didn't even mention. *I just may have to shut down the whole damned rubber industry because you boys are so rotten stubborn.* You chew on that a while before you start eatin' Skinny Walker."

Then they left. The telegram reached Skinny that night: GOODSTONE CORP. RECOGNIZES LOCAL TWO. SIGN TOMORROW. MARSHALL. They had knuckled to Skinny Walker—thirty days before Pearl Harbor.

Felix Grazzio deposited his daily report in the mailbox, not without pride. It read as follows:

Your Operative No. 26 staked out the Subject at the Dollar Hotel 6:06 A.M. on the morning of Friday, March 11, 1942. According to the desk clerk who was on duty all night, Subject retired shortly before dawn. Estimated retiring time: 4:30 A.M. Since said clerk was not prone to divulging facts to strangers.

Subject first seen in lobby at 7:25 sharp. Was shaved, wore a white shirt, no tie, and dark colored coat-sweater. He walked east on Market Street to the Lenox Cafe where he ordered breakfast of ham and eggs (two) while making indecent remarks to the waitress who served him. She appeared to consider this part of the terms of her employment. Six people addressed him in passing but nobody, except aforementioned waitress, engaged in discussion.

At 8:03 A.M., after really insulting the waitress (who pretended not to mind) and leaving her seventeen cents tip,

Subject walked west on East Market Street downhill, over the Erie bridge to Case Avenue intersection. There he was engaged in conversation with City Patrolman Badge No. 398. Topic of conversation not known. Both Patrolman Badge No. 398 and Subject were seen to wave greetings to a known prostitute in second story window at 8 South Case Avenue. (This may be of interest.) Prostitute unknown by name. (Perhaps Judy?)

Blue 1938 Chevrolet (Lic. No. 892-004) pulled to curb headed south on Case Avenue (where Western Cut Rate Store is located) and Subject crossed street to engage in conversation with driver. (About 40 years old, white, wearing cap.) Topic of conversation not known. Subject appeared upset at one point in discussion (this may be of interest) and appeared to be threatening driver of 1938 Chevrolet.

At 8:31 A.M., Subject entered Union Offices at 27 North Case. Six or seven men were waiting for his arrival, at least half of them (or three) were in advanced drinking condition, evident by loud noises and profanity. It is custom of fourth shift men to drink from 6:30 A.M. throughout morning. Subject seemed to take all in stride and was soon closeted in private office where all telephone calls were monitored and appear in separate Report for April 11 (headed Telephone Report).

10:14 A.M., a violent fight broke out in the waiting room wherein one chair (folding) was broke up as well as one leg from a bench, and two men (tirebuilders) required medical attention. Subject heard noise of fight at its outbreak and was seen directly by your Operative to join the battle. He struck one of the men involved very sharply and was heard to yell loudly, "Get out in the street for your fighting!" The man, later identified as Patrick "Red" Coyne, went to the hospital instead. Subject broke Coyne's jaw in full view of your Operative although the official report attributed the "accident" to the man he was directly brawling with before Subject interfered. That man, known as "Spangles," (no last name found out) was also hit by Subject but suffered injuries

118

when leg from broken chair (folding) penetrated his groin.

Subject arbitrarily ordered all witnesses off Union premises (for reasons best known to himself) and your Operative took up the stake on street until 11:56 when Subject next appeared in company of two girl secretaries and man by name of Gibbs. This foursome was followed to White Front Cafe, 12 South Case Avenue, where they were observed from 12:02 until 12:59, eating lunches (wherein Subject imbibed 4 glasses of alcoholic beverage, namely beer).

Leaving the White Front Cafe (12 S. Case) at precisely 1:00 P.M., Subject told passerby the following words, "I'll be back about 4:30. I've got a meeting at Mahogany Row." This referred to a Management-Labor meeting scheduled for 2:00 at Goodstone Tower. Your Operative assumed this was a good time for his own lunch and acted accordingly at the same abovementioned White Front Cafe. From auxiliary reports and careful back-tracking, however, your Operative can report that this turned out to be not so good a time for lunch as previously figured.

Subject arrived at Goodstone Tower not until 2:47 P.M. which caused distress to the many men of both parties who were waiting for him. It appears that he stopped at the Dollar Hotel and was entertained by one of the Arlington Restaurant waitresses (identity unknown) in his own hotel room, thereby delaying what can only be considered a major meeting. During the meeting taking place in Conference Room AA, your Operative took pains to doublecheck Subject's whereabouts which caused the delay. Please note: the waitress did not leave Subject's hotel room until 4:15 P.M. to pick up her split shift at the Arlington Restaurant.

Due to this slip-up, Subject was tailed very closely when leaving Goodstone Tower at 4:25 P.M. back to Union premises, 27 N. Case. There he was met by one Patrick Coyne who was wearing bandages on his head and over one eye and engaged Subject in what appeared to be a friendly conversation. Subject was overheard to say, "You silly s-- o- a b---,

119

are you sobered up enough to have a drink?" The two of them visited the White Front Cafe where Subject bought the injured Coyne several shots of whiskey, while partaking himself.

Strictly at 5:02 P.M., Subject returned to his private office and made phone calls which were monitored as usual (see separate report). By 6:28 P.M. a group of 21 tirebuilders had gathered in the large meeting hall and were joined by Subject at that time. They were second shift men coming directly from Plant One. There was much discussion and Subject appeared to be listening more than talking, although from time to time he was saying something (nature unknown).

Tirebuilder's meeting broke up about 8:00 P.M. and Subject himself retired to Dollar Hotel arriving there at 8:17 P.M. by walking. He evidently showered and changed clothes because shower was heard running and he appeared in lobby at 8:56 P.M. with shirt, tie and suit clothes on.

Your Operative followed him close again, out Highway No. 8 in the direction of Canton where he stopped at roadside establishment called Green Hornet Lounge at 9:15 P.M. Here he was greeted by manager (Dom Granata by name, no police record) and engaged in conversation with two ladies of the establishment, one being Rosemary Cladd, featured enter-tainer, and the other unknown at this time. Soon after he was served a steak dinner and was observed imbibing a series of whiskey shots (seven in number through the course of his meal).

By 10:30 P.M. the Green Hornet had perhaps 18 customers not counting Subject (or your Operative) and abovementioned Miss Cladd performed her number which was both singing and dancing but mostly dancing during which she removed practically all her clothing. This was a spectacular performance and may be of interest to the County Sheriff if not already under observation.

(When doing shadow work such as your Operative is engaged in it is a custom of the trade to melt into

120

surroundings as much as possible which is why four beers and steak dinner appear in today's expense account. Also—if any Sheriff's man was present and perchance should have witnessed your Operative applauding Miss Cladd's indecent exposure, even whistling once or twice, just tell him it is a custom of the trade.)

At 11:34 P.M., Subject and Miss Cladd left premises. In following, your Operative found air let out of four tires on Operative's car in parking lot, which ends the report for this day.

22

A young man in bed with a loving woman is like a bear in a berry patch. His muzzle and his paws will drip with the fruit juices of his spoils. Hunger turns effort into workmanlike intensity and every movement is directed toward greedy consumption. More and more and more—because this is the *last* bear in the *last* berry patch until the end of time. Or so it seems.

Older men are different. Their appetites are stronger, really, but memory regulates their consummation. They take time (as young bears never do) to wonder just how the berries may prefer to be devoured? They even have time for comparative reflections—never forgetting other berry patches, other spoils. They carry a tragic view to bed with them in a sense, because old men know it is *not* the last time, and will *not* go on forever, no matter how complete the illusion of eternity may be for a little while.

Skinny Walker (with no advice from any YMCA counselor and no reading at all in the literature of Sex Hygiene) was a young man with an old man's view.

The rubber shop was responsible. He had taken his strength to the tirebuilding machine and the machine had given him back a sense of discipline that never deserted him. He always addressed himself to the succulence of a loving woman with the regulatory mood of "making out." The culture of work has thus shaped the sexual rhythms of our century and many of Skinny Walker's gals were thankful for it.

In addition to this, he was alone. Mac and Burke and Alabama were buddies, but they weren't *close* in the sense that young fraternities build closeness. In his late twenties, Erskine Walker needed to break the solitary shell which kept him too much to himself, within himself. He needed *intimacy*—a person-to-person contiguity that would prove he was part of humanity. He needed to renew his compact with the human race in order to remain superior to the damned machinery he was at war with.

Woman-loving did this for him. He could lay a big hand on a curving hip and all his disciplinary evocation would go to work. With hands and lips and loins, he knew how to build a communicative union. Know one more thing about Skinny Walker and his way of coupling with womankind: *he had good taste.*

How many bad movies have you sat through, only because you had paid your admission price and had nowhere else to go until the movie ran its course? How many senseless television programs? How many cigarettes have you brought to your mouth and smoked to the bitter end—despite the fact that the first puff had offended you? This is the kind of *bad* taste that Skinny Walker didn't have.

Taste is a matter, simultaneously, of selection and rejection. You pick out the good shows, and you stay out of the bad. Skinny Walker was very strong esthetically because good taste with a refined selection-rejection mechanism is after all, a matter of opportunity.

If that were the *only* movie house, the *only* TV program,

or the *only* cigarette at your disposal—then you may forgive yourself for bad taste. Your crime is putting up with lack of opportunity. Skinny never had a bad time in bed. He always had excellent companions. Invariably, he did well with the good material at hand. His taste was good and he deserved it.

It would happen like this. . .

He'd be having a cup of coffee at the Arlington Restaurant when a new waitress would approach to serve him. She was so new she didn't know him. (So don't discount the act on the grounds of his reputation.) Her name was Lolly Angsters and she had come by bus from the farmed-out region of West Kentucky.

Skinny looked at Lolly well, because that was his habit. In one, quick saber-blue appraisal with his eyes, he saw soft skin beneath the lobe of her left ear, the back of her knee (with no stocking) showing the faintest blue tracery of vein, and a forearm with blonde fuzz that would turn dark when moistened.

Other men, lesser men, see other things. They saw in Lolly the rise of her breasts, the aquilinity of her nose, the sculpture of calf to heel, and, it goes without saying, the proud movements of her backside. Skinny's view was subtler.

"Good mornin', Peaches," he drawled to her. It was a soft, polite, warmly friendly greeting. Ordering, at any time, was an occasion for sociable dialogue, never perfunctory. Even the homely waitresses had a kind of intercourse with Skinny Walker when they brought him coffee. And this Lolly wasn't homely.

"Mornin'," she responded. Her eyes met his directly because Kentucky has always been like that.

"You're lookin' like you got yourself up before breakfast, old gal. Didn't you sleep easy?"

This is how it was. He'd not set eyes on this woman before, and yet he could fabricate the sincere inquiry of a brother, a spouse, a family doctor, and engender a response of the same order.

"I didn't sleep at-tall," she answered. "I rid the bus all night just to get here."

Skinny sipped his coffee at the counterside. At the moment he looked blank-faced and inattentive. Having lured the girl into this intimate disclosure, now it appeared that he couldn't be more disinterested. She served other men and came back to offer Skinny more coffee.

It was as if he had kissed her and then ignored her. Something in her was defiant and maidenly, brave and compulsive and she stood there. She felt summoned.

"My name's Lolly," she announced abruptly. "Call me Lolly, mister, should you be wantin' something."

Her voice was frail and delicious, not wanton in any way. She was eighteen years old, weighed one hundred and twenty-two pounds (without stockings) and her name was Lolly Angsters, from Wayside, Kentucky. She had ridden a bus all night for the sole purpose of meeting Skinny Walker at the Arlington Restaurant and she didn't want the ceremony to be nullified for lack of a name. This is how opportunity presented itself to him. How can anything *except* good taste prevail when this occurs?

"That's Skinny Walker, sister!" a man called out from two stools down. "He's *allus* wantin' *somethin'*!" The counter laughed a ribald laugh. Lolly stood there. Skinny sat there. The laughter rolled over them like pollenated scent.

In bed that afternoon, he looked down at her wide, bruised breasts.

"Peaches," he told her, "You're like an orchard in the Springtime. . ."

This is how she was and how he was.

They lay together closely clasped, and Skinny joined Lolly and rejoined her—serving her with rough gentility, young enough to rejoice in the opportunity—old enough to savor it and tend it, without solipsism or unnecessary cruelty. She held him tightly, meeting his demand for intimacy as fully as it can possibly be met.

125

"Skinny Walker," she breathed. "You're sure beautiful, you are!"

And that's the other specification for the type of love that Skinny offered. He was disciplined as we have mentioned—modifying the flow of his passion to the requirements of the moment. He was lonely and aspired to overcome that loneliness with the closest union human beings can ordinarily achieve. It was not wholly physical. Over and above these considerations, Skinny Walker matched the lovely qualities of Lolly Angsters with a beauty of his own.

Good love, without the complications of the money factor or unnatural lust, makes angels out of brutes. Radiant and clean-skinned, muscle against muscle, paired in unqualified rapture—this Lolly and this Skinny were something more than brutes to start with.

There were Lolly and Trudy and Janie and Bess. There were Marge and Delores and Red and Marilyn and Becky Lou. There were Liz, Annie, Barby, Trixie, Rita, Connie, Rosemary, Doll-Baby, Sally, Evelyn, Marlene, Winney May, Big Gert, Teddy, Caroline, Louise, Patty and Nancy-Girl.

Some of these were "Peaches" in their time, and some were other soubriquets. Some were "orchards in the Springtime" and others were "honey dew melons," "blossoms in the moonlight," "a glimpse of heaven in the morning," etc., etc., etc. All of them were good.

Like Lolly, they eventually went back to work (in restaurants, or factories or five and ten cent stores), or to their husbands or to other towns. It wasn't that they were destroyed or demoralized. You can say that they had been startled, or alerted for unexpected events. They'd never stop looking up in surprise when a new shadow might strike their doorways from that time on. Because they could never, from this time forward, relinquish the foolish notion that Skinny Walker would come after them; knowing truly that he never would.

Skinny Walker's sweethearts were like a basic mood of

126

Akron itself, which still looks sharply at the hillbilly kids fresh from Boogerhole Junction; thinking it may be another Skinny Walker, which it never is. . .

Lolly (like all the rest) had her bitter moments, standing by the coffee urn at the Arlington Restaurant. It is not easy to reconcile oneself with the final knowledge that love cannot be held forever by locked thighs and blonde hair that turns dark when it's moistened.

Bitter at times she was. But she remained, in her heart, a friend of Skinny Walker's. If only his beloved women, and no others, had been allowed to cast their votes, Skinny Walker would have remained President of his Union forever.

Which shows you the power of good taste.

23

Ira Watkins submitted a report to his Central High School journalism teacher, headed

MY INTERVIEW WITH A UNION BOSS
By Ira B. Watkins, 11-B Journalism

It was some surprise to me as I arrived at the Case Avenue headquarters of the American Rubberworkers Council to see if I could get an interview with Mr. Erskine Walker, its President. In the first place, this establishment is very dingy. To read about the Union in the newspapers (non-school papers) we would be led to believe that the Union is a very impressive thing, or at least I was. The entrance way was not very clean and is certainly far from impressive.

However, this was not my biggest surprise. I went to have my interview prepared with a telephone appointment, fully expecting to make my presence known to a secretary and being called in when my turn arrived. This was not what happened at all. I couldn't find a secretary or receptionist. I looked around the main meeting hall and spied an open door

128

from which I could hear men's voices.

There was a man half-asleep on a wooden bench in the meeting hall and I asked him where I could locate Mr. Walker's office. The man was sick or in an alcoholic condition because he acted like he never heard of any Mr. Walker.

So I walked to the open door and looked in where I observed a group of men, one of whom was Mr. Walker himself. He was in shirtsleeves behind a desk more or less yelling at some of the men sitting around. Occasionally one of them would yell back. It was not the kind of conversation to be reported in the Central Forge. I thought for a moment or two that I would witness some union-type violence but this did not come to pass. Perhaps my presence saved the day.

Mr. Walker noted me standing in the door and he waved to me, inviting me to "Come on in, Kid." I accordingly entered and introduced myself as a representative of our newspaper. Mr. Walker commanded the other men to leave. What he said, in fact, was "Get out." Then I was seated.

The Interview Itself

Erskine Walker is as young as some of our younger men teachers such as Mr. Bryant (Civics) or Mr. Stewart (English). He is very informal as well as coarse in his language. I must say that he was gracious with me and did not evade any of the pointed questions I pointed to him. He is hard to understand because his way of speaking is country-style and because it is heavily sprinkled with unprintable matter. He asked me, for example, something that I finally understood was, "What department does your Daddy work in?" I suppressed a smile and explained that my father was in the real estate business, not a factory worker by any means.

My first question was, "How did you get elected President of this Union (Local No. Two, ARC)." His answer rambled quite a bit but I have pieced together the following (indirect) quotation:

"Our Union was in such bad shape that none of the usual

office-holding types were really interested in running." (Mr. Walker referred to such types as "Porkchoppers.") "Some boys put my name in nomination and it was a runaway. I think it was because older men who founded the Union backed me up. I think they backed me because they were very mad at Goodstone and figured that it would teach Goodstone a lesson to have to deal with me. I had no family and was a little mad myself." (Note by Ira B. Watkins: I have cleaned up this indirect quote for obvious reasons.)

Second Question: "What has your administration done for your members?"

Answer: "I have kept them mad."

"What do you mean by this?"

"I mean I have made it my business to expose the squeezing tactics of management."

Third Question (a very suggestive one): "Have you been guilty of encouraging wildcat strikes?"

Answer: "If I tell you not to eat any green apples and you eat them anyway, am I guilty of giving you the bellyache?"

Question: "Don't you recognize the right of the owners of factories to set the standards within their own property?"

Answer: "I recognize the right of a horsefly to bite me if he can get away with it. I also recognize my own right to smash him before he does."

Question (a real dynamite one): "What if Goodstone should move its plants out of Akron and leave all your members without jobs? Aren't you getting the horses and the horseflies mixed up?" (He did not relish this question.)

Answer (much cleaned up): "There may be horseflies that think they are horses. Where Goodstone goes the Union goes. It will cost them .more to move than to pay decent wages. They can run their factories any way they want if they don't use manpower. When it comes to manpower, we are going to have some say about how it is run."

Question: "Are rubberworkers really able to judge how they should be used in the factory system? How much experience do they have in running anything?"

Answer: "Even a coalmine mule runs itself to a degree. (Here he made unpleasant references to your reporter's father. No offense was taken.) Gum miners are some smarter than mules. We know what hurts and what doesn't hurt even though all of us have not been to Central High School." (No offense here either.)

Note by Ira B. Watkins: A couple of thoughts during this part of the interview: Mr. Walker answered these and other questions from a 16-year-old without regard for age. He used the word "Kid" but aside from that he spoke to the point and without looking down. He seems to have no fear of quotations. Three times during the fifty-five minutes I was in his office his telephone rang and he spoke to the party on the other end without regard for my being there. After the first ten minutes of private talking I got so I could understand him fairly well. Not knowing shorthand (apologies to Mr. Chenot) your reporter simply wrote down key words and later put them together. I am not ashamed to say that on two points I thought Mr. Walker was made over-excited by my pointed questions and would come to the brink of actual physical assault against me. I was not exactly made afraid but I was worried. He speaks very strongly. A further comment: he often refers to himself as if to another party and always as "Skinny," never as "Mr. Walker."

Question: "Are your members better off as a result of your policies since you have been in office?"

Answer: "I don't know. (This was a surprising answer.) We have got recognition all right and the check-off of dues. But other things have offset these gains. Our average wage pattern is up but so is the cost of living. The number of grievances increases more than 10% every month. Either this means things are getting worse or the members are getting smarter. I don't really know."

Question: "Will you be re-elected next election? Will you move up to the International Union level?"

Answer: "The only ones who know who will be elected are the tellers when they count the votes. You can bet your life I'll run. I'll run because I wouldn't like to think that Goodstone can get me out before I'm ready. They may get a meal but I'll get a sandwich. (Which was a mysterious statement.) As far as the International goes, we'll cross that bridge when we get to it. (Another mystery?)"

Question: "Did you ever think you'd be a Union President? Are you happy at your work?"

Answer: "I didn't know a Union existed when I was your age, and I sure didn't know they even had Presidents. I didn't set out to *be* anything at all, which is what I turned out, I guess. I never figured to be a tirebuilder either. Once I made that, I guess any tirebuilder can be a union president. (Note by I. B. W., A true statement.) Yes, indeed, I am happy any day that I can get up, get by and go to bed. I'm especially happy when bright young reporters stop by to visit."

At the end of the interview, Mr. Walker asked me if I thought my story would get printed and I assured him this time had not been spent in vain. I assured him also of a fair treatment in the traditions of American journalism, high school or other.

Interpretations

From this first interview of mine I can say that the man Erskine Walker surprised me in many ways. He looks very much like his newspaper pictures. He is very sincere. I think he is highly intelligent in spite of his speech defects. Seeing him in his own nest, so to speak, leads me to believe that factory workers elect officials who can do better than most of them in the duties of the office. Mr. Walker deals with members, with management, with the Government, other unions and reporters, such as this one. He has had no training for this or any such position but he manages to carry on.

It appears to me that he has been put out in front to do a job for people pretty much like himself. He is not a

132

Communist in this reporter's opinion as rumored. He puts more into his job than he gets out of it. (My father's office is a hundred times more presentable.) He is bitter in attitude toward employers generally but he should respond in time to reason and logic if the upper management is so inclined.

He is still in his twenties and will probably one day emerge as the strong man to be reckoned with in U.S. unionism. I will always remember this interview.

Inscription by Miss Ruth Simpson, journalism teacher:

B+

Very good, Ira. You were most professional in your questioning and thorough in your reconstruction. Of course, the piece is much too long for publication and it would be wrong to cut it. In the Spring, I would like you to interview the Mayor. Perhaps we will be able to print that.

R.L.S.

24

On alternate Sunday afternoons Skinny met his men. In Akron, Ohio, "the Meeting" was an occasion of some substance. Rubberworkers went to "the Meeting" twice a month with a civil solemnity. At Goodstone Local, they trooped up the stairs to their second floor auditorium, surprisingly well-groomed in go-to-meeting clothes; the lampblack scrubbed from their pores, the smell of soapstone almost washed away, and the stiffness from "making out" all week softened by drinking bouts the night before.

Not all of them went. The Hall held only six hundred persons on wooden folding chairs and these were rarely without a score or so unoccupied. Gum miners work six days a week (when the mills are running full) and Sundays are not so lightly given over to the parliamentary drudgery of administering the Union's affairs.

It was different when a large issue crowded the agenda and at those times the Armory was hired to accommodate the several thousands who would turn out. But on these Sundays only those who are moderately dedicated attend, those to whom the business of the Union is fairly precious. There are committeemen, stewards, departmental representatives and the local union officialdom. The "ins" are well-represented, and there are a few "outs" too. Goodstone Local's politics were clearly articulated those days and the opposition caucus was not much in evidence. "The Meeting" was Skinny Walker's meeting, and the ones who came to it were, mostly, Skinny Walker's friends.

The Hall itself was a dull place. The officers were on a raised platform behind a plain table and the flag stood dutifully behind them. The room was long and wide, with plain walls, like a low barn.

Skinny sat in the President's chair, amiably watching his people arrive. They waved; he waved back. Many came to the platform to exchange greetings before finding their seats. More than a few were women and Skinny joshed them about their Saturday night adventures. Occasionally a cantankerous old trucker or Banbury operator will come to the dais and complain.

"They're getting out of line again, Skinny. Ain't there *nothin'* we can do?"

"There's always something to do, Shorty," Skinny will assure him. "Just what did you have in mind, exactly?"

"Oh I wasn't thinking of *nothing*, Skinny. It's just how they're acting snotty-like, and kind of spitting on the Union, like. You know?"

"Spitting on the Union? Did you write up a grievance? Make a report? Give me the names, Shorty, and we'll all do us a little spitting!"

There's nothing amiss in Shorty's department, and Skinny knows better, but the ferocity of the President's reaction tells Shorty that his problems are important, be they real or imaginary.

"Damn it, Skinny. I can't make a report on just their *attitude*, can I? What I was thinking was this: What would do the *most* good? I said to the boys: just what would sit them back on their honkers and make 'em act just a mite respectable? And the boys said ask Skinny to say a word. Y' understand?"

Of course, Skinny will say a "word." The point was that Goodstone management listened to Skinny Walker—or so the rank and file believed.

He watched them file into the Hall on Sunday afternoons, ritualizing their belief in his leadership and massing the consolidated weight of their followership. The meeting was opened with a reading of the minutes after Skinny had dropped his gavel and announced, "This here regularly called meeting of Local Two is *now* in session!"

After the minutes were "approved as read" there was an induction of new members. The Obligation was read to them, as they stood in a separate group—probably forty of them at such a meeting.

In unison they repeated their pledge of fidelity to fellow union members, widows and orphans, and at regular intervals the full assembly would chant in response:

"We bear witness!"

Which is why they all came to the meeting. To bear witness that the Union was intact, that Skinny was their leader, and that the barons of the rubber capital had cause to proceed with caution.

Then the Treasurer made his report and it was moved that the vouchers be drawn and the bills be paid. Flowers were ordered sent to ailing brothers and sisters.

Skinny watched his meeting progress. This was his church and many of its rituals derived from Pentecostal rituals. He, too, was dressed up. A tie, a suit, a clean shave and his hair brushed slick on his skull. He sat there and permitted the drab trivialities to take place, with the present reminder that it all revolved around *him*. The Chairman of the Grievance Committee gave a long, tedious report on actions which were being processed, compromises which had been made. You

136

could hear the irritating clank of arbitration's machinery as he narrated the last fortnight's activity.

There were educated persons in the meeting; many had high school diplomas; not a few had been to the University. There was an articulated dignity to the meeting, a sonorous fluency. Skinny Walker presided.

From the back of the Hall he looked like a youthful cleric who had been invited to say the benediction. He didn't intervene often and in this respect, he was a good President. During "Good and Welfare" (that portion of the meeting where any member of the assembly could speak his mind for "the good of the order") Amy Horton would begin her usual ranting against Sunday meetings. Amy was a fat, fortyish bandbuilder and her religious scruples brought her to meeting for the sole purpose of seeking to schedule it on a weekday.

Sunday was the only day when all four shifts were available. Skinny gave Amy what he considered her just due, and he caught her in mid-sentence with a sharp rap of his gavel.

"Thank ye, Sister Horton. We will now get on with the Meeting."

Following his own instinct (or artfulness) he saved "The President's Report" for the last point on the agenda. Waiting for it to come, Skinny sat at the presidium table, staring at the hundreds of his people, working his big hands now and then, toying with the gavel, laughing when Ike Wheeler answered Amy Horton. . .

"The Good Lord don't give a good damn when we meet so long as we walk upright and keep the Goodstone Company at bay!"

When he rose to address the meeting, it might have appeared as if his thoughts were prepared ahead of time. Or as if he had used the hour and a half preceding to organize his remarks. He hadn't. When Skinny Walker spoke to the Sunday meeting, he heard what he had to say at the same time his audience heard.

He understood the logic of the meeting. He knew his people were here to "bear witness." That their purpose was to "Keep Goodstone at bay." That the meeting was some part of the church-going pattern. And that he was expected to sermonize. He allowed the rhythms of the meeting to emerge and he tried his best to sort one out and tie a ribbon to it. Skinny knew he was expected to "say a word."

When the floor had been crowded with too many of the leftist politicians, for example, and he felt uncomfortable from their polysyllabic phrases, he'd talk about it, in this way:

"Brothers and Sisters, I sure love an education. This good Union of ours needs all the schooling in it we can get. Down in old West Virginny we can always tell a learn-ed man. We can't tell him much (laughter) because he already knows it all."

When Amy or other women got carried away under Good and Welfare and added a strident female note to a meeting, Skinny would pontificate on this, too:

"There ain't no barnyard without the hens. The question is whether they're cackling so loud because their eggs are plentiful, or because they want the rooster should know where they are. . ." (Laughter.)

Along the way, some moderate would stand to plead for understanding. Preacher Thomas was like this, and would wait for the opportunity to suggest that management was ready to conciliate, if only the Union would realize that such an understanding was possible.

The President would answer him thusly:

"I heard Preacher Thomas asking for 'understanding' again. I sure respect that Preacher. Only two things about him are his faith that management is really sincere, and his memory to repeat *exactly* what he said the last time. (Laughter.) I like to talk back to the Preacher because it's so blame easy. He talks and talks about 'understanding' and if I shut my eyes I might be took in. But it happens I carry a piece of paper in my pocket."

At this juncture, Skinny took a scrap of envelope from his jacket pocket, and held it up.

"I save this here paper just in case Preacher Thomas tries to make me believe Goodstone is turning all sweetness and light. There's only two words written on it. . .(Here he unfolded the paper and squinted at it.) Why that's peculiar! There ain't but a *date* on it! (Very slowly and quizzically) *May, Nineteen hundred and thirty eight*!!

This was the dreadful date of the Goodstone riot and Skinny took pains to see that his people never forgot it.

The meeting was where Skinny Walker met his people by the hundreds. He met his lieutenants in his office. He met management officials in their offices. He met his women individually, wherever they could be best met, usually in bed. At rare intervals, he met himself. He'd come around a corner fast and bump into a familiar form, his own, and he could hear a voice, his own, trying to save him from something or other. He'd mostly listen during such a conversation:

"You're cleaning up a mess that somebody else has made. These people would rather go to a meeting than fight for their rights. . ."

"They've been with me on a picket line. . ."

"That was a long time ago. They've turned a picket line into a church social, and they'd like to turn you into a deacon."

"I'm no deacon—"

"You can say that again. And when they really wise up to that, they're going to throw you out."

"These are my people—"

"You're drunk, Erskine Walker. These aren't your people. They're using you for what they can get, but not for long. They let you sit up in front because if the place goes up in smoke it will be your butt first. They let you talk a lot, but they listen to a lot of talk—and it's a lot finer talk than *you* can offer."

"I *know* these people—"

"Then you know they're not like you. They've got homes. They've got families. They go to church and they're looking for the long run. Where's *your* home? Where's *your* family? Why don't you get off this crap?"

"Because they *asked* me to sit up front."

"You going to wait until they ask you to get the hell out?"

"Maybe."

"What you going to do until then?"

"Get laid."

"Need help?"

"All I can get."

"I'm with you."

"Right."

Which is how Skinny Walker pulled himself together after a confrontation with his wiser self. He had no mentor, no coach, no counselor. There was no book or philosophical source to advise him. The best he could do was to look the question in the face with a quick honest answer and then get back to battle (or to bed).

After the meeting was over, he'd look around for a girl, a friendly widow or a whore, if she were truly nice. He'd make love with the strength of two men and he would wink in the darkness of a close embrace. He'd wink at the irony of his life and his mission. He winked at Love's navel and it winked back at him.

He bore his own witness on the witnesses. . .

Transcript of testimony by Dr. Leon D. Shrank before the Senate Committee on Irregularities in the Labor Movement, November 14, 1955.

SHRANK: Well, Mr. Chairman and distinguished gentlemen of the Committee, I'd like to begin with the explanation that my doctorate is in Philosophy although I have a Master's Degree in Psychology. Some of my publishing credits are listed in this edition of the University catalog. (Catalog entered in record.)

Now, I've been attached to the University for several years on a part-time faculty arrangement which dates back to the war years. At that time I was studying the trade union movement, summations of which appeared in my Harvard Press book, "Coercion Versus Compulsion In the Industrial Format." It was about this time too, that I made the acquaintance of Erskine Walker, called "Skinny," who is now the subject of your Committee's attention.

Since I have been invited to make this statement by Mr.

Walker's attorneys, I assume that I am what could be called a "friendly witness." (Laughter) By the way of response, if not rejoinder, let me say that my expressions will be uniquely my own and have not been influenced in any way.

With your permission, I'd like to frame my contribution in a somewhat eccentric manner—I'd like to present what I call, if you will, "*The Political Anatomy of Skinny Walker.*"

THE CHAIRMAN: I understand you to say that you were not a medical doctor. (Laughter.)

SHRANK: Yes, but it's my notion that your Committee will better understand the subject of your examination if he is dissected, bit by bit, and identified with those facets of our political-cultural traditions to which he has some derivative connection, however fragmentary. . .

THE CHAIRMAN: Please proceed, Doctor. We'll do our best to be enlightened.

SHRANK: At the outset, I want to establish the grounds for my conviction that we are dealing with more than a single man, that Skinny Walker is no less than a phenomenon. Let me submit that I, personally, feel very friendly toward him. What I have to say is addressed to the phenomenon, not to the human being, or, let's say, not to the single personality. . .

Origins are of vast importance, and this man begins, or originates in the closest condition we have to an American peasantry. This is the so-called "hillbilly." I am fully aware that a peasant class, in European or Asiatic terms, should be wedded to a simple version of an agrarian economy. Peasants should be wedded to arable real estate, in a sense. Our Appalachian type, the so-called hillbilly, has been declassed, or made rootless, stripped of any productive land connections.

The paradox, of course, is that a peasant should be some kind of a farmer, but our hillbilly probably never was a "farmer," or at least no closer than a self-sufficient pioneer. His autonomy then counted on a spinning wheel, a forge, a still, and casting pots for bullets—as well as land enough to farm and hunt.

142

Some of the characteristics of a traditional peasant economy are its acute cultural isolation, its alienation from the sophisticated capitals. This makes it almost a "deep freeze" of ancient attitudes. Skinny Walker comes from this Anglo-Saxon patch of society which, in a sense, hides in the hills and resists the encroachments of modern times.

Akron, Ohio, as you know, has a higher ratio of this contingent than any city in the United States. This is one of the peculiarities which drew me to Akron from the East. Akron's demographic profile reads Anglo-Saxon, white Protestant, semi-rural and so on. But these factors don't quite communicate the ferocity with which this cultural spore holds onto its own ingrown social traits and mores.

While it is not a propertied group, in any sense, and certainly not a productive farming group, Skinny's kind are very close to the land. They identify with the wilderness and in the city's absorption of the group, which will come to pass very shortly, the passion, violence and untrammeled attitudes of the wild condition will cause more trouble for social workers and police authorities than from any other immigrant authority—pound for pound.

THE CHAIRMAN: Dr. Shrank, we have heard very little about Mr. Walker.

SHRANK: Yes, yes—I know, but permit me one last word on this characteristic. Another of its contradictions is that this hillbilly group has a highly developed sense of individualism, but that it is generated within the "gens" social organization—the extended family structure, commonly called the clan. The only political organization to claim their allegiance in recent years has been the Union. So it is not strange at all that Skinny Walker should have moved into the union environment and blossomed there as an insurgent leader.

In terms of a political vocabulary, Skinny Walker is a "Know Nothing"—perhaps the last of the category. He is a non-philosophical follower of a non-philosophical tradition, which is basically "populism" in the American idiom. The Populist Party of the last century, as well as the Industrial Workers of the World in the First World War epoch represent the only massive expression of the Know Nothing phase. Skinny Walker is simply a vestigial remnant of the trend. He would have admired Big Bill Heywood more than John L. Lewis, and he would have felt more at home with Bull Moose Teddy than with Franklin Roosevelt.

THE CHAIRMAN: Are you telling us, sir, that the man Walker is simply unassimilable? Is that what you're saying?

SHRANK: Mr. Chairman, I am trying not to make any such value judgments. I'm trying to show among other things that this man Walker has nothing in common with the Mafia or the Comintern or any of the imported variants of underground organization. I tend to think that his is rather a splinter of authentic Americana. If he has, as your Committee bias has it, committed acts of a criminal nature which I know nothing of, let me say even so, that his is not a criminal type by definition. He has no desire for confinement or no innate thirst for revenge against established institutions. He just doesn't have the psyche or emotive equipment which makes for personal corruptibility.

For all of these reasons, he is "out of time," and "out of place." I am almost finished. If he were more corruptible, rather than less so, and more criminally-inclined, rather than less so, it is my earnest opinion that he would be in less trouble, much less trouble, than he now seems to be in. I suspect that he finds it impossible to adapt to the patterns of corruption which prevail in his environment. As a hillbilly and a Know-Nothing, he is motivated by only one drive—to adapt to his own needs, sieved through the screen of his gens-type culture, pragmatically and specifically, ignoring as far as possible the transitory pressures of his exterior environment.

THE CHAIRMAN: Are you finished, Dr. Shrank?

SHRANK: Gentlemen, honored Senators, you are sitting in some kind of judgment of this man, and for all I know, his

144

history may warrant your judgment. I have watched him with more than academic interest for a number of years. My best advice to you is that the phenomenon of Skinny Walker has no visible historical roots. He is a conjunctural derivative of a peculiar period, because the rubber shops of Akron, Ohio, became a meeting place for the hills of West Virginia and the worn-out banner of Populism. The tattered, segmented serpent-flag of the rebel colonies which flouted "Don't tread on me" is out of fashion. It has no future, just as Skinny Walker has no future. He is like a Mexican general, one of many hundreds of Mexican generals, who sits for a moment in the President's chair, and when he leaves, there will be no mark on the marble to remember him by.

I am his friend and I say this. Thank you.

THE CHAIRMAN: Thank you.

Once he was in motion, you had to move fast to keep up with Skinny Walker. The FBI knew it. Their two-man details complained among themselves of the pace he set. The Goodstone Corporation knew it because he wore their bargainers out in many midnight sessions. The Communist Party knew it too...

Which was funny, because Communists (by reputation) are hard to tire out. The Party is supposed to be something like a Big Ten football team, working by platoons. Big Alex Scheiderman was the "theoretician" of the party in Akron and his most grueling assignment was to convert Goodstone Local's President. He just wasn't man enough for the job. He sat in Skinny's office in 1942 with a briar pipe, a pamphlet, and the look of a Josef Stalin fresh from the YMCA steam bath...

"Skeenay, the proposition is basic. Property relations dictates the social relationships. Don't *forgedd* that. Don't forgedd either that classes are organized by property

146

relationships. The Government is the executive committee of the owning class—."

Skinny enjoyed the Communist approach to things. To him, the foreign-flavored gibberish of their theory was as funny as a comic strip. They were a burlesque of many things. They were so glib and yet so stereotyped. They all sounded alike. They were so steeped in book learning and their books were so shallow.

On the other hand, they wallowed in a doctrine of force. They preached "the revolution as the mid-wife of history"—and they were so unforceful. He lay back in his old swivel chair with his feet on the desk, a grin curling at his mouth. Here was Moscow strained through Warsaw strained through the Bronx—trying to win over Devil's Own! It tickled Skinny. Much as an old farm dog would be tickled by exotic fleas from the city as they tried to puncture his leathery hide.

"Tell me, Doc," he asked the Communist spokesman, "why in the hell does Goodstone hate Roosevelt so much?"

Alex drew on his pipe and practiced twinkling his eyes, as he imagined Stalin must look while chastising his Politburo.

"This is a factional difference, Skeenay. Only factional. You find factions within classes, just as you have the A.F. of L. opposed to the C.I.O. Don't forgedd that. As the crisis deepens, however, the capitalist class will close ranks. The class war will intensify—."

"*You pot-bellied word-chewing pimp!*" Skinny abruptly sat up. He was bored with the eye-twinkling bit. "You ain't talking to some sharecropping nigger. I'd like to see you when your class war gets hot. Did you ever shoot off anything except your mouth?"

"I have seen violence," Alex blinked. His pipe had gone out.

"Where was you the night of the riot? I don't recollect seeing you when the bridge was under fire—?"

"Our comrades was there. I had my assignment. . ."

"You had an assignment! Listen, Doc! This here is Skinny

Walker you're talking to! Tell me how many votes you got in the Union. Tell me *that*"

"Our faction is very strong. . ." Alex was deciding that theory had exhausted its possibilities. He composed the phrases of a report to the Parallel Center as he stared at the Union President. . ."Power mad bureaucrat". . ."rank and file demagogue". . ."class-collaborationist."

"You got three party members on my Executive Board, that's what you've got." Skinny laughed at the commissar. "I don't need any votes you got, Doc. I don't need your pamphlets neither. Why don't you go home and send a cable?"

Alex Scheiderman went home and sent a cable.

Within a week, by using a short quorum and a forgotten section of the by-laws, Skinny dumped all three of Alex's men from the Executive Board. The party men were fairly good Board members and not (at the time) overtly opposed to the Walker regime. He dumped them just to show Alex who was running things.

The word got out and it traveled a long way around. It went from Akron to Cleveland to Pittsburgh to New York to a Swedish freighter to a Baltic port. (Alex didn't actually send cables.) It traveled in microfilm and it was really read in Moscow. There were people in Moscow who were much concerned with the CIO, the rubberworkers, and the goings-on in Akron, Ohio. (They were more interested than you were.)

With all the superiority of dialectical doctrine and of soviet history, the word came back. The word was: *Get Walker.*

The word tried to get Walker. It checked his bank account (there was nothing in it). It went through his private files (nothing there either). It interviewed his bedmates (they all talked but there was nothing new). The word finally followed Skinny Walker to a Case Avenue saloon. . .

There wasn't a Communist in the joint. (Alex Scheiderman was home in bed.) Skinny was at the bar between a drunken tirebuilder and a crippled bum. Skinny Walker was besotted.

148

He was in the stupor that comes from drinking too much whiskey in too short a time. From living too much of a day with too little sleep. From being too much involved in life with not enough real reward. . .

The bartender was Frankie Besso who loved Skinny Walker. He knew that getting drunk was Skinny's best release from tension. He intended to see that Skinny got home safely to his room at the Dollar Hotel.

"You tol' 'em, eh, Skinny?"

"I told him, Frankie." Skinny's head wouldn't sit erectly on his shoulders, and his eyes were unanchored. His speech was slow and effortful. He held himself to the bar with the automatic strength of his fingers. "I told him. They had reports on ol' Cooley. Ol' Cooley's butt was cooked in those reports. Absent? Jeescry—was that ol' boy absent. . ." His speech slurred into nothing and Frankie waited.

Up came Skinny's head from its pool of incoherence.

"Three hunert eight-fie days inna year. Right, Frankie? And ol' Coole was absent forty-six. An' they wanted fire him for ab-shen-tee-ishm. Wouldn' that kill ya?"

"So what'd you tell 'em, Skinny? What'd you tell 'em?" Frankie polished a glass like crazy. All day tomorrow he would repeat to his customers whatever it was that Skinny had told them.

Skinny gripped the bar and squared his shoulders.

"I told them—so the man was drunk? Who the hell *made* him drunk? *Goodstone made him drunk, I said*! And Goodstone's gonna keep him on the job. . ."

Frankie laughed at the deliciousness of the story. That's the kind of union man they needed! "Who the hell made him drunk?" Frankie repeated it with a chortle. "Goodstone made him drunk. . .that's who!" His hero slumped across the bar.

Two men came forward from the back of the room. They looked like workingmen but their hands were soft. They were from Buffalo and they had been waiting for just this moment. They didn't know one union from another, although they were on a Communist Party assignment. They knew what Skinny Walker looked like and they had good reason to believe that he was worth money to them dead, but not alive.

"We'll get him home," one said to Frankie.

"I usually just call a cab," Frankie remarked as they lifted Skinny from the stool.

"We'll call a cab," the man said.

"Just so he gets to bed, that's all," Frankie insisted.

"He'll get to bed."

"See he does, you guys. We like Skinny Walker around here."

The two strangers had the limp figure between them. (One was thinking: *Where do they get this "Skinny" stuff?*)

"We'll get him to bed. We like him too."

"So all right," Frankie said. "Just a suggestion, fellows."

If you don't know Case Avenue, it won't seem possible, but it was. They hauled drunken Skinny Walker down the street and with no embarrassment at all (under a streetlight!) they unlocked the trunk, lifted the turtle-back—and stuffed his sodden body in it...

If they had known the town better they would have driven right out Arlington to Triplett Boulevard and found the lakes within twenty minutes. As it was, they made too many wrong turns, argued among themselves and had two drinks from a bottle. This all took more time.

Skinny was a big man in that turtle-back. He was crowded. The going was rough and bounced him violently. The important thing was that his face was resting against a brand new spare tire.

Tell this to Alcoholics Anonymous, will you? If you ever want to revive a drunken tirebuilder, let him breathe the pungent aroma of fresh rubber. It is sharper than ammonia, better than a shower. It brought him to full consciousness. When (after testing) he knew that the trunk couldn't be opened from the inside, Skinny shifted his position and worked his big hands to get the circulation going. And just

150

waited. . .

By the time the hoods had found their lakeside spot and had another drink, their would-be victim had it all figured out. He had reconstructed the ride, and knew everything about his kidnappers except their names. His consciousness was such that he recalled the soft hands in his armpits and the flat voice, "We like him too."

It was quiet in the country when they opened the trunk.

Skinny kicked the first one in the groin so effectively it ruptured his spleen and three other organs. (He died the next day in Canton.) Two tirebuilding hands found the other man's head and choked until he sputtered into asphyxiation. Then Skinny clubbed him with a fist. Just for good measure. While the first assassin thrashed and screamed in the long grass by the beach, Skinny dropped the partner over him for company.

He borrowed the car (which carried New York State plates) and drove into town. He made no police report. He didn't bother to check with the sheriff's office about the bodies. He made one resolve: *never to get drunk on Case Avenue again*. He never did (except once) and Frankie Besso never understood why.

Scheiderman's "word" was still out. The FBI didn't quite put together all the pieces of that night's puzzle. (It was a very long day—keeping track of Skinny Walker.) But Moscow had many messengers. The next event in the conspiracy to "*get Walker*" occurred in his hotel room. He was sober that night.

As he usually did, he took off his tie in the elevator. Nobody objected because Mr. Walker was the Number One guest of the Dollar Hotel. He opened his door and switched on the light. He noticed immediately that somebody was in his bed. He observed that it was not a man. Without a grunt of recognition, he removed his jacket, threw it over a chair and went into the toilet where he made water very noisily.

The only thing that surprised him as he studied her from the bathroom door was that she was so damned good-looking.

151

"You got no room of your own?" he asked her.

Where they find women like this is their own secret. They call little gangsters from Buffalo and beautiful whores from God knows where. (It shows what connections can do for you.)

"Hello, Skinny Walker," she said to him. She threw back the pale blue blanket and sat in Skinny's bed with all of her nude body showing. It was the work of angels. Angels who were blinded afterwards so they could never repeat such perfect handiwork. It was the kind of a body that turns up once in a decade in Hollywood. Every so often in the form of a New Orleans half-caste. Now and then on some Hungarian declasse. Her body was dark and lissome with a musky brunette quality. Breasts like living instruments. Legs growing out of a shaven mons veneris above an organ so eloquent it could say its name. . .

If you were part of a "Parallel Center" plotting to bamboozle a country boy who stood in your way—this body would have seemed like the answer. In the Party's book, it showed great respect for Skinny Walker. This was no chorus girl. This was top-drawer special material usually reserved for important attachés in foreign capitals. This was rich, heady stuff. You cannot sneer at what Skinny did with it.

He stripped to the bone. (It was his hotel room, after all.) He placed a loaded pistol on the night stand table and he didn't turn off the light. He straddled Miss Whoozit as if she were a python and he speared her to the quick. He felt as if the whole convulsing earth were within his thighs and he rode with the tidal torment like a master before the gale. . .

He relished the prize that had been tossed him. He respected the power of the political force which could summon such a lure—*just for him*. The more he labored at enjoying it, the more he rejoiced. A fierce pride welled up inside him. To think that a little old barefooted boy from West Virginny would be worth a prize like this!

He had her good. He had her in a variety of ways. She

stayed with the game because her chemistry was made to respond. Her mission was to please and to ensnare. It wasn't her fault that this was no gullible member of the Diplomatic Corps.

Please she did. When the day clerk came on duty and rang Skinny's room to waken him, the master threw the strange woman out of his room and her clothing after her. He didn't even let her use his bathroom.

It was hard to keep up with him in those days. Once he was in motion. . .

27

"I walked into this town with six bits in one pocket and a stiff horn in the other. . ."

Betty Marshall held her martini glass by its thin stem and watched Skinny Walker's face intently as he told her this. The big long face with its dark eyebrows and Indian cheekbones looked pleasantly Satanic to her. His squinted eyes had a look of intelligent aggression which distracted her from looking deeply into the eyes themselves. They were astonishingly blue, and Betty very much wanted to look into them.

"A stiff horn?" she asked amusedly.

He allowed her to look into the blue eyes while she deciphered the phrase for herself.

"*O-oh!*" she exclaimed as the meaning came to her. She felt a hot flush creep forward on her temples. They sat in the livingroom of Bennett Marshall's townhouse apartment. She was perched on a drum-like hassock and the transparency of a glass cocktail table permitted him to study the silk-sheathed lines of her legs. He sat forward on the divan, two big hands

154

wrapped around the glass he held. The glass was already emptied. (Bennett will wonder about his liquor cabinet, she thought.) The blue of Skinny's eyes was almost a cobalt and it drew her glance in and in. (To hell with Bennett, she thought.)

Betty had come from a small town on the edge of Cleveland. She had successfully avoided scandal through a bachelor's degree at the Lake Erie College for Women. She was not a virgin at the time of her elaborate wedding to Bennett Marshall but she was the next thing to it. Bennett was six years older than she, and already making twenty thousand dollars a year when she'd been chosen. When they married, he knew this much about her: she mixed excellent martinis and she spoke French with a suave incoherence. Even after their honeymoon, she knew very little about herself.

She rose to take Skinny's glass and felt his blue eyes study her long, lithe torso. The crepe afternoon dress didn't hurt her figure a bit, as she and Oleg Cassini knew. It hugged the top of her thighs and treated her bottom as if it were a bouquet. The fluff at the bosom was simply an interesting distraction (she just wasn't large in that department). The wine-colored ensemble made her blonde coiffure all the more daring, all the more expensive.

"Do you still have the six bits?" she asked over her shoulder as she poured new drinks.

Skinny knew this was expensive stuff. He'd sat across from Bennett Marshall at the bargaining table often enough. The man had expensive tastes. Marshall was a small dark man with small dark hands and custom-made shoes. Skinny had the notion that Marshall could pay for his tastes a lot easier than he could satisfy them. . .

He watched her pivot from the bar and move across the carpet toward him. Her rear end was good enough to eat. Did Bennett know that?

"Six bits don't mean a thing," Skinny replied. He took the glass she offered, drank it in one efficient gulp and threw the glass to the floor, not a drop left in it. Her eyebrows (oh, so carefully groomed) arched themselves in conjecture. "I still got the horn," he said, and reached for her. Which wasn't the way she had it planned.

Skinny was right. She was expensive stuff—if exquisite grooming and precious planning are the criteria. Betty had taken three hours to prepare herself for this tete-a-tete. She had tubbed and showered, creamed and powdered, stroked and caressed herself before full-length mirrors. She had gently applied oils and perfumes to her private parts. She had toiled with precision with tweezers and clippers and little scissors. When she had answered the bell she had walked with arrogance and cunning (knowing by prearrangement that Erskine Walker had come to pay his respects while Bennett was in New York City). She had never intended that he might grab her roughly as if she were a bar maid. . .

So she resisted. She resisted in the only way she knew—by dropping her hands to her sides, stiffening all of her body, turning her head. And saying, "*Please!*"

She said it with refinement. With just the right touch of indignation. Whenever she used this act with Bennett he would lose his last masculine urge and retire to his own room. She had perfected it years ago with football players from Baldwin-Wallace. They too had responded properly—by withdrawing their advances.

In Devil's Own, West Virginia, the act meant less than nothing. She felt herself being lifted. (If he tries to kiss me, Betty vowed, I'll bite him.) Mrs. Bennett Marshall, society matron, 34 years old, svelte and charm-schooled to the armpits, was being carried to her boudoir by a strange man. She was in no immediate danger of being kissed. In Skinny's mind, kissing was for friends. (He hardly knew this gal.) He considered it an act of chivalry to take her to the bedroom— the carpet was plenty good enough.

At this point, Betty would have screamed but it would have been unseemly. She had nothing yet (really) to scream

156

about. I'll scream in a minute, she promised herself. *I'll teach this brute some manners. . .*

He kicked open the bedroom door and paused. Skinny had never seen such a chamber in his life. The windows were covered with curtains so fine and feminine they seemed indecent. The floor was chalk-white with a pubescent fur. The bed was round and hooded, taffeta-trimmed, with dolls scattered over it. In the afternoon light, the fol-de-rol of the room made it look like a toy shop to him. The place had a baffling scent of powder and oil and cosmetic. He kicked the door shut behind him, studying the place with wonder and dismay.

Betty decided to bite him before he dared to kiss her. She raised her perfectly coifed head and closed her teeth on his neck. She had never bitten a man (or anyone) before. Her teeth were sharper than she suspected. She was gripping him with all her might and swallowing warm salty blood before he dropped her on the bed among the dolls.

This rendezvous had been scheduled at a chance meeting. Betty had delivered Bennett to the airport and Skinny Walker had been introduced to her in the lobby. He was returning from somewhere.

"My nemesis," Bennett had said, presenting him—laughing, as a gentleman should. Betty recognized the labor man from newspaper pictures. Skinny recognized expensive stuff when he saw it. He lingered at the limousine station until Mrs. Marshall returned, her fur stole fluttering.

"Can I drop you?" she said brightly.

"Sure can," Skinny said, meaning something else altogether. On the ride into town this afternoon's session had been arranged. Betty wasn't certain what it all implied. Her husband didn't demand that she show much interest in Goodstone affairs. He expected her to look well at buffets at Goodstone Manor. To keep up her membership in the best social clubs. (Akron didn't have many.) There were no children, after ten years of marriage, and this left one's life so uncluttered. . .

157

Now she found herself in bed with Skinny Walker bending over her. Her arms held him tightly. Her mouth was drawing his blood. She gasped and let go.

He didn't move in. He turned his back to remove his jacket and trousers. Lying there, in genuine astonishment, she had all the time in the world to scream. Instead, she savored the blood-taste in her mouth. She wiped a hand across her face and saw the streaks on her palm. Would he take time to undress her?

He would not. Naked from the waist down, he swept some rag dolls from the bedspread and sat beside her.

"You bite mighty hard," he commented.

"You bastard," she said, stretching her arms toward him. "Let me bite you again. . ."

There was never anything to really scream about. Moan—yes. Cry out—yes. But never to scream for help. No help was needed.

When darkness came she served him broiled steak in the livingroom. He was dressed again, except for a tie. She wore only a French maid's apron. (She was saving it for something. Until today she hadn't known for what occasion.) It was tied in a little bow at the small of her bare back. Its cuteness covered perhaps a square foot of her forward surface. Skinny enjoyed the sight of her long legs and dimpled buttocks as she brought the filets on wooden platters.

"You give this kind of service to Bennett Marshall everyday?" he asked her, with steak in his mouth.

She sat cross-legged on the floor beside him, a platter balanced in her lap. There was a wild flicker in her eyes. She was drunk with martinis, with unaccustomed fatigue and with having fully experienced a man for the first time in her life.

"Every time I get the kind of service you gave me," she laughed. There was wickedness in her laugh.

"About once a week, eh?" he taunted her.

"*About once a never!*" she answered bitterly. She collapsed on the floor, spilling her platter and the grease. She began to sob. She covered her face with the froth of the little apron and wept over many things.

Skinny Walker finished his steak, relishing every bite. He drank his black coffee slowly. The sound of her crying merged with the muted hi-fi console which was playing music he had never heard before. (It was the Scheherazade.) He had a peasant's wisdom about women and their crying didn't bother him. Somehow he divined that she needed the tears. He knew damn well that he needed the steak.

When he was ready, he pulled her relaxed form away from the spilled platter. One soft light in Bennett Marshall's livingroom gave Skinny Walker a huge black shadow that fell across the fine furniture and covered Bennett Marshall's nude wife like a stain that would never wash off.

Skinny took her on the carpet and converted her sobs to healthy anguished gasps for consummation.

At midnight she regained her great lady's composure and had covered herself with a hostess gown. Skinny finished the decanter of Chivas Regal and knew she was about to ask him to go.

"It's been great fun, Mr. Walker," she said, flatly. Never expect gratefulness from the expensive type. Skinny picked up his hat, his tie and the topcoat.

"Don't mention it, M's Marshall."

She followed him to the door.

"I'll consider it a favor if you forget the apartment number," she announced. "If you ever return, I'll kill you. . ."

Girls from the suburbs of Cleveland shouldn't speak that way to Skinny Walker.

He hit her once while she was standing. A wide-armed slap that drove her across thirty feet of expensive carpet. Now it's time to scream—she thought in desperation. When at last she opened her mouth for the scream she had been hoarding, he picked her up and struck her again. The scream was frozen in her eyes as he hit her the last time. She lay unconscious on the floor when Skinny Walker left.

He had whipped her because this is what a man must do when he's insulted. He didn't feel unkindly toward her. His open hand would leave bruises hard to explain but he didn't reckon that any bones were broken. (Which was right, unless you counted a ruined bridgework.)

He considered the afternoon and evening well spent, despite the fact that he missed an important caucus meeting of all the local unions. Knowing what Bennett Marshall kept at home was important to Skinny Walker. Drinking his liquor and exploring his wardrobe were more enlightening than laying his wife.

Betty, the girl, had been lively and delightful. First, in how surprised she'd been when he lifted her off her feet. Finally, in the little apron with the steaks. She had become Mrs. Bennett Marshall only with her display of snobbery at the door. Skinny wished her no harm. (He wouldn't have returned if she had insisted on it.) But from this moment on, he felt a great contempt for Bennett Marshall, Goodstone's vice president in charge of operations.

At the hotel desk, the clerk handed him a telegram from the caucus chairman.

SKINNY BOY WE NOMINATED YOU FOR INTERNATIONAL PRESIDENT ITS A SURE THING YOU COXMAN YOU

The Western Union clerk had accepted the message from Alabama Gibbs without a question. She thought "coxman" was some office in the union hierarchy. Perhaps it was, in Skinny Walker's day.

Skinny Walker didn't make the mistake of currying favor from his friends. His strength in the shop came from the militant aristocracy—his fellow tirebuilders. Accordingly, he paid close heed to the needs of *other* departments. His staunchest supporters were the Southern-born contingent (probably seventy percent of the shop). He went out of his way, therefore, to woo the Slavs and the Italians and the colored.

Ultimately, he would stand or fall on his home base, which was the Goodstone system. His plan was to carry his name and his banner into the other plants of the other rubber firms.

Akron was so interwoven that this was an easy matter. Skinny did it with family meetings at the Armory, with picnic rallies at Summit Beach Park. He used the radio because it reached them all.

Nothing he did had the look of tradition. Everything smacked of an emergency. This was how he wanted it. His radio time was never scheduled well in advance; he paid premium rates and came on when no one expected him. Then his partisans would yell from porch to porch. *"Turn on the radio! Skinny's givin' 'em hell again!"* The speeches were better. Not because of Vicky (she had been replaced three times by now). They were better because they were closer to being "pure" Skinny Walker. The "pure" formula was always the same: pick an issue, tie it to your people and give it hell.

In 1942 his issue was the contract and its limitations. No sooner was the ink dry on Goodstone's capitulation than Local Two went after the agreement, hammer and tongs. (Any other president would have been resting on his laurels.) Skinny Walker treated the new contract as if it were the cruddiest pact he had ever seen. The clause that offended him the most was the one dealing with *"management pre-rogatives."*

This was the sensitive ground. All of American business was shaking over this issue. While the laboring man was enthusing over "worker rights," the management group was rallying to defend its "prerogatives." The stump jumpers of Akron, Ohio in the summer of 1942 didn't know a prerogative from a pomegranate. Skinny Walker brought the issue to them. . .

The beauty of the issue was that it was not, specifically, a Goodstone issue. It belonged to everybody. It was a very good issue for a man running for President of the International Union.

"You may not know a *pree*-rogative," Skinny told everybody over the radio. "But a *pree*-rogative belongs to management. Labor just better keep its dirty hands off. Mahogany Row out at Goodstone knows its pree-rogatives. Out at National Rubber they know. Over at Universal they know. So I figure it's time you uneducated gum miners knew, too.

"Just you hear me out now! Back in '34 when you lost your house because you lost your job because the plant shut down. . .Remember that? I thought you'd remember that. Well, that was a pree-rogative. Management decided to shut the plant down because they had the pree-rogative to shut it down. They want to be able to use that pree-rogative any time they feel like it—whether your house is paid for or not. That's a *pree*-rogative, friends—that's what it is.

"And in nineteen hundred and thirty-eight when the bullets and the poison gas was thick out on the Market Street bridge—whose pree-rogative was that, do you reckon? That tear gas costs a lot of money. It takes money to pay for pree-rogatives like that. Let me tell you good people—management pree-rogatives are too expensive to put up with. We can't afford 'em! We got a right to our rights, and they've got a pree-rogative to their pree-rogatives. . .But hear this!

"This is Skinny Walker saying this! If any one of their soul-less pree-rogatives so much as forecloses one home of ours or so much as clubs one of our womenfolk down on our streets, then I say the rights of labor shall rise in wrath and descend upon these pree-rogators. The retaliation shall be severe. . ."

Somehow, for a long time after such a broadcast, all of management personnel would be referred to as the "pree-rogators."

His speeches sounded a lot better than they read now. His voice always had an excited, arousing quality to it. Rough around the edges, with the beginning of a whine at its high points, like gears going into high. . .His manner and inflections had just a touch of the Southern evangelist, but not too much for the time and the place. It was a pleasure to listen to Skinny Walker. It was amusing. It was also dangerous—because a quarter-million people were listening too.

It was a pleasure, too, to watch Skinny on a picket line. He was made for the picket line. His form blended perfectly with the rest of his men, except for little nuances of differences. The way he held his head. The way he walked. The way he gestured when he had something to say. Even the way he threw a fist—which happens on a picket line every once in a while. Skinny was *with* his men (made of the same substance, for better or worse). But he was not *of* them. He called attention to himself. In the alloy of his personality there was a drop of foreign matter. It may have been good or bad (you name it) but it was exceptional. . .

At the annual election in September 1942, Erskine Walker was elected President of the International Union of Rubberworkers, representing something like 175,000 dues-paying members. He was twenty-seven years old; still unmarried. He hadn't built a tire in nineteen months but he was as hard as a brine-soaked fist. He still lived at the Dollar Hotel on Market Street.

In many ways the International Presidency changed his life. It pulled him out of East Akron, for one thing. His first official act was to appropriate eight thousand dollars to redecorate the President's offices. This provided him a bachelor apartment—adding a private den (with bed, shower and bar) to the office proper. The action that kept him in physical shape was the action that took place in that den.

Skinny's taste in women was wide and pioneering. Shop women made it a point to bring certain grievances direct to their President. He was always good for some form of satisfaction. There was *noblesse oblige* in the way he found himself unable to turn down a gal from the shop when she wanted to throw one.

Akron was full of waitresses just arrived from the hill country. Thick-spoken, narrow-waisted, high-busted, long-legged, supple-backed, sharp-eyed kids who would mate with an active man before, after or even during a meal. Skinny liked them.

In his more exalted office, he traveled more—to Detroit, Atlantic City, Denver and to Washington. He never found any reason to refine his basic technique with women anywhere. You grab 'em, you buss 'em, and you lay 'em. (If you're in a hurry, don't buss 'em.)

164

His attitude toward women was exactly the same as his attitude toward the factories. You will understand him better if you understand this. Born in fear, this feeling of his could only take shape in a conquering intent. It was not a guilty fear (any more than a man feels guilt for being a man when he walks through a jungle, or a beast feels guilt for being a beast when it finds itself in city streets). Skinny's fear came from his unceasing astonishment that women were women. They were an alien breed, and their differences in dress, anatomy, texture, speech and mind were forever fascinating to him. They invited conquest. So he conquered. It didn't come from any special sadistic ambition. It was simply his way.

He didn't mean his conquest to be destructive. If destruction happened to come, it was always a by-product of his relentless drive to conquer. He might slap a woman, but only if it strategically fitted his plan to subdue her. Never out of spite or blind anger.

When she was his (and many were truly his) he didn't slap her. He treated her with tenderness and flowing passion—at least for a while. He was not by nature an abusive man. He was however a fighter. His fists were always cocked for action, as was his mind (and also his genital equipment).

Skinny Walker never slept on his sword arm. He was never dismayed when an owner, a politician, a rival organizer or a lover turned on him in betrayal. There was no betrayal in Skinny's kind of war. Only raids and maneuvers and tactical thrusts. He carried himself ready to respond at all times to absolutely everything.

This is what made him dangerous—to men and to women. It made him masterful. His quality of aliveness and curiosity and intelligence and energetic readiness made him responsive to life in its totality. As a result, his centralized drive (inevitably) was mastery. Only through mastery could he achieve *his* kind of security.

If a woman still twitched, Skinny knew he had work yet to do. And he did it.

In Washington a famous syndicated woman columnist had decided to do a "profile" of the young labor leader. Her publishers looked forward to an article full of sophisticated venom. (Goodstone's Public Relations Department was prepared to run a million reprints.) Shirley Faber was no novice in her trade. She had interviewed absolutely everybody in her time (she was about forty), including kings and princes, Hollywood stars, Senators and some four husbands. Shirley had been around and bedded down (just for kicks) with many of her subjects, including three of the husbands. Several qualifications made her a better than average reporter.

Martinis didn't faze her. (She knew where the body was buried in every major capitol.) Her formidability came from yet another source: *sex didn't faze her.* No kind of sex—some of the Hollywood stars had been women. These tested traits made her valuable to her reading public. Shirley always came through with the story. . .

Over cocktails at the Willard Hotel, she saw Skinny Walker as a crude, strong, unscarred young fellow—very cocky, very quick in his adjustments. He was wearing a ready-made suit and a badly knotted tie. He ordered straight rye whiskey. She marked him as a man who would never make it.

"Mr. Walker, let's start—," she began.

"—You call me Skinny, doll," he adjured her. "That's how we'll start."

"Very well, Skinny," she smiled a tired, world-weary smile. "I want to know what you're after. What *are* you after?"

His blue eyes opened wider than she had yet seen them.

"You mean my Union? Or you mean me *personally*?"

Shirley had to laugh at the quaintness of his expression.

"I mean *personally* you."

"You're not talking about contracts or rates? You don't care about any of that?"

"No." She gave him a long, hard look. "Do *you*?"

"Hell, yes." He laughed at her. "We got a program you can read up on. Honey child, just what is it you and your paper

166

care about?"

"One hundred and eighteen papers," she reminded him. "We care about Skinny Walker. What makes him tick? Why is he doing all of this?"

After dinner they went up to his suite at the Statler. As a hard-boiled journalist, Shirley should have noticed that she was doing all of the talking. To her surprise, once they were in his room, he removed his jacket, tie and shirt. The wide flat muscles of his shoulders were startlingly prominent as he lounged on the settee. Light blue veins traced their way across his chest. She could smell his body-sweat.

"Walter Reuther is obviously political. He has a social-democratic set of purposes. Harry Bridges is political on another level. What about you, Skinny Walker?" To meet his standards of informality she kicked off her shoes. (They pinched her toes, anyway.) There was an interruption while a bellhop brought in a bar-on-wheels and served more drinks. When he had gone, Shirley Faber lay on Skinny's bed, feeling like a combination of a den mother, a marriage counselor and a city editor. Very, very sure of herself. . .

"You're only a kid, Walker. Where will you be in twenty years? Another John L. Lewis? Or are you feathering your nest? What's in it for you?"

He drank his rye slowly. This infuriated her. She sat up in bed and crossed her legs in exasperation.

"For Christ's sake, boy! *What makes Skinny Walker run?*" she yelled.

He stood beside her with a hand on her slightly disheveled hair.

"City woman, there's one thing I like to know. Comes sun down, I always like to know who's going to warm my bed for the night—."

She was amazingly pliable. (Any price for a story—she reasoned at first.) His rough hands were abrasive on her flesh. The piece work tempo made her limbs quake and shudder. The mountain terror of Devil's Own made her heart leap. Skinny Walker reached within her and turned her inside out.

167

Not once and not twice only. (During the night, when she was quite haggard with the effort, she still thought: this is for the book. I'll put it in my memoirs.)

She lay supine. She twisted in counter-violence. She tossed like a horsewoman. She dangled limply over the side of Skinny Walker's bed, murmuring, "Go, boy, go-go-go!" Bryn Mawr's mild antics were forgotten. Drunken exercises in a hundred hotels (Vegas, Athens, Cairo) were soon obliterated. She was a shred of passion caught in the flywheel of American industry. Skinny showed her the pit, the tire room and final assembly that night.

Shirley Faber's admirable column, *A Woman's Washington*, never carried the story of Erskine Walker. She couldn't bring herself to write it, not even in her memoirs. It was hers and hers alone. Skinny's women were conquered, but you must remember that they insisted on it.

Skinny Walker winked at the moon—in Washington, New York City and San Francisco—wherever his new duties called him. From convention to conference and back again he learned to be somewhat at ease when the take-off came at the airport and to travel with a modicum of style. (The girls in the bead room collected enough money to buy him some hand-tooled luggage.)

But he always came home. Case Avenue, the Silver Dollar, the union hall, the common whores—these were home to him. All in Goodstone's brick-red shadow, with the smell of soapstone pervading it.

You mustn't think he didn't have contact with greatness. . .The Vice President of the United States (whoever he was at the time) had a select group of labor statesmen to tea and Skinny was among them. There were so-called "Labor-Management" banquets where Skinny sat next to some urbane magnates of industry (but not too close to Harley Goodstone).

He had one dismal unsatisfactory session with Walter Reuther in Detroit. Reuther reminded him of a cold ball of pudding. They discussed events in the CIO and their discussion was evasive, indirect and deliberately vague. Reuther's reputation in Akron was good but Skinny knew of certain undercover alliances which weren't savory. . .

"What about Aircraft?" he asked Reuther. "You got commies in your local out there till Hell won't have it. . ."

The Aircraft plant on the edge of Akron wasn't in the rubberworkers' jurisdiction. As a unit of the automobile workers, it was booming now. It was also a nest of intrigue and a thorn in Skinny's official side.

"C.P.-ers?" Reuther nodded to his lawyer to make a transcript of his remarks. "You don't confuse leftwingers with the Communist Party, do you?"

"I don't confuse nothin' with nothin'," Skinny rebutted. "I said commies. *I mean commies.* What the hell is a left-winger up here in Detroit?"

"Up here in Detroit," Reuther told him, "We don't confuse ideology with party alignments. A *leftwinger* could be any number of ideological splinters. It's a matter of philosophy. The Party, on the other hand, is a monolithic structure of trained agents."

"Well, kiss my butt!" Skinny exclaimed. "You mean you can't tell a commie without he's got a party card?"

"Our union doesn't stoop to red-baiting tactics," Reuther stiffly responded. "Why don't you file a formal report on activities in the Akron area?" Then he added, meaningfully, "—Without butting into any other union's private business?"

"I've done filed my report," the rubberworkers' leader said. "I filed it right here and you answered it. Just do me one more favor, will you? Pass the word down the line that Skinny Walker will break the legs off any commies that get in his way. . ."

Reuther smiled patronizingly and pushed a button. The interview was over. Which was fine with Skinny. He had absorbed about as much of this kind of "greatness" as he could stomach. It wasn't that way at the United Mine Workers office in Washington. In Akron, the name of Lewis towered above Reuther's like a mountain over a beetle. . .

"He's done it again!" a girl on a bias machine would yell to her partner. "Ol' Johnell is raisin' bloody hell!" Froggy the plycutter said to the watchman, "There's one bastard ain't afraid of nobody." The watchman agreed. "Biggest man in this country!" Roscoe the elevator operator grinned. "*Bigger'n the whole damn Sue-preme Court!*" "When ol' Johnell shut 'em down," the trucker from Czechoslovakia confided, "Ain't nobody open 'em up *except* ol' Johnell!"

"Godallmighty but couldn't we talk to Harley Goodstone if we had that Johnell to do our talkin'?" Tommy Poole the bandbuilder remarked to Shorty Matthews. "Skinny Walker talks fine," Shorty retorted, "Don't think he's very far from old Johnell!"

And he wasn't—at least in spirit. He knew that under the smoke from a million headlines, a half-million coal miners supported the effigy of that grand personage, John L. Lewis. The gum mines were populated with old men from the coal pits. They had brothers and cousins and in-laws among that great shadowy mass which upheld the statuesque Lewis with his grim, unflinching face.

Skinny Walker shared the allegiance his people held for this gruff old Welshman. When he sat in Mr. Lewis' oak-paneled office he knew for sure how much he respected the old boy. It was a restrained respect, nothing wild and wooly. For one thing, cantankerous old Johnell didn't cater to it. (You never saw him ask for public affection.) Skinny could see that he was vain; he was overfed and too well clothed. His cigars were on the rich side too. He didn't lift one damned finger to demonstrate how lovable he was.

Skinny sat there and admired him. By God, here's one real man—he told himself. They can't buy him—he's all *ours*. For all his ugliness, he belongs to us. He thought: this son of a

171

bitch struts his big manhood and doesn't bother to camouflage his vanities. Through it all, as through a haze, Skinny could see the *Miner*. In the person of Mr. Lewis he saw every coal digger there ever was—in his force and in his rage.

"Mister Lewis," he told the UMW chieftain, "They're moving the government in on me—all over the place. They've got labor-management pacts and they're trying to get me tied up with a no-strike pledge. I need advice. . ."

Lewis talked to him in a rumbling-throated, frowning fashion, much as a man talks to a half-ignorant boy.

"Mr. Walker," he said. "You are just seeing the beginning of it. American labor has sold its soul. This war will finish the emasculation. Your milk-fed Reuthers, weaned on Das Kapital, won't lead you out of the wilderness. Gutless Phil Murray will have you all dancing on a string, calling each other 'labor statesmen.' I remember Akron well and fondly and I have one message for you. The United Mine Workers will be the last union to go down—*and we will go down fighting!*"

"I'm with you, Mr. Lewis!" Skinny Walker said. Knowing while he said it that he didn't have this kind of strength. No half-million miners, united like a fist. No voice like summer thunder. No chauffeur. No cigar. No wild, ferocious eyebrows. . .

He told Burke Danver and Henry MacDougal what Lewis had told him.

"It looks like one hell of a fight coming up," Danver said.

"One *hell* of a fight!" MacDougal agreed.

"So, what the hell?" Skinny told his lieutenants.

He went down to the Silver Dollar to find his own kind of strength. He embraced the crowd there, one by one, and bought drinks for the house. He too drank, being careful not to drink too much. Frankie Besso was overjoyed to see him.

So was Ruthie Rastek. Ruthie was (if anything) the low, dark, prideless spirit of Case Avenue. She was a two-bit whore.

"Let im alone!" Frankie hissed at her as she edged toward Skinny at the bar.

"Shove it!" she hissed back and made her way to Skinny's side.

Ruthie had been hustling since she was thirteen. She was diseased and scarred and not very clean. She had accommodated as many as thirty men in a single night. Her body was tired and beaten and beyond caring much for anything. She was almost twenty years old. Skinny Walker attracted her as a flame draws a moth. . .

"Drink?" Skinny asked her.

"Beer," Ruthie answered.

Skinny talked to the nameless people of the Silver Dollar about John L. Lewis and Walter Reuther. He talked loud and ramblingly about the war and Goodstone's use of it. While he talked, Ruthie fitted her body to the curve of his hips. From time to time, he noticed this.

"Need me?" Ruthie whispered to him.

"Why not," Skinny Walker replied.

His salary was twelve thousand dollars a year at that time. His expense account (if you included everything) was perhaps twice that much. He knew what expensive womanflesh smelled and tasted like. He had feasted on the prize sluts of his day. Why did he acknowledge poor little Ruthie Rastek? Not because he was a gentleman. She was as tattered and lonely and misbegotten as you can get. Not because he was sorry for her. Skinny Walker was very seldom sorry for anybody. . .

He took Ruthie out of the Silver Dollar and they went to her room on East Market Street (where the bedbugs were crawling in triumph). He lay with her and by some magic they gave each other pleasure that night. Ruthie almost learned how it feels to be a woman. Not quite—but as close as a miserable wench in a bottomless pit can ever hope to see the light of love. She had nothing to offer Skinny Walker except the absence of fear. He had been to the palace and he

173

had seen all the kings. He had flown through the sky and viewed the clouds which threatened him. He lay with Ruthie Rastek because he was lonely that night.

Ten days later he knew that she had given him something to remember always. He was clapped up so bad he felt like screaming every time he made water.

The war was moving in fast. By the fall of 1942, Skinny Walker had a difficult time ignoring it. He resented its presence. He had his own problems, and the war interfered. First it came when so many young bachelors turned in their tools to answer draft summons from their "neighbors." Then it came with the loss of real rubber. Tirebuilders were confronted with a bastard stock made of some tacky, soul-provoking substance called "synthetic."

The war began to take on the character of a Goodstone plot. It seemed as if all the basic strength of his organization was at stake. For the first time (in Skinny's history) the famous six-hour work day of the rubber industry was imperiled. The Communists began yelping it up for "collaboration" and a management-labor "truce." Alex Scheiderman's boys began to really work out on the Walker regime. They hoped that the war would do what their goons from Buffalo had failed to do.

Skinny's attorneys warned him of "contractual obligations." His Executive Board was unenthusiastic. Governmental representatives crowded his reception room, seeking to implant their message which was, simply: *take it easy, Walker—there's a war on*. . .He determined not to take it easy.

There were armies in Africa but the chancellories could not dissuade Skinny Walker from pulling the switch. Just to show the Goodstone Corporation that certain hard-won standards were not easily to be rescinded. He sent the word and called out the tire room. He knew this was the heart of the shop and contained his most loyal cadre. (They didn't like Winston Churchill, anyway.) Out they came.

There were millions of soldiers massed in a terrible

174

momentum across the world. Their weight bore down on these few hundreds of Skinny Walker's boys who dared to act as they chose to act. There were U.S. Army training units garrisoned in the Dollar Hotel across from the Willard Street gate. Skinny was to be the picket captain for this walk-out.

At 5:15 A.M. the first shift workers were unloading from buses, ready to ring in. They were stunned at the sight of Skinny Walker and his picket squad in front of the black gate. *"It's all down and it stays down!"* Skinny called out.

His edict circulated among the crowd. Many received it obediently. Many stood in squinty-eyed unrest. Perhaps a thousand gathered there in indecision. Then the police swung open the iron gate, inviting them to challenge Skinny Walker and go in to work. Now Skinny, and Red and Paul and Alabama and Henry MacDougal (shoulder to shoulder) became a substitute for the gate.

"It ain't like the old days, Skinny," Red Cameron turned to tell him. "Look at those bastards standing around—half of 'em wanting to go in!"

"That other half is hanging around to see that they don't," Skinny replied.

A knot of soldiers appeared among the blue-grey swarm of workers on the far side of the street. "Hey, you S.S.!" they gibed. "Who's paying you now—the fuhrer? You four-effs on parade! You get overtime for sabotage?"

Skinny's blood went hot and lively. "Get back to your bunks, you snot-nosed Napoleons!" he roared. "Let your lieutenant tell you to wipe your noses!"

A fatty, old-faced man came rushing from the crowd, bouncing up against Skinny.

"I go in!" he shouted. "My boy over there! This strike is bad for the boys over there!"

"I ain't even sure you got a boy," Skinny advised him. "There's too much slack in your britches. Take a walk and cool off. . ."

"There's a war going on!" the man sputtered.

"You ain't in it," Skinny said. "And neither is Goodstone until it starts acting right about union standards."

They all went home and Skinny's picket line remained on guard. The newspaper carried its biggest banner head to date (ten points larger than the Pearl Harbor headline). It read: *HITLER'S AGENTS! WALKER'S GOONS CRIPPLE WAR EFFORT.* Despite this, the Goodstone management finally conceded. They agreed to abide by written standards. By this time, Mahogany Row was determined to "get Walker." Washington, D.C. resolved to "get Walker." The Communist Party had reaffirmed its own "get Walker" program.

The only person to really reach him was Ruthie Rastek.

Great issues rolled across the land while Skinny Walker walked the stage like Tom Sawyer in an atomic laboratory. He carried a jackknife and they wanted him to understand a reactor. He wasn't interested in atomic reactors, but he understood two things his critics would never understand. He understood the spirits of Huck Finn and Becky Thatcher.

Tom Sawyer was no dope. As Mark Twain conceived him he was (and still is) a vigorously bright kid with enough mental energy to outwit the forces of his own time and his own place. The thing about Skinny's predicament was the awful chaos of his time and the volatility of his place. He did pretty well, armed with only a jackknife.

You know what he looked like and how he slept, drank, fought, bossed his organization and made love. You may well wonder: how did Skinny Walker *think*? What went on inside such a man to drive him to the decisions he made, the expressions he uttered, and the policies he fought for?

Nobody "thinks" the way some books describe it—as if a

careful tape recorder (inside a character's head) was set to "play." The horrible truth is that this process called "thought," for the most part, is a mask to cover up the decision-making action (whatever the hell *it* is). Mr. Reuther had a gaudy Pandora's box of ideological reflexes to draw upon. This made him, comparatively, the rich boy on the block—with more toys than anyone, as far as "thinking" goes. Mr. Lewis was essentially a mystic, receiving portentous concepts in the dead of night, then lacquering them with the lore of his lavish historical perspective.

Skinny Walker was too simple for all of this. Too brutish. Too honest. He was so directly and efficiently organized in his mental ways that he became complicated to everyone except himself. Just for the absence of over-rationalization, his mind in many ways was sharper and fiercer than the minds of Messrs. Reuther and Lewis combined. (And don't even mention Jimmy Hoffa, who had no mind at all, only a muscular ego that knew enough to keep moving.)

There is thought beyond words. Some of it is in pictures; some in other forms of sensibility. Still other thought is beyond both words and pictures, and it is so far out that it requires a formidable mind to bring it back as usable material. This kind of thought needs a mind as tough and well-developed as a tirebuilder's hands—just as strong, just as clever, and just as deformed, too, from the job it does. . .

Skinny looked at a factory, a mass organization, a war, and an entire society—all in a logical, perceiving, action-directed manner. He was no "intellectual," as you know, but not because he lacked the capacity or the schooling (although he lacked both). The jackknife of his mind was clean and quick and saber-like.

He was never interested in the pedigree of a thought. He never allowed himself to get between him and a bona fide idea. This is why he couldn't be an intellectual. Intellectuals are breeders of ideas. They are dedicated to genealogy and the class fashions of the dog show set. Their ideas are contrived and must wear blue ribbons.

He couldn't be an intellectual because he never pretended to understand, or sympathize, with an abstraction. All thinking was very *personal* to him.

Skinny thought with his whole person, not with a corner of his mind. In this sense, his mind ruled his chemistry, because once any idea struck him strongly he would yield in his personal behavior to accommodate it. In the same sense, the chemistry of Skinny Walker's make-up was the vessel for his mind. If you should begin to *act*, or allow your every thought to actively influence your actions, in accordance with your thinking—then your thoughts too will become as direct and unencumbered as were Skinny Walker's.

There was no elaborate superstructure to justify, appease, and counterbalance *counter*-thought. No need for it. There was no trick vocabulary to varnish over contradictions and conflicts. There was no fabricated morality for service as a deodorizer.

There was Skinny—one man with one view—acting in concert with his thoughts. So perfectly in unison that shadow and substance were inseparable. This was how Skinny Walker did his thinking, inside his being.

He came to the Union because he had walked into Akron and into the gum mine and there the Union was. (As the factory hand says, "I was lookin' for a job when I come here." Meaning: he can go right on looking if you say the word.) The Goodstone factory was a *thing*, as well as an *idea*, and so was the Union. The idea impinged on the existence of the thing.

When this happens, something has to give or be mated. Skinny eventually decided the Union-idea was a good-thing. What did this mean? How did it happen? It came about once he was able to visualize *himself* inside the Union; once he had conceived of the Union as being an extension of his *own* existence. All things met this test, their conjunction with the basic idea of Skinny Walker, a person.

179

If *this* Union was a good idea (and Skinny believed it was), then somewhere the idea of a collection of similar Unions was born. Skinny Walker's mind was germinal. He wanted to reproduce a good idea—over and over and over.

He was very particularistic. He could never, in any degree, think in the hypocritical generality. When other men talked of "prostitution," Skinny Walker thought "whore." And he could only think, truly and specifically, of *this* whore or *that* whore.

He couldn't tolerate the abstract idea of "means of production," (which the Reuthers understood). He could conceive only of Goodstone or National or Youngstown Sheet and Tube. He never entertained the glib slogan-ideas of "classless society" or "mixed economy" or "collectivism." Every idea he ever had was immediately wedded to any step he ever took. It was an indissoluble chain of predetermined consequence.

He had walked into industry because he was a man and a man had to work. You can't get much more basic than that. His premises were so simple they hardly bear repeating. A man has to work. He needs a good Union, since his work is in this time and place. He must fight to keep it good. The War was a bad idea because its real effect was harmful to the Union.

A man sometimes has to soldier as well as be a worker. Skinny's fatalism accepted the inevitable succession of "wars and the rumors of wars." Even so, he had a jurisdictional dispute on with World War Two. It was encroaching on his personal good idea of the Union, and he wasn't having any part of it. If they could have fought their war without bothering his Union, they were welcome to it.

This is how he was. God, for another example, was real to Skinny Walker. Not an idea-God. . .a real God. Skinny felt that it was unfitting to think about God. Such thinking was for doubters, in his view of it. Thinking about the nature of God and His purpose would have been (to Skinny Walker)

180

like dissecting a vagina under a microscope. That wasn't *his* department.

God was the great Scorekeeper. As far as anybody knows, he also handles the "fix" for the game's outcome. This really wasn't Skinny Walker's affair. He played the game as if it were on the up-and-up. He watched the scoreboard without resentment. When he lost a goal, he winked at the Scorekeeper.

His wink registered his acceptance of all terms—fair or foul. He might hope for a fair shake in a tight squeeze, but he didn't count on it.

His wink was his good-natured laugh at the game itself, and at his own involvement. No man of such humor can be utterly stupid.

As it was, nobody paid much attention to the mind of Skinny Walker. Mostly they worried about his trigger-finger. Would he shoot the War Effort? Wound National Unity? Mostly they thought about him as a potential assassin, not a thinker. If they had examined him more closely, they might have seen that the only ammunition he had to fire was the essence of himself, the solitary person.

That essence, though, was high-powered stuff.

31

On December 14, 1942, he received an odd letter (which his secretary set aside from his official correspondence). It was postmarked Parkersburg, West Virginia. It was from his father. It read:

Dear Erskine—
I seen your name in the papers. I was in the Fifth Division of the first war. Honorably discharged with sergeants rating. Your grandad Walker and your grandad Mitchell both served the War between States. Are you going into service? Just for my own information.

J. B. Walker

Skinny, at that moment, was operating under an "essential deferment" accorded to certain labor leaders. He had already been treated to an offer from official sources. A man named Coggle had called on him. Although not in uniform, Coggle had claimed to represent "the Secretary." (Skinny wasn't sure

182

if it was the Army or the Navy.) Coggle was most authoritative.

"A commission can easily be arranged," he announced in a cloud of cigar smoke. "Choice of branch and even theater, for that matter. Not above the rank of Captain, I'm afraid. Lack of formal schooling, y'see. Anyway, Captain just to start with. . ."

"Hell, I went to common school for six whole years," Skinny told him, exaggerating his West Virginian brogue.

"Yes—humph." Coggle swallowed some cigar smoke. "You can *write*, I assume?"

"Oh hell, I write some ever' day. . ." Skinny boasted.

"Well, I can guarantee you a commission. Let's not worry about the grade, just for the moment." He puffed meditatively on his cigar.

"I surely want to thank you, Mr. Coggle," Skinny told him finally. "And I want to return the favor. You just go into any saloon in Akron. Mention my name and give the boy fifteen cents. You'll get yourself a bottle of beer that way." Which was his own way of saying Thank You Very Much Kind Sir.

Despite J. B.'s doubts, Erskine Walker was very much an issue of his grandsires Walker and Mitchell. His attitude toward the war and the military establishment was strictly a good homespun frame of mind in the American tradition. He didn't look up to soldiers. He wasn't afraid of war; he simply didn't want any part of it. The Hitler business bored the hell out of him. Skinny didn't read Walter Lippman and his mind wasn't cluttered with issues far removed from working conditions in the rubber shops.

As patriotism became more and more the vogue, union meetings took up a pledge-to-the-flag for their opening ceremony. President Walker very much approved of this. (It didn't take a war to make him feel kindly toward the flag.)

He told the membership, at one such meeting, a story from his own childhood. It concerned some miners on strike and their reaction when the mine operators planted the American

183

flag in front of the mine to entice them back to work.

"Those old boys marched right up and saluted," Skinny related. "They said—Old Glory, we love ya. We'll fight for you and we'll die for you. *But we'll be damned if we'll scab for you!*"

The story didn't go over very well. It was, of course, received politely. (He was the International President.) The cold fact was that not many chuckled at the reminiscence. It was January of 1943 and there were Gold Stars hanging in Akron's windows. . .

Skinny Walker's attitude was American, all right. It was just a little out of date.

He held his union aloof from the No-Strike Pledge that gallant Philip Murray had unctuously offered the National Association of Manufacturers. He conspicuously stayed away from the Labor-Management teas. The Navy wanted to offer certain plants an "E" for effort. Skinny told them to go ahead but the rates had to hold up. "My boys ain't working for banners," he told the Navy. "They work for wages." The Navy wasn't happy about this. Neither were Henry MacDougal and Burke Danver. The rank and file were never polled for their opinion. Skinny Walker didn't give a damn whether they approved or not.

He did care about one thing. His father's letter (on blue-lined note paper) really mattered to him. He had it in his wallet one night at the Mayflower Hotel. He and an airline stewardess were standing in the lobby about to go up to bed.

(The word went around afterwards that Goodstone had engineered the beating. This is highly unlikely. The facts speak for themselves.)

Four soldiers, pretty well-liquored up, saw a young-looking man and a pretty girl. The airline uniform (which was saucily tailored) made Skinny's civilian attire all the more conspicuous. If she hadn't been so cute, so obviously un-married, and so apparently willing to bed down with Skinny—the affair might not have developed. But it did. (If

184

Goodstone management took the rap, it was fair enough. It made up for other episodes of violence which they had actually sponsored.)

The soldiers clustered around the girl.

"Hard up, honey?" they inquired. "Cant'cha do better than a four eff?"

Skinny measured the first one and broke his nose in two places. This splattered a lot of blood around. It didn't prevent the injured fellow from jumping in with his three cohorts once they had Skinny down the lobby floor. One of the group was from New York City. He used his elbows on Skinny's face to good advantage. Another was from Steubenville and he knew nothing better to use than his fists. The other two, however, were from Texas. They used their boots with savage effect.

It was a good little time before this lynching in the Mayflower Hotel could be broken up. It was wartime, you understand; a highly embarrassing episode. By the time they got him to City Hospital, Sergeant J. B. Walker's son was a pulpy mess. He had the usual share of broken ribs—one of which punctured a lung. His skull had been fractured on the marble floor. His testicles were ruptured. (Texan boots are stern.)

Pauline Danver collapsed at his bedside.

"Oh, Skin-nee! Skin-nee!" she moaned in gurgle-throated anguish as Burke tried to contain her with his hands on her shoulders. Skinny heard her grief through a red fog of pain and puzzlement. She sounded like a mother whose child was lost.

They came often to his bedside, bringing gifts as Skinny came back to life. Once, in Pauline's absence, Burke told Skinny something he hadn't told him before.

"It hits her hard," he said. "Since that night at the Water Works nine years ago—you see—*I've never been a man to her. . .*"

Skinny lay in bed and thought about it. ("I'm a

185

professional wife," she told him.) The Mayflower beating did not render him impotent, as Burke Danver was warning. He proved this to himself (and to a homely night nurse) before he was released.

It did accomplish one irreversible thing. In the Spring he went to the Army recruiting office (with his father's letter still on his person). They stamped his application "Volunteer" and sent him through a corps of examining physicians. He didn't make it. As far as the Army was concerned, Erskine Walker was unfit for service. How could you communicate this to Devil's Own, West Virginia or to a pair of grandfathers dead and powdered in their graves?

There were a great many Erskine Walkers in the Army and nobody wrote any books about them. A high percentage of them died in combat. (They were prone to be first scouts or tail gunners.) If the Army had not been so choosy about Skinny's left testicle and other defects, Mr. Coggle could have killed him off without wasting a commission. It could have pulled him out of the labor movement and made life easier for the Murrays, Reuthers, Careys and Alex Scheidermans.

But it didn't. Skinny still had some stones to throw.

By now he could muster a vote among his International's membership with the efficiency of a Tammany chief. If he wanted a strike vote, a wildcat, a dues assessment or a convention delegation—he knew the boys and exerted the pressure. This always produced the results he wanted. In five years he had leaped from the status of a kid tirebuilder to a Big Boss. He was a full-fledged bureaucrat.

He had a couple of hundred thousand workers nursing him in his role. He was not a boss by temperament. (If anything, he was a first scout by temperament.) He ran his executive board with a whim of steel. He was persuasive, but his associates insisted on being persuaded. His nonconformity to the war effort set policy in his union. His rank and file (despite their private feelings) ratified it. He controlled their votes—but their votes were easily had. He quelled the

186

opposition but the opposition was never very much. . .

When all his wounds were healed (from the Mayflower fracas) and the American armies were in France, Skinny Walker was entrenched as a trade union power. He lived in his office-apartment and flew between Akron and Washington at regular intervals. He was known and despised as a "die-hard" by the "labor statesmen." He was feared and followed by the federal gum shoes. No one was to appreciate his real power for another five years. (Which is the way it is with things. It takes so long for the starlight to reach us, we are saying "*Ooh!*" when the star is already cold and dead.)

His heavy-handed rule (dictatorship, the papers called it) was the result of three things. First of all—his people loved him. As much as they could love any man they put in the top position. When his union conventions gave him a standing ovation and cried with a thousand-throated voice, "Skinny! *Skinny!* SKINNY!," you couldn't deny the roots of the man. This made it difficult for him to resist power. Even you can see that. . .

Secondly, the war caused him trouble. It was a big war. Through it he steered a certain intransigent course—a highly individualistic one. He was uncorrupted by the fashions of the moment. Watering-down standards, debasing rates, selling out partisan causes. He remained a labor champion when his own rank and file had gone over (emotionally) to the other side. This left him high and dry. He had no choice but to wield his power pretty much as he, himself, decided. Don't talk about "democracy" when the leader is that much alone.

Thirdly and above all—Skinny Walker was scared.

Just when the newsreel audiences were taking his scraggy countenance for granted, he was seized by alarm that it all had happened. When he heard his membership roar in adulation he felt the chill of the hunted. Because he knew they were not with him. And this being so, they might be after his scalp before the cheer died down. . .

In questions of power, he was running scared. He mended

his fences and battened down his hatches against the day when the beast of approval would turn. The conspiracy of the times (the war, especially) made it easy for him to conquer the source of his fear. He had to conquer his share of the labor movement just as surely as he had conquered everything else since he first set foot on Case Avenue. The befuddlement of his friends as well as his enemies assisted him. They helped make Skinny Walker a bureaucrat in the worst sense of the word. He became an owner in a feudalistic sense—not of property but of chattels. . .the men and women in "his" mills.

His grand vizier Henry MacDougal smelled danger in the wind. He tried to caution Skinny. MacDougal was General Treasurer for the Rubberworkers International. (Henry's real job was keeping Skinny in line; a department of girls handled the dues checks from the contract companies.) He made the mistake of cautioning Skinny. That was all he did—simply caution him. . .

"It looks to me like the boys like Roosevelt more than Walker," he said.

"Roosevelt ain't president of the Rubberworkers Union," Skinny answered.

"No, and Skinny Walker ain't President of the United States," MacDougal told him.

All of which was a mistake. Henry "resigned" shortly after that. He left his controller's suite and returned to the Willard Street gatehouse. Back to work as a trucker in the tire room. He didn't whimper when Skinny gave him the word. He was tired of signing checks anyway. It had been a long time since the MacDougal caucus had plotted the building of a union. His daughter, on the other hand, took it in less grace.

Helen MacDougal confronted Skinny in his private room. She had been there infrequently under more pleasant auspices.

"How come you put Dad back to work?" she demanded.

"He likes to work," Skinny said.

"Shouldn't you keep one honest-to-God union man around the International office? *Just one?*" Her entreaty was obvious.

"Why don't you get a slate together and run him for President at the next election?" His taunt was flat and cruel.

"Why don't you kiss my butt?" This was the height of her eloquence. He opened his blue eyes widely and smiled at her.

"MacDougal," he told her. "Your butt is getting old."

This is the way a true bureaucrat talks. Skinny Walker was always this way.

32

Red Cameron and Alabama Gibbs stood in Skinny Walker's office defiantly. They were like a pair of oak trees soliciting the wind.

"It ain't the Company, Skinny. Can't you get that through your skull? It *ain't* the Company!" Red growled.

Skinny sat in his leatherbacked chair, holding his hands pensively. "No?"

"Hell no!" Alabama exploded. "It's the *Government*! Any jackass can see that!"

"You're thinkin' I'm a jackass maybe?" Skinny asked him with a menacing calm.

Alabama was unapologetic. "When you're a jackass, Skinny Walker, you're the biggest damn jackass as ever was!"

"Any man can be a jackass if he tries hard enough," Red added.

The beleaguered man stood up. He walked around to confront his accusers. Red was a shorter, full-torsoed man; Alabama towered over Skinny from a height of six foot four.

190

They were a formidable couple. They had nursed their grievances for a long time now.

"Just who the hell are you all—to be calling me a jackass?" Skinny's question was taut with royal arrogance. They refused to fall back in the face of it.

"We represent the Executive Board," Red replied.

"That's who the hell we are," Alabama supported him.

"What do you bindlestiffs know about this Government you're talking so big about?" Skinny paced in front of them. "You're telling me about the Company and then the Government. Who the hell is running this Government? Is it a Company Government or what is it? What makes you talk so all-fired big about the Government?"

"It's the only Government we got," Red answered solemnly. "It's the United States Government. That's what it is."

"Nuts!" Skinny shouted. *"It's a Goodstone government!* You lie in your teeth if you talk about anything else!" He calmed down abruptly and leaned against his desk. "Boys, when Goodstone had the red apple Assembly, it was the only union we had, wasn't it? Somebody talk then like you talk now, and we'd know him for a red apple. Ain't that a fact?"

"No, that ain't a fact," Cameron spoke belligerently. "Goodstone's Goodstone. The Government is something else."

"Your mother is something else!" Skinny told him. "Is Bob Taft your man or is he a Goodstone's man? If they send a Navy commander in to run a plant, is he going to be our man or a Goodstone man?"

"This is a big war, Skinny," Alabama argued. "This is the biggest war we was ever in. Our Union has got forty thousand members in the Armed Forces. You can't be hardheaded about that, man."

Skinny stood again. Very erectly. A great wrath was churning itself inside him.

"I'll be just as hardheaded as I damned well please! I don't need any slewfooted hillbillies giving me advice! Take your red apple Government and your red apple soldier boys and get the hell out of my office!"

His two lieutenants stood stunned with the outcome of their counseling.

"You talkin' about us?" Alabama asked plaintively.

"You sayin' we're red apples?" Red asked.

"Finks! Stahlmaters! Scissorbills! You make me puke! Get out of here before I throw you out!"

In some refined circles you can talk like this without dire results. Not in Akron, Ohio. Alabama Gibbs threw a heavy, long, wide-armed round-housing fist and struck Skinny Walker such a blow it knocked him to the corner. There he sat with a trickle of blood from his mouth. His eyes were opened wide in surprise. Alabama took a step forward, confusedly.

"Christ, Skinny!" he gasped. "You shouldn't of called us red apples."

Red stepped forward too.

"We kind of figure this is our office, too."

Skinny rubbed his jaw and smiled languidly.

"OK boys. Just give me a second to get up, will you?"

They nodded in commiseration. Skinny winked as he pulled himself up. Red remembered that wink afterward and realized that it was the signal for danger. At the time however he saw Skinny stand and felt relieved (foolishly) that the unfortunate episode was over. It had really only begun. . .

Skinny's arms were like red-burning bars of steel. His fists were mallets. He clobbered Alabama where he stood and caught Red before he had time to move. He was a battering ram of retribution. He slugged and he walloped and he clouted. Once they sensed the violence of his reprisal, they were far from passive. But the two of them (415 pounds together on the hoof) were no match for Skinny on a rampage. Not in his own office.

They gave him some good licks of course. When they happened to move in concert against him, his knees came up like pistons. His eyes were wild with blue vengeance. Alabama finally fell heavily against the paneled wall. One eye had been thumbed—gouged deeply. He decided to sit and hold his head, trying to contain the great pain. (He lost the sight of that eye as a result of this fight.) Red Cameron called on the full strength of his shop-forged muscles and drove into Skinny like a stubborn bull. Skinny beat and beat him. Fist after fist. Clubbing him, crashing thunderously on Red's head until his legs lost the message and he sank to the floor.

The victor panted over him, waiting for him to rise. Red couldn't rise. But he wasn't out. He watched Skinny closely, towering ten miles above him.

"It's still the United States Government," he mumbled. "Ain't nothin' you can do about that. It's our Government. . ."

Skinny kicked him in the head. That shut him up for a spell.

It cost twelve hundred dollars to repair the office. Red and Alabama went back to the factory. Skinny Walker initiated the biggest purge since John L. Lewis ran the Communists out of the mine workers union. He used every arbitrary power of his office. He staged kangaroo courts for suspensions, expulsions, retirements and demotions. He cleaned out his field staff of organizers. He eliminated every one of his old-time cohorts.

Except Burke Danver. Now old Burke (with the carved face and the show of bitter blood in his eyes) faced him in the redecorated office.

"Say your piece, Burke," Skinny invited him.

"Not much to say, Skinny. You know you haven't got a real rubberworker around you anymore."

"Except you, Burke," Skinny reminded him.

"Except me. And I don't understand that. Why don't you railroad me, too? I don't belong anymore."

Skinny stared at him through a mist of memory and pathos.

"I'm not going to knife you, Burke. I want you here after

I'm gone. You put me here and you clean up the pieces."

"I don't belong," Burke said. "There's nothing here for me. You don't need me and I don't need you."

"You're asking me to blast you too?"

Burke grunted ruefully. "Might as well, Skinny. You're king of the hill. . ."

"King of *what* hill? I ain't going to do it. You want to tell the papers that you're as far out of the union as a Chinaman walking the streets of Hong Kong. I'm not doing you any such favors. As far as I'm concerned—you stay."

"Then I'm getting out on my own, Skinny. The hill belongs to you."

For the last time in his life Burke Danver went back to the shop. He returned to tirebuilding on the graveyard shift. He did this for three months until a heart attack smote him down. It was just before dawn and he fell into the revolving drum of his machine. (They carried his battered form to the dispensary. According to the insurance report, he died "en route to City Hospital.")

Skinny called Pauline Danver when he heard the news.

"What can I do, Pauly?"

"Just forget the whole thing," she replied. Her voice was like death over the telephone. "Forget Burke and forget me. Just forget it all happened."

"Can I help—?" He was as sincere as he could be.

"Just forget it. *Forget it!*" That was all.

Skinny wanted to go down and get drunk on Case Avenue but he didn't dare. Case Avenue had changed and he had changed. Its shadows were the shadows of danger and dark alien forebodings. He wanted to go inside Goodstone and build one more tire on Burke's machine. It was impossible. He wanted to find Pauline Danver's wide bosom, damp from the tub. He wanted to bury his face in it, whispering, "Li'l mother, li'l mother!"—but she told him to forget it. . .

He wanted to walk into town all over again and be

twenty-three years old once more. To make love on Mac's front porch with MacDougal snoring in the upstairs bedroom. To be a picket captain at the Willard Street gatehouse just one more time. At dawn to stare at a thousand men and to snarl, *"Get home, boys. What's down stays down."* But it couldn't be.

It was 1944, a tormenting year for any man in any country. Skinny's "country" was something more (or less) than the continental borders of the United States.

He had the hillsman's pervasive sense of identity with his environment, a pantheistic interunion with the things and forces, the senses and shapes immediately around him, directly in his view.

His universe was the tire room with the Goodstone empire surrounding it and his Union was his way of dealing with such forces. He was dealing very well. Only twenty-nine years old, six years a resident of Akron, unchallenged ruler of his social unit and its "pecking order."

You may not like his social unit. Nobody asked Skinny to like it. There he was, immersed in it, forced to do something about it. And don't forget, he didn't create the damned thing...

He'd walked into the game and worked his way up to bat. Now he stood ready for some kind of a homerun and the umpire was shouting, "Sorry, Skinny—*the rules have been changed.*" You may appreciate his consternation at this point. But—you may object—he turned on his own kind, his particular brethren, the Burkes and Reds and Alabamas. Where then was his primitive loyalty, his militant bond of fraternity?

Skinny Walker was a hillsman. There was a wildness about him which won't easily fit your discreet morality. A wild creature caught in a trap will chew its own limb free in order to escape. It will gnaw at its own flesh in the compulsion not to be held prisoner. The paw in the trap belongs to the trap. If thine eye offend thee, pluck it out.

He had followers but no friends. His cohorts had cursed

him with the crown of leadership. It was a mean crown with blood on the rim but he wore it as well as he could.

Akron had given him the respectful confederation of many men and willing women. In Henry MacDougal's poor parlor, the kid Erskine Walker had saluted his fellows—"All hickory"—standing strongly in a forest of integrity after the storm.

So now he had chopped down a few of his own. But not until they offended him. Only after *their* assault. Only because they had become part of the trap. . .

And the wild dog slinks in the forest of time, one limb torn and the eye of the hunter on his trail.

Roosevelt was a fine thing. He was big, handsome, happy, rich, eloquent and well-mannered. He was like a fine whiskey. He knew what he was doing. To Skinny Walker's kind, American government became close, friendly and understandable all through the person of "Pres-i-dent Rewz-e-velt." (They didn't think of him as "FDR" any more than they could think of him as "Frank.")

The President was large and strong and had a big homely wife and a flock of big sons. So it didn't matter that he was supposed to be an invalid. The hillbillies of Akron, Ohio heard all the talk about leg braces and about his being a "hopeless cripple" but they ignored it, really.

Skinny heard every broadcast speech the President made. He knew that Roosevelt had a corps of "speech writers." He sometimes suspected the truth, which was that Roosevelt could pick up a speech draft, sight unseen, and read it to his millioned-massed people, changing national policy in the course of the reading of it and not knowing its contents

197

before his audience did. . .But Skinny knew the man could sure talk. Words turned into song in Roosevelt's speeches—what the hell difference did it make who wrote them?

And his diction was a splendid, freakish piece of finery, unlike the talk of any man that Skinny Walker had ever heard. The broad "A's," the open "R's" and the sophisticated phrasings all were accepted, along with the cigarette holder. The sum total made him a real person—so real you could smell him. And you could trust him, too.

Until the time of Roosevelt (which was also Skinny Walker's time) the President of the United States had no existence in the immediate universe of the rubberworkers—no identifiable existence that impinged on their sphere of recognition. Until Roosevelt there were two kinds of presidents—the great dead ones of long ago, like Lincoln, Jefferson, Washington—and all the rest.

Among the nameless mediocre line was Herbert Hoover. He was a roundfaced slob and they thought enough of him to despise him faintly. (Only faintly, because he was never the object of popular scorn that the Communists made him out to be. The fact is, these same workers had also despised Coolidge, Harding and Wilson, but until Hoover, nobody bothered to ask them how they felt toward the White House.)

There was a picture of Franklin Roosevelt in Skinny Walker's office. He had shaken the President's hand once during a campaign stop-over at Union Station in 1940's election. He liked the man and approved of him. He figured if the United States was going to have a President, this big happy man with the golden voice was just about the best available. (Skinny couldn't go along with old Johnell when he turned Republican in 1940.) Third term or fourth term—it didn't matter in any excruciating way.

Skinny was out to keep Goodstone in line, and he wasn't of any mind to tangle with Roosevelt, if he could avoid it. The President had his own shop to run, and let him run it,

Skinny thought. Cheer for him at the newsreels, vote for him at election time, and defend him from the few Republicans you might run into. Even so, don't take him too seriously.

Roosevelt could drink, smile, curse and charm all he wanted. There was one fine-line distinction between him and Skinny Walker which rose like a mountain barrier between them and no amount of prestige or persuasion could ever level it.

Roosevelt had never built a tire. He was down there in Washington, or at Yalta or Teheran (wherever they are) and it wasn't bad that he was there because he wasn't a slob like his predecessors and he looked like a President anyway. But not like a tirebuilder.

Then he died. On the day in April, 1945 that it happened, Skinny became a lot older. He didn't feel as badly as some of the Hunkies and the niggers felt. He aged a lot that day.

Roosevelt had been a big man before Erskine Walker had ever thought of leaving Devil's Own. The Roosevelt kids had grown up on Pennsylvania Avenue before Akron, Ohio really took off its hat to the kid from West Virginia. In Skinny's album of public figures, there had always been a Roosevelt and now they said he was being laid away.

You learn to live with the great looking down at you—knowing they remain, marks on the landscape and totems to good luck. The giants of sports, the Ruths and the Gehrigs and the Dempseys. Hollywood's greats—the Beerys, Gables and Barrymores. Don't take them away too abruptly. You will feel a shock as if your life line to your own youth has been severed. Which is how Skinny felt when Roosevelt died.

The evening of the day it happened, he made love to a school teacher, name of Ella Stauffer. They were in her apartment on East Market Street, being very quiet during the antics of intercourse because her neighbors might hear. And then talking loudly between sessions as a reward to themselves for the burden of restraint.

Skinny had never bedded down with such a talkative female. Ella was in her early thirties, surprisingly plain and frumpish with glasses over her blue eyes and fully dressed; surprisingly ripe and good to behold in the nude, striving to be quiet as Skinny sought to overcome his surprise.

She talked and she talked, about her experience, her new attitude toward "the climax" and how she justified this encounter with Skinny. It was almost as if she talked in order to provoke Skinny into renewed activity, which it did. And she talked even then, although not in any way that could have been recorded in the PTA minutes.

Skinny found his several hours with Ella were good, although they bored him. There was no liquor in her apartment and she talked too much. To love a school teacher, however, had a certain incestuous lilt to it, and her untutored body was grateful in an animated way. The effort to keep the bed from vibrating the entire building called for a caution that added to the piquancy of the evening.

It was the evening of the day that Roosevelt died. Skinny lay spent for a moment, wondering how a fully grown woman could smell so much like a fifteen-year-old girl, and Ella inevitably said, "Oh what's going to happen, now that FDR is dead?"

Skinny cupped a big hand over her soft, quiet flesh and winked at the luminous alarm clock which ticked petulantly on Ella's bedside table. He could imagine this gal, gripped at the height of a climax between a screech and a sweat, thinking desperately about the tax structure of upper Mongolia. The warmth and shudder of her flesh made him tolerant of her silly expressions and he answered her, "First thing's going to happen is this damned war is going to stop."

He wanted the war to be over. So did a lot of people. In August of 1945 the Second World War ran down like an engine which had petered out of fuel. Mussolini was dangling by his heels with his mistress dangling beside him. Hitler was gone. Franklin Roosevelt had given all the Skinny Walkers

200

their *"rendezvous with destiny"* and called it quits. (A yellowed parchment figure at the end.) Stalin and Truman were meeting in far-off places. Two little grotesque men with big ideas. Skinny Walker was still on his hill. Still king. . .

He celebrated the Cease Fire by pulling out of the CIO. He established the American Rubberworkers Council, declaring himself free of all the namby-pamby encumbrances of the parent union. It was part of his last ditch campaign to build a real union beneath his feet. It was a cunning strategy with one chance in a thousand for success.

He met the returning veterans at the train. He pulled them back into the union by firing all of his resources toward their camp. The rubber companies had figured on reabsorbing the discharged soldiers in a leisurely, economical manner. They had reckoned without Walker and his Union Veteran's Program. Skinny organized educational sessions at the union halls—with films and free beer. He made the rounds as vigorously as if an election were in progress. No company, under any pretext, was allowed to discriminate against a returned veteran. The Union gave the men something that amounted to "super-seniority." These ex-GI's were hard and energetic and less than inspired. Once they saw the un-inhibited power of the Walker program they rallied to it. In this way Skinny built himself a secondary base when the war was over. He fought for veterans' rights within the shop more militantly than an ex-soldier would have fought. (Nobody called him a four-eff anymore.)

Now and then at a Union meeting, some old-timer would stand on an aggressive point of order and make an anti-Walker statement. The *union vet's caucus* would make short shrift of such dissidents. The younger men were impatient with any criticism of Skinny Walker. Sometimes there was violence. It subsided when the older men were evicted.

Every union hall had a bar now. Skinny made it a point to drink with his supporters. He politicked a lot at these bars, with a cluster of young ex-soldiers around him. The drinks coming like a bombardment. The talk by the boys was of strange places and important events—of Manila, the Huertgen Forest, and the Rapido. While they laughed and recapitulated these battles, Skinny drank with them and remembered his own. *He thought of the riot in 1938; the boys from Buffalo who had taken him for a ride; the lobby at the Mayflower Hotel. Mostly he remembered Red and Alabama on the floor of his office...*

It may have been the war's end. Or it may have been a change in his personal chemistry. At any rate, he found himself hungering after younger women. Girls much less his age—eighteen or younger. Their nipples were pinker, their backsides smoother. And they didn't know as much about anything.

He woke up one morning in his office-apartment with a young girl who called herself Teddy. She sat up beside him with her nipples glowing like strawberry gumdrops.

"Where in the world are we?" she wanted to know.

"We're at my place."

"*Your* place?" Her blankness was incredibly sincere.

"Yeah. Right off my office," Skinny answered. "It's in the Buckeye Building, right downtown."

"Why on earth is it *here*?" She walked across the room, sniffing the air. Touching the furniture. Her bare body was long and graceful and uninformed. She walked on her toes.

"This is where I do my business, that's why." Skinny was impatient with her, but he enjoyed the way she walked.

"Just what *is* your business, Daddy-o? Are you in the rackets?"

It was a trifle too thick for Skinny, even as she climbed in beside him and snuggled up.

"No. I'm a labor man. This is a union office."

"I've read about *them*." Teddy whispered in his ear. "What's a union, Daddy-o?"

"Oh for Christ's sake!" Skinny murmured in disgust. He clutched her to him and stopped her mouth. She was young

202

of course and sweetly ignorant. Perhaps this is what he wanted. About all he could do was to make her forget where she was. This he did.

Pauline Danver now—*she* really knew what a union was. She knew all there was to know about unions. Skinny Walker was forgetting her. . .

34

He was a good looking man, strong-faced, with eyes that looked directly from their fortified positions like friendly sentries. Black, close cropped hair, an unprepossessing mustache above a generous mouth. Henry Robinson was probably thirty years old. He had a rich, throaty voice which he used intensely, vigorously, in his conversation with the Union leader.

Skinny watched and listened with an easy air, part candor and part ingenuous amusement. Henry was a man who warranted listening to. He had been an All-State football player in an Akron high school a dozen years before. He had been briefly on the city police force. Now he represented a few hundred workers in a National Rubber department. He was well-spoken, militant, and had always been a Walker constituent.

Henry Robinson was a Negro. Skinny Walker's attitude in 1946 toward Negroes was made up of exactly the same set of biases which he brought with him to Akron. Henry wanted to know what these implied. FEPC and various egalitarian movements had brought him to the point of show-down. They were talking in Skinny's office; it was late in the evening and there was a bottle of whiskey on the desk.

"Just where *do* you stand, Skinny?" Henry inquired. "I mean I can support you for your protection of standards well enough. As a worker I understand you. As a Negro, I've got to know more than that. . ."

"Robby, I ain't lynched a darky since I come to town," Skinny laughed.

"It's no laughing matter! The days of lynching are over. It used to be we darkies had to know who our enemies were. Now we've got to know our friends!"

Skinny poured himself a drink, straight Early Times with no mix and no ice. He pushed the bottle toward Henry. By this time (in his bureaucratic career) he had been confronted with irate rank and filers so many times with so many protests that he had grown to enjoy the confrontation.

"Unfortunate thing, Robby, is I got only one kind of union membership. I want your support as a member of the bargaining unit. I ain't soliciting votes according to color."

Henry was intelligent, articulate, handsome, muscular and well-coordinated. More than that, as a superior person, he had learned to pay no attention to his particular superiorities. He was a black man. He leaned toward Skinny, rejecting the new drink for the moment. (He had drunk many times with white men; it was not a thrilling experience for him. On the other hand, his father had *never* done it. Henry's father had been six foot four and had died on a New Orleans dock when a derrick chain snapped to let fall a two ton bale. Henry's father kept on dying in Henry's mind.)

"The time's here, Skinny, when you're going to get your votes on the basis of your attitude toward color, whether you like it or not."

"What the hell *is* my attitude then?"

"That's what I'm here to find out."

"You better drink a little then—"

"All right, I'm drinking." Henry poured himself a fresh shot. He was getting overwrought, he knew, because Skinny Walker perplexed him, antagonized him, and fascinated him, too.

"You are a hillbilly, Skinny. Let's start by admitting *that*."

Skinny smiled. "The rubberworkers' union is ninety percent hillbillies. I'd look pretty silly trying to deny it. . ."

"—And you're *basically* sold on white superiority, the White Man's Burden, and the last-hired, first-fired practice, aren't you?"

"Robby, you're a good man and you talk well. But you talk a lot of bull when you run on too much. Who the hell took your people off their brooms and give 'em a chance in production jobs?"

"I pushed a broom at National for two years before I ever heard of *you*."

"Yeah, but you're building tires now, and you heard of me *now*, because this is my office you're sittin' in."

Henry knew this was true. He also knew that he was talking to Skinny Walker man-to-man; that the "hillbilly" wasn't thinking of him as a colored man. He wanted more than anything to drop his disputative manner, forget the race issue altogether and drink as if he had found a new friend. But his father kept on dying. . .

"You're evading the issue, Skinny. You really are. You know as well as I do that the war-time shortage of labor is what took us off the brooms. Don't horse around with me. You wouldn't want your sister to marry a Negro, now would you?"

"I ain't got a sister—just for your information, in case you're countin' on it," Skinny chuckled. "But you know the answer to that—I'd just as soon see my sister dead, allowing that I had one, and allowing that she'd take up with another race. . ."

"Well, that's the attitude that's got to go," Henry

Robinson snarled. "You're a bigot in your heart, no matter how you keep the bosses in line. You're a Kluxer, when it gets down to cases—"

"I'm a white man, Robby, that's what I am—"

"A white man! Is that your excuse for second-class citizenship to ten million Americans? You're a *white man*? What does that make me?"

Skinny Walker's eyes were very blue as he drained his glass and looked his antagonist in his black-pupiled eyes.

"I spec' that makes you a nigger, Robby."

His voice was flat and inevitable, honest and cruel as an executioner's. Henry Robinson caught his breath. He wanted to reach across the desk and strangle this cracker. He wanted to drag him at the end of a rope. He wanted to burn him in turpentine and scream in the night as the flames lynched the once-white, scorched flesh and his father perished again on a tarred wharf.

He allowed Skinny's words to echo in the room. He drank slowly to let his heart be quiet. His eye met Skinny's and they smiled at one another. After a moment, he was able to speak.

"I wanted to kill you for that statement."

"You asked for it," Skinny said.

"And you gave it to me. . .Now I don't want to kill you at all. I'm over the feeling."

"That's a good thing—"

"Not exactly, it isn't. What I want now is to see you run out of office. I want to see you torn down and stripped of all your power. I think you're a bad symbol and I want all the niggers in the rubber industry to turn against you. That's what I want now."

"No harm in wantin'." Skinny this time poured Henry's drink for him, in a conciliatory gesture.

"At the same time, I respect you more as a human being. Not as a labor leader. Not as a politician either. I don't suppose a politician would have talked to me like that at all?"

"Maybe not. I'm talking to you straight. I'm talking to you as a human. You buy it or you don't."

"I don't buy it, Skinny. I can't. And it confuses the hell out of me. You remind me of a cracker I whipped one night. You know I used to be a cop?"

"I heard tell you was on the Force."

"I really was. I had the Howard Street beat. You know, it fits a nigger cop to have a nigger beat."

"There's more than blacks on Howard Street," Skinny reminded him.

"That's how I had this trouble. There was this cracker, fresh from Georgia, and he was drunker than sin, this one night. I was extra polite to him, and I really didn't want to run him in—"

Henry drank. Skinny sat there.

"I told him to move on, with extra politeness. I had on a new uniform, freshly pressed, buttons shiny, all that. And he looked at me with great surprise. 'Why, you're a nigger!' he told me."

Skinny grunted in amusement.

"Yes, I told him, but I'm also an officer of the law. You look at my badge and not my face, and you just get on out of here. Now—get!"

"Did he *get*?"

"You know he didn't. He kept telling me over and over, as if he couldn't believe it, 'Why, you're nothing but a *nigger*!' So I called the wagon and I threw him in. But I didn't take him directly to the station—"

"Where'd you stop?"

"In a vacant lot. I had it backed in and I started to work out on this poor white trash. I was real mean to him. I'd bash him and pick him up and bash him again. He was little and he was drunk, and I came close to killing him in that parking lot. I didn't even worry about marking him—a thing no good cop ever forgets. I worked him good."

"Did you ever shut him up?"

208

"No. The last thing he said to me, he lifted his bashed-in face up from the floor of the wagon, just before I closed the doors. He could barely talk, with his teeth caved in, and lots of damage. But I understood him. 'No matter what you do,' he told me, 'you're *still* a nigger. . .'"

The two men sat with the whiskey bottle growing empty. The office was quiet and they felt very close.

"I'm glad I didn't kill him," Henry Robinson told Skinny Walker. "Killing wouldn't have helped. And it wouldn't help to kill you either. . ."

"No, it wouldn't help," Skinny agreed. "And I suppose you're going to join up with all the hypocrites that talk fancy to you."

"I suppose I will. Even though I know it's fancy talk. I'll probably join up with them."

"You'll be leaving men who are truly friends—"

"I suppose. I guess we'll have to work with enemies for a while. But we've got to. This whole thing has got out of hand. You can't put a darky in a uniform and go on calling him a nigger."

"Start calling him something else, and you're liable to forget he's a man—"

"Could be. But that's the way we're heading, Skinny. And that means I'll be out to defeat you next election."

They sat together that night. Two straight strong men, each representing a social issue, social forces that were relentless and imponderable. Two men, who in the ordinary course of things, could talk well to each other.

Skinny felt sad about it.

"I worked with your race in the fields before I came to the shops," he told Henry. "I been on the picket line with you. You'll never have a better buddy when the fightin's thick. You know that?"

Henry shook his handsome head.

"I know that, Skinny."

"And you know something else, Robby?" Skinny poured

the last of the liquor.

"What's that?"

"You're *still* a nigger."

"Yes," Henry Robinson admitted. "Yes, I am." And his father died once more.

In 1947 a lot of people were worried about Big Labor. A country lawyer-type by the name of Robert Taft joined up with a nondescript Congressman (whose name was Hartley) and they sponsored a bill which (in a country lawyer's eyes) was designed to curtail the encroachments of Big Labor.

It was a hard bill to read. (Herman Boettinger couldn't make sense out of it.) It would be even harder to enforce. But it really wasn't what Philip Murray called it—"*a slave labor bill*." Taft's bill made a big thing of financial statements and stopping secondary boycotts. It proposed a elaborate system of cooling-off periods and the like. What it wanted to achieve, mostly, was to put the labor organizations into the hands of their lawyers. . .

But, a slave labor bill? Hardly. John L. Lewis knew a thing or two. He knew that if one lawyer gave you bad advice, you merely hired another one. (There are lots of lawyers.) His lawyers told him to ignore the Taft-Hartley legislation. This is exactly what he did, even after it became the law of the land. *He ignored it.*

On the other hand, sanctimonious Phil Murray decided to make a big name for himself. He wanted to be known as a *militant* labor statesman. So Murray's crowd fed the rank and file snake oil and whiskey. They denounced the Taft-Hartley bill, then coming out of committee. They beat the war drums and growled ferociously. They didn't fool Senator Taft. They didn't fool Harley Goodstone or John S. Knight. They fooled the hell out of their own membership. . .

Skinny Walker didn't know any better. He didn't bother to read the fine print in legislative proposals. If the boys in Washington said it was a slave labor bill, he was willing to believe them. The word went whistling through the rubber shops—"*Wait for word from Skinny*! Let 'em talk in Washington. Skinny will lower the boom when the time is right!"

Rubberworkers are direct descendants of coal miners. They know how to prepare for a strike. When the shutdown comes they will tend to their gardens, paint their houses, put a new driveshaft in the family car. They don't know a great deal about politics or labor legislation. They know how to work. They know how to strike. They were ready.

Although the American Rubberworkers Council was technically sundered from the CIO, poor Phil Murray had many Skinny Walkers on his hands. A caravan of local labor leaders mobilized itself in Los Angeles. It intended to drive East, shutting down all CIO-controlled industry as it came. This was to be a monumental showdown. American labor was not going to accept a slave labor bill without fighting back!

The caravan never crossed the desert. Murray stopped it as soon as he knew it was a serious venture. The decision was to let the lawyers handle everything. . .

In the rubbershops, Skinny Walker was doing without legal advice. He ordered "gate parties" and "dues checks" in every plant under his jurisdiction. These were, in fact, miniature picket lines. No one was allowed to pass without showing a union card and proof of good standing. Skinny's strategy

212

(which was effective) was to deliver a 100% union shop before any law could be signed.

A bespectacled fellow appeared in Skinny's office, representing Philip Murray and representing him very pompously.

"If you consider yourself part of the labor movement, Mr. Walker," he announced, "you'll pay attention to the CIO's program. We aren't interested in any violence. We don't want any stoppage—."

Skinny interrupted him. "I thought you boys were going to resist this *slavery* to the bitter end?"

"We'll handle everything from Washington—."

"You say you will, eh?" Skinny asked disrespectfully.

"We know what we're doing, Mr. Walker. You hold your men in line and this unity will win us more respect than any wildcat strike."

"Is that so? You're out to win respect from these slave-herders?"

"—And Mr. Murray wants you to know that the rubber-workers will never be allowed back in the Congress of Industrial Organizations if you ignore our decision in this matter."

Skinny didn't throw him out because he was only a stooge, and not a very bright one. (Skinny himself had stooges who looked just like this one. They're reprehensible but they don't warrant being touched by hand.)

"You tell *Mr.* Murray," he said at last, "that we're handling our men all right. You tell him that if his buddy-buddies pass this here law, Skinny Walker's shutting down everything he can lay his hands on!"

"Are you talking about a *general* strike?"

"I ain't talking about any little old walkout at one gate!"

And he wasn't. They passed the Taft-Hartley Act but they will remember Skinny's reply. It was only for twenty-four hours but it was a remarkable demonstration of strength. He closed Akron down as tight as a drum—rubber shops, newspapers, milkdrivers, plumbers. *Everything.* Six other industrial cities (with Skinny's connivance) did the same thing. Murray and his gentry were more horrified at this "anarchism" than they had been by the "slave labor" law...

Nobody was quite sure what the strike accomplished. It was Skinny Walker's strike and he enjoyed it. It put his picture in a lot of newspapers and his name on millions of lips. If his public relations department had schemed in the night for a *cause celebre* they could not have done better. The "Walker Strike" had been so devastating in a concentrated way that Skinny's fame (or infamy) broke all the barriers of insularity. For a while, any kind of a work stoppage was colloquially called, *"taking a Walker."*

Now the American Rubberworkers Council was dramatically poised for a wide organizing drive. The headquarters staff of the CIO was convinced that Skinny had planned it. Budgets were increased hysterically in order to resist raids on CIO locals. Skinny Walker was ready to raid. He was now prepared to launch a new coalition of labor.

He hadn't planned it this way. His resistance to the Taft-Hartley law was entirely sincere. He had exploded into national prominence only because of one grievous fault: *he had believed Philip Murray's warning.*

When the dust had settled, he found himself (unlikely as it seemed) at a banquet in Hollywood. It was nominally in support of some obscure charity. Actually it was to lionize Skinny. Most of the men were in formal wear but the "lion" was in a grey business suit. His company included some noted writers, bohemian commentators, assorted politicians and various distinguished representatives of the film industry.

Irene Dunne was there (representing the United Nations). Melvyn Douglas was there (Eleanor Roosevelt missed it, having taken the wrong plane). Errol Flynn, Mickey Rooney and a host of Hollywood luminaries were there. One of these was a most glamorous film star.

Her name was Gloria Morrow and she had frequently starred with Gable. She sat next to Skinny Walker, telling him

214

about it.

"Clark often mentions Ay-kron, Ohio," she exclaimed. "So powerful! So primitive! He worked there, you know, in one of your mills, I believe."

"Good for him," Skinny grunted. "I used to work there myself."

Gloria extended one long, peach-velvet, much-braceleted arm and clenched his wrist excitedly. "May I ask you a *personal* question, dear? You promise me you won't be offended?"

"Hell no," Skinny assented. He figured she was ready to flop.

"You seem to be rather husky. Why do they call you '*Skinny*', dear? Is there some frightfully quaint reason for it?"

"My given name is Erskine," he explained. "Er-*skine*. Y' see? That's the way it is with my people. They give you a nickname for any reason at all."

"Oh *charming*!" she whooped. Turned to clarify this to her neighbor at the table. Far down the line, a reporter by the name of Shirley Faber took note of this animated display. (*Skinny-boy gets crushed ice tonight*—she thought.) Gloria whispered to Skinny, "What would your people call me, I wonder?" She shuddered in anticipation.

He surveyed her rich opulent figure. The alabastrine shoulders like moulded sherbet. The breasts bursting from their satin decolletage—like molten torpedo-heads. "You really want to know?" He opened his eyes widely for her. . .

"Hmmn-*hmnn*. . .I do, I do!" she grimaced deliciously.

"We'd call you *Booby*, I reckon."

"*Booby*!" She clutched her breasts eloquently and whooped in ecstasy because he was so very, *very* provincial. For the balance of the dinner (at her request) he called her "Booby." She made a big thing of it. Describing the marquees with that title for her star billing. How envious Monroe and Russell would be. . .

Gloria Morrow was an overpowering creature for Skinny

Walker. He could hardly breathe in the atmosphere she exuded. The swishing majesty of her gown awed him. The avalanche of her bosom made him gasp. (It was said at the time that the wide screen was invented just to accommodate Gloria Morrow's mammary glands.) She wasn't Mrs. Nick Charles (alias Myrna Loy) but she was in the flesh, not on the screen of The Strand in Parkersburg, West Virginia. That made a big difference.

A section of the party retired to her manor in the country. Skinny went along for the ride (and because Gloria insisted that he come along). Her glamorous home was fake Monticello with a swimming pool as big as a polo field. There was a polo field too. The establishment reminded Skinny of a resort hotel with no room clerk. . .

However it happened (and it wasn't because he had any initiative in the matter) he found himself in a suite of rooms which he took to be Gloria's private chambers.

"I'm so hot!" she confided. "Aren't you hot? Isn't it beastly tonight?"

Skinny was hot. He admitted this, and that he, too, thought it was beastly tonight.

"Would you like to shower? Is there anything more refreshing than a shower? I mean *really*?" As she made her invitation, she was removing her jewelry. To be honest, Skinny Walker wasn't thinking about a shower.

A maid came in. She was a slight anonymous girl with a flat Swedish-looking face. Ignoring Skinny, she assisted her mistress to disrobe. The gown and its appurtenances demanded more than the wearer to dismantle it. Gloria's white billowing flesh slowly revealed itself like a fountain above the fabric.

"Well, *do* hurry, Skinny!" his hostess urged him. He stood mesmerized by the event. "If we're going to shower, dear—let's do be ready!"

He thought: *so that's the way the wind blows. . .*

"OK Gloria," he said, whipping off his jacket. The maid didn't blink.

216

Gloria held her great milk-white, pillow-like breasts in her hands. The faintest blue-lace of veins accented their whiteness. The aureola were pale too. As big as small saucers in diameter.

"Call me—you know? Call me *that* again!" Her maid was briskly rolling down a feathery foundation garment.

"Booby?" He was beginning to feel like an idiot. Holding his hand, she led him to a mammoth shower stall with frosted glass cabinets and white marble benches. Each spigot was a golden swan's neck. The tile was a tapestry of cloven-footed satyrs. To Skinny's surprise, the famous star presented him with a bar of scented soap and a luxurious wash cloth. She closed the door behind them—pressed a button which brought forth a gentle stream of warm water over their heads. It was precisely warm enough. . .

Humming softly (with a contralto voice known to one hundred million movie-goers), she began to soap herself. He stood back to admire the voluptuous quantities of her body. A film of beaded foam traced its way down the sculpture of her torso. Her navel was a sentimental engraving on the unblemished face of her belly. The waist was the neck of a goblet overflowing with goodness. Her thighs were formed of gleaming flesh, whitely luminous with the murmuring cast of pink.

Skinny couldn't bring himself to grab her. It would have been like spitting in a national shrine. She turned and swiveled beneath the flowing water. Polishing the contours of that magnificent body. Because he couldn't decide how to act in the situation, Skinny Walker soaped and washed himself too. *They sure are clean out here*, he mused.

As they dried, he placed a tentative hand around her unbelievable waist.

"Booby, girl?"

"Yes?"

"Are you ready for me now?"

She glanced down and noticed (evidently for the first time)

how thoroughly ready he seemed to be.

"Oh *heavens*!" she gasped. As a good hostess will when discovering an oversight. "I'll ring for a girl, Skinny. I'm *so* sorry, dear."

He pulled her close to him.

"Never mind no girl. I was thinking that you and—."

She pulled away with a savage intensity.

"No!" She laughed in un-hostess-like contempt. "It's just not for me, really. *Really*, dear. Please let me ring for a girl."

He allowed her to ring for a girl. He never returned to Hollywood. He had been introduced to the world of celebrities, and that was enough for Skinny Walker.

There was a sitdown in another "Hollywood," the bandbuilding department at Goodstone, so-called because it housed the largest congregation of female employees in Plant One. It was a minor work stoppage and in the ordinary course of things, Skinny Walker would never have known.

One afternoon in late February, 1948, he stopped at the Lenox Cafe to have a shot of whiskey and to feel the nearness of the Willard Street gatehouse across the way. It was a cold winter's day and the Lenox should have been almost deserted in the middle of the second shift.

It wasn't. It was crowded with girls still in their work clothes, slacks and cotton dresses. They were loud in a holiday mood, but it was a mean-tempered holiday. Skinny pushed his way to the bar before they recognized him.

"Cock o' the walk is here, ladies!" one broad woman called out, strong enough to be heard above the din. The title was more truth than satire and she smiled in a friendly fashion.

"Skinny!" someone else saluted him. "Skinny, doll!" the chorus echoed and he was swarmed.

"How come you're all here?" he asked.

"Because we're tired of working beside a rat," a familiar voice told him tartly. It was Helen MacDougal, with a kerchief around her head and blood in her eye.

He bought seventy girls a round of drinks and listened as Helen told of their trouble. A new girl was refusing to join the Union.

"Been through her break-in period and just told us to shove it," Helen reported.

"Just a dumb-assed kid," Bertha Crowley added. "Can't be more than nineteen years old."

"Where is she now?" Skinny wanted to know.

"In there. In the department. Probably laying all the supervisors," Bertha answered.

"That one girl's in there? All by herself?" Skinny's question showed his disapproval. "And there's seventy of *you* out in the street?"

"What's your recommendation, Mr. President?" Helen spat at him, "We supposed to work right on side by side with a red apple rat?"

"How about that, Skinny?" somebody else called. "We always had 100% in Hollywood. What's the new policy— ninety percent?"

Skinny heard the taunting undertone of their replies. He drank his shot and wiped his mouth with the back of his hand. He felt like working. This was the first Akron bar he had ever patronized, the night of his first day in town. He had himself been a kid at that time. . .

"I'd think it'd be a lot easier to keep one gal out than to take all of you out. And a damned sight more sensible." He looked around to find out why. There was a pause of silence.

"We tried that yesterday, Skinny," Helen admitted. "Four of us met her at the gate."

"She whipped us, Skinny, and went right on in."

"She whipped *you*?" Skinny stared at Bertha in disbelief.

"She whipped Bertha, Helen, Babe and me," another girl announced. "She's seven foot tall and she's got three arms."

"Where the hell'd she come from?" Skinny asked Helen. "The circus or where?"

"She comes from the hills of Tennessee," Helen said, "and by God, Skinny, it's up to management to get her out of there. None of us is going back until they do!"

"Tell 'em that, will you, Skinny?"

"I'll tell 'em," he promised. "What does this circus gal call herself?"

"She calls herself Janey Graham," Helen said. "She's a rat, Skinny. Make no mistake, doll, the Department's shut down until she's shipped somewhere else."

All of which prompted the International President to an unprecedented visit to Plant One in the middle of the day. He conferred politely with the plant superintendent, the shift foreman, the division representative and in due course he came face to face with Janey Graham.

She was not seven feet tall. She had two arms only. She was not, in any way, a "circus" gal. She was nineteen, she *was* fresh from Tennessee.

Charlie Morrison, the foreman, had explained the company's position to Skinny.

"It's not our baby, Skinny. Join or not join, it's her own affair. I don't even know what her beef is. For Christ sake, the department is solid anyway. Look around you and you can see how many other non-union girls there are."

The floor was empty. Janey Graham sat in a four-wheeled truck, as if she were waiting for a train to arrive at some wayside station. Her hair was very black, with a Cherokee luminosity, and her face was bland as she saw "the big shots" conferring.

"You're going to lose a lot of production, Charlie," Skinny advised him. "Your Hollywood girls are getting drunk over at the Lenox and they look like they're set to be drunk for more than one shift."

"It's your job to get 'em back to work," the super-intendent argued. "I'm not going to lose my quotas just because you can't control your own members. If I have to, I'll bring new labor in from off the street—"

"No you ain't," Skinny told him, with the blue of his eyes exposed. "You're talking big now, Charlie, when you should be listening. We both of us got a problem here. Has the squaw woman got a man anywhere?"

They assured him she was without family and, as far as was known, not promised to any man around.

"I guess it's up to me to talk to this Janey Graham," Skinny grunted. "I sure hope she don't feel like whipping me."

He walked over slowly to confront her. She surveyed his person insolently and stood when he was a yard away. Within an inch or two, she was as tall as he, broad shouldered, full chested, and with sloe-eyes like an Arabian.

"Southeast Tennessee," he drawled, by way of greeting. "Eighty miles out of Nashville. . ."

"Possum Wallow," she admitted.

"Janey Graham by name?"

"That's right, Mister. Are you the man I'm working for?"

He sat on the truck, to leave her standing before him. She talked like a boy, straight and candid, but her eyelashes were long enough to hang by.

"In a way I am," he grinned. "In a way I'm not. I'm here to find out why nobody will work with you at all."

Her face darkened. She placed her hands on her wide hips and pursed a sullen lip.

"They tried to force me into their Union. I did no harm to *them*."

Skinny knew that she supposed him to be a company official. This had never happened to him before, and the situation delighted him.

"What if *I* told you you had to join the Union in order to hold your job?"

222

The young woman narrowed her eyes and deliberated a moment.

"The job ain't worth it now, I suppose. The girls are down on me even if I joined. I don't see why I should. If you was to tell me that, Mister, I'd go to the locker room and get my clothes."

"Why don't you do that, Janey?" Skinny said softly. "This job really ain't worth it. And I'll meet you on East Market Street. I'm driving an Oldsmobile convertible. . .

She looked in his eyes reflectively. Without a word she walked toward the girl's locker room.

He drove her to Cleveland that evening. Street clothes tamed her a little, but every bar they entered was stricken by her appearance. They had a long dinner in a wood paneled German restaurant near the lake.

"What does Possum Wallow have against joining the union?" he asked her once.

"Possum Wallow don't pay no union no mind," she said. "It's Janey Graham that won't be pushed around, that's all. Especially not by silly old bags trying to make like gangsters."

Skinny Walker respected Janey Graham. He was ready to defend her right to keep aloof from the Union. Her personal liberty became a high principle in his eyes. He was ready to do many things to her and for her that night.

Devil's Own and Possum Wallow were only ten years apart. She was a big girl but big girls didn't frighten Skinny Walker. They talked about her home and family and the boyfriend she had left, in order to find her fortune in Akron, Ohio.

"He's a farmer. If he was anything else at all I would have stayed and married him for real. But farmers make me sick. Don't know why. I think it's the way they turn everything into a stable. . ."

He concentrated on pouring whiskey into her. She drank everything he ordered, as if it were tea. By two o'clock he faced the unalterable fact: she was *never* going to get drunk. So he decided he'd have to lay her sober.

"You coming to a motel with me?" he inquired—which was a most genteel manner for him to employ.

"Might as well," Janey Graham assented. "The night's half over, and I've got me no job anyhow. Besides, you don't smell like no farmer."

He was less sober than she. He signed his own name on the motel register and had trouble untying his shoelaces. He leaned over to fumble with them as she came out of the bathroom, with her clothes on her arm.

She made Gloria Morrow look like an old fluffy-laced Valentine. Her naked body was lean where it should be, the waist, the ankles, the long neck above the lithe back. And it was full-contoured in the breast, the rump and the long thigh muscles. He never saw her face again.

From a height somewhere above her belly, which was a tawny slope leading to a neat furry formidable vortex, her voice reached him as he wiggled his bare toes.

"Just what do you do for Goodstone, Mister,? Do you *own* the company like?"

With his trousers still on, he lay back across the bed to laugh helplessly at the thought. This beautiful hill gal, with nothing to her name except the treasury of her pelt, was led to believe that he might be Harley Goodstone himself! And ten years ago he had been as bare as she and not nearly so lovely. . .

"*Christ no!*" he roared, with his eyes closed in the mirth of it. "I'm head of the damned Union!"

It must have been the lamp. It lay on the floor when he awoke in the morning—the bulb smashed, the shade demolished and the wire frame twisted from the blow.

His face, seen grimly in the bathroom mirror, was puffed and bruised where he'd been hit. But he had no memory of it. Simply the explosion—the swift, savage impact of her rage, and his drunken sleep to follow.

Janey Graham was gone for good. The girls in Hollywood were grateful for the power of the Union, and management was pleased with how efficiently Skinny Walker had resolved the dispute.

Skinny himself had a wry smile for the episode.

"It's like Babe Ruth said," he told himself shortly afterward, while pulling a razor over a sore cheek. "You just can't hit 'em if you can't see 'em."

And he felt like a fisherman who is secretly glad that the big one got away.

37

Akron, Ohio carries a wallop. It has a habit of spawning big things. If not big, at least terrible. You mention Akron on a vaudeville stage and it is always good for a laugh. . .

Vulcanized rubber has a lot to do with it, of course. And being a one-industry town at the beginning. . .As well as being abandoned in the commercial geography of Northeastern Ohio and being forced to develop canals, trucking and air transport because it didn't lie on any major rail artery.

But these can't be important reasons. The hangar for example? So big it snows inside. . .And the two dirigibles? The Akron and the Macon so ghastly big they made the sky quaver. . .(Just forget they didn't fly very well.) How do you explain these?

Akron was big in its toughness. At the high point of the crime scandals (when Chicago was making all the headlines) Akron had more pimps, pickpockets, prostitutes, bootleggers and cutthroats *per capita* than any city in the United States. They all holed up here—Pretty Boy Floyd, Dillinger, the Moran gang.

226

Jim Thorpe played with the South Akron Awnings. Before that, George Sisler went to Central High School. How big can you get? Even today, Murder Incorporated uses Akron as a way-station. . .

John Brown lived here and he was one tough hombre. His home is still a museum on top of one of Akron's hills. (And who remembers Harper's Ferry?) Wendell Wilkie made it here. Jumped right into the headlines and the Philadelphia nominating convention (but not quite into the White House). Alcoholics Anonymous was founded in Akron. Dallas Billington organized the largest tabernacle in the world here. On the edge of Akron you could have found a gambling casino bigger than anything in Las Vegas.

You will understand Akron better when you know that its bondsman was a character by the name of "Whisky Dick." (A bondsman is the entrepreneur who goes your bail and then your life belongs to him.) Whisky Dick built a home on West Market Street. A fine, expensive home in the Italo-American tradition (with much stone work and cute little canopies). This home was the mark of his achievement. A consort of criminals and the demimonde had really made it. This wasn't enough for Whisky Dick. . .

He caused a useless traffic light to be installed in front of his home. When it was red (at least half of the time) all of West Market Street's traffic was halted to admire Whisky Dick's fine domicile. Akron was like that.

Its police force, at one time, was a thick-headed buccaneer crew which made Chicago's clout-heavy cops look like an Epworth League troop. They came into Akron from all over—half of them from Pinkerton rejects and the other half thugs without ambition. They were brutes, in their way—well-trained in the simpler exercises of sadism. They were tough too. They thought law was a fine thing but broken bones were quicker. One police sergeant made a career of driving his motor bike into picket lines. (He saved the splinters of night sticks he had broken over rubberworkers' heads.) He was Akron, too. . .

So was Judge Aloysius Riley. A big, flamboyant man whose daily chore was to make it up to his courtroom bench without falling flat on his face. (Many times he made it.) He was drunker every day than Churchill and W. C. Fields put together. It was wonderful to hear him (in near-stupor himself) sentence the Howard Street and the Case Avenue winos. "Stay away from that dago red," he would admonish them—with a fifth of booze beneath his robes. His moment of glory came every year on Bastille Day. Then he would free the wretches in his courtroom—turning loose his share of Akron's jail birds. "Out wiz ya!" Judge Riley would roar. " *'Tis Bastille Day in Akron!*"

Akron was big as an underground station during the Civil War. It became a capitol for the Industrial Workers of the World in the terrible strike of 1913. (When hillbillies carried the red flag behind Big Bill Heywood and Russia was yet to be heard from.) It was a headquarters town again, ten years after that. This time it was the Ku Klux Klan. . .and the red flag had been traded for some frowzy sheets. The fiery crosses burned and Akron's Jewry increased their donations to the ADL. The papists kept on playing bingo and waited for the sheets to wear out. Which they did.

The CIO was born in Akron. It happened in the sit-down strikes and on the longest picket line in the world. This is true, no matter what Detroit says. Detroit always was a lying town. . .

Where did Akron get such a wallop? Nothing but a tough little town in the shadow of Cleveland—surrounded by the fat-necked farmers' communities of Canton and Medina and Mansfield?

In the first place it was the gateway to the North. The map won't prove this to you. John Brown's home and the K.K.K. are strong evidence for this contention. In the thirties it had the highest proportion of white native-born Americans of any American city. Its hills brought them in from the border states and the deep South. The tire machines brought

228

them in. Goodstone's labor recruiters brought them in. The tides of history brought them in. . .

Just as they brought Skinny Walker in. Skinny Walker was what made Akron mean and tough and somewhat terrible. In the gum mines, the term for speed-up (the man-breaking tempo of piece work) is "raw hide." Raw hide makes a man mean. Raw hide makes a city mean.

The long-headed ridge-runners who poured into Akron were mean enough to start with. . . They hadn't been citified to the point where they could make peace with decadent hypocrisy. They had energy and purpose and a gallused dignity that wouldn't shut up. They were tough because they weren't sophisticated enough for fakery. The raw hide system kept them from vegetating on Tobacco Road.

Skinny Walker was nothing. Akron *made* Skinny Walker. It made him a force to reckon with. There was some of Skinny Walker in half the population.

For better or worse, Erskine Walker (President of the American Rubberworkers Council) was an American. He was masculine. He was authentic. He was an active product of his place and times. They were very active times—but *not* inspiring ones. He continually reacted to new events in a dynamic and an interesting way. This is quite a trick when the fabric of your times is falling apart with a bleak depression and a bleaker war. And you happen to be a kid from the backwoods. His peculiar career as a labor leader wasn't caused by a lack of morality. His lack of morality was caused by his career.

Akron was his environment. Skinny changed his environment—creatively as well as negatively. Changed the hell out of it. He fashioned a world for himself. It was a world which had not existed before he came along. He helped release giant impulses which went sailing through the world like drunken boomerangs. He was no crumb bum crooner picked up by a press agent and "created." He was no synthetic fluke. Whatever happened to Skinny Walker, he worked for it, and he deserved it.

He wasn't elected to his position of leadership because of any contrived "program." In all the years of his career he was never guilty of having any kind of program. Not a real program. He was elected to power and he stayed in power (for an exceedingly long time) because of one accomplishment. *He was Skinny Walker.* You could depend on that.

In 1950, two big things happened to him. One made headlines for Akron. The other was an obscure event known only to Skinny himself. In the first case he issued a call for a new and independent confederation of unions. His general strike record had established his name across the land; the response to his call was immediate and impressive.

The nominal basis of the call was to unite all unions on a platform of solid aggressive wage increases. No Reutheristic hokey-pokey about "fringe" benefits—just real dollars per real hours worked. This may have looked like a "program" to you. It wasn't. Skinny's invitation to unhappy A.F. of L. and C.I.O. unions was saying, in fact: "All those who are sick unto death of the craven policy of their present International—come on and get in line!" More than this, it meant: "If you like Skinny Walker, *here's your chance to join up with Skinny Walker.*"

About a million of them liked Skinny Walker.

Not that they knew him. But they knew and they disliked the Reuthers and the Careys and the Hoffas and the MacDonalds who currently were running their affairs. A million of anything is something to deal with. A million of organized Skinny Walkers was a big event, indeed.

It warranted many headlines and attracted Senatorial attention. Akron got credit for it and Akron deserved it. Akron had nurtured Skinny Walker. But remember that behind Arkon you had the tough, bitter, recalcitrant memories of John Brown, Judge Riley, Jim Thorpe, Wendell Wilkie, Dallas Billington, Pretty Boy Floyd, the Grand Klaxon and Whisky Dick. As well as two generations of tobacco-chewing mountaineers who knew in their tendoned guts what raw hide meant...

230

The new labor movement called itself the *"Joint Labor Congress."* By this time the rubberworkers included the cork, linoleum and plastic divisions and represented 250,000 dues-payers in their own right. They were the heart of the JLC.

This new amalgamation kept Skinny hopping for several months. It broadened his range of activity and it bored him too. He wasn't designed for the tedium of negotiation. The tit-for-tat bargaining that goes with pulling so many strands together. Picket-line-unionism is one thing; business-unionism is another. But he kept at it. It was started and he intended to see it through.

Among other distractions, the JLC pulled him out of Akron for longer intervals than usual. He was losing track of things in his own hometown. He was being consumed with hotel parlor parleys and horse-trading sessions to see if the farm implement workers would swing toward Detroit or "go Walker". Whether or not the electrical workers would carry Communist spores into the JLC—if they came. . .

On one such occasion (back from a six-week organizing drive in the Rock Island territory) he felt moved for an excursion of anonymity. He elected to stop in a little South Akron cafe for a shot of rye. It was a dark and dreary spot between shift changes. Its neighborhood patrons didn't look up when he came in. He kept his hat on and sat at the bar. His slouched loneliness merged with the maudlin bar. The proprietor served him without comment or recognition. Down the bar, two rubberworkers were talking as rubberworkers will. (Their discourse is laconic. There is no arm-waving animation about it. Their speech is slow and gnarled, dried out like a weed; pungent like tobacco.)

Such little joints are the Union League clubs for gum miners. They go down to the corner for a beer every night. They may watch the fights on the television set high above the bar mirror. They may just sit there and look at the scarred table. If they should feel like it, they will exchange opinions in their way. This is what Skinny overheard that day:

"*What the hell is this Joint Labor thing?*"

"*It's Skinny Walker's new deal. Something he dreamed up.*"

Silence for a spell. . .

This was the other big thing that happened in that year. Skinny never read editorials. When Raymond Moley excoriated him, he wasn't touched at all. When his union competitors printed handbills and called him names, he received no personalized impact. War was war and the ammunition of invective was an expected part of it. If a woman should throw her mane in a drunken rage (as many of them had) and screech at Skinny Walker about what a lousy bastard he was—he felt it not a bit.

Since the falling-out with his old comrades, not much in the form of criticism had reached his ears. His toadies insulated him from that. On this night, therefore, it had an other-worldly effect on him. He sat in petrified attention to listen. . .

"*What do you think Skinny's up to now?*"

"*Skinny's up to nothin'. That's what he's up to.*"

More silence. Every man cares what other men think. Every fighter needs to know that his banner is honored among his legions. Be as tough as Skinny Walker if you want to, but take care not to eavesdrop on talk like this. . .

"*Nothing going to come of it?*"

The men at the table sipped their beers in unison.

"*What the hell can come of it?*"

"*Maybe Skinny knows. . .*"

"*All Skinny knows is where to get laid.*" The speaker snapped off a chunk of plug tobacco. "*That's all he knows.*"

Skinny hunched his shoulders at the bar. While his critics (not knowing and not caring that he was there) carved out his obituary. He winked silently at the bottom of his empty glass. He paid for his drink, took a long look at the undistinguished men who'd been talking, and left. . .

232

It was cold on South Main Street and no cab in sight. (There's never a cab in sight in Akron, Ohio.)

At that moment Skinny Walker didn't even know where to get laid.

Alone in a hotel room in Toronto, Skinny was trying to write a letter. He sat at a little desk with the Gideon Bible and a ballpoint pen—staring at the embossed crest on a sheet of hotel stationery.

It was almost twilight on a Wednesday, March 12, in 1950. He had sobered up, with a series of showers and a short sleep, after a night of drunken revelry with some of his Canadian cohorts. There was to be a banquet in the evening.

Now, after an afternoon of solitude, transfixed with the feeling of being out of joint with everything, Skinny Walker was moved to make a mark on the paper. He had three hours to kill, and he was alone—except for the desk, the pen, and the unmarked paper. Writers have been born from lesser opportunities. . .

It seemed to be the time to write some fragment of his story. He thought of it only as a transient impulse, an itch to scratch, not as any kind of literary composition. If he had sat down with the determination to write a comprehensive declaration, it would have been different, requiring different vanities than he had on hand. He knew he was no writer. But he toyed with the pen and felt the private urge to leave a clue, much as a captive (being borne away by his enemies) leaves signs along the way, in the hope that his rescuers will follow.

Just a note, he thought, of where I am and how I got here. And then I'll mail it to somebody, anybody at all, just for the record.

That's all he wanted—to write a letter to anybody at all. He could talk it better, but there was no one to hear. Not in this Toronto hotel, or in any hotel anywhere in the world. He could have dictated it to a public stenographer, if the itch he felt hadn't been so private.

The pen looked like a slender reed in his big hand. It's astonishing how a man's handwriting freezes at a certain scholastic age. When Erskine Walker had last been a pupil (in a one-room country school) his hand had been small and awkward in its relation to a pencil. Now it was big and awkward, but the handwriting was the replica of his handwriting then. He made each letter separately, rigidly linked with the next to follow, and the O's were very rounded and the crossing of the T's was absurd. He wrote:

I should of kept on walking

The only reason I came to Akron at all (he thought, with the pen poised over the hotel stationery, with his first thought already written, staring back at him) was because I heard of a Goodstone recruiter and how they paid anyway two dollars an hour. It seemed like a good amount for a boy with no schooling, and in Devil's Own there was nothing doing at all. If I'd stayed on there I'd of been married in a month and broker than a nigger sharecropper the rest of my days. . .

but Akron looked mighty big to me in them days

He thought: it froze my balls and that's a fact. It was pitiful is what it was. I thought Akron was the whole wide world and the tire room was the heart of it. What the hell did *I* know? For Christ's sake, I never was anywhere else, and I wasn't the only one who thought it was so damned big. The boys, they thought so too—even Mac, who was born and brought up there. . .

besides I wanted Burke Danver to run for President in the first place.

Old Burke would vouch for that if he was living—or if you could get to him, wherever he is. I didn't want one cotton-picking thing they ever had to offer. I was a green kid, looking for two bucks an hour and discount whores. I didn't know a point of order from a triple ply. I made no pretense that I knew. It shows how moonstruck a bunch of guys can be. That first election in '40 was a freak, that's all it was. I didn't campaign. I didn't even control the tellers, for Christ's sake!

It was him that put me up and is responsible if anybody is. His missus will vouch for that

Oh yeah? Old Pauly would testify to the hanging, that's what she'd testify to! I should of loved her instead of talking about it. Been better for Burke and a damned sight better for me. But I didn't know Burke was crippled at the time and she sure as hell didn't let on. His heart might have got him *any* time and I'll burn in hell before they ever prove it was me that sent him back to the shop. He's the one guy that walked out on me—just plain walked out, that's all.

if she only will.

If I had turned back the night she kicked me out when she was standing in the front room naked as a snake, I could of hosed her on the side until Burke cashed in. Then, by God, I'd have married her for real! Then I'd have me something, something to hang onto. . .

I give the Union what I give and no complaint of any kind. I don't blame it because I never made myself a home

The tire room was my home. Case Avenue and Frank's Cafe. The Union Hall was home. How did I know what the hell home was cut out to be? Pap's shack in the hills was as much a home as Bennett Marshall ever had. By a damned sight! Home is when and where you bed down. Plant the old horn and hold on until you make out—that's what the hell home is.

what's more I owe not a damn excuse for anything that came my way

Whatever came my way? A free drink? An easy lay? I didn't need no union to bring that on. I've got no bankroll laid by. I don't own any farms or motels or government bonds, either.

I can go back to work tomorrow and earn my wages with any man.

So why did I ever let myself get bumped from the tire machine? I let Burke and Mac and the rest of them hustle me into the Presidency—for what? Not because I wanted out of the shop, looking for idle time. By no means! I was prime to give Management a whipping, and that's why I let myself get pulled off the machine! That stupid damned rag-picking Mahogany Row was asking for a fight and by God and by luck Skinny Walker gave it to 'em!

Upper Management made so damned many mistakes that all I made won't tip the scale. I made a few I suppose

The whole thing is fish or cut bait. You can't hold elective office or sit down at the bargaining table without being a goldplated liar and a two-bit cheat as well as a double-talking, conniving bastard. I don't care *who* you are! Which is really why Burke put me up for office and wouldn't run himself. *He* was too damned good for it. Let the kid take the rap, he figured. Well, I took the rap, and his rap and I'll take any damned rap they can deliver . Screw them, I figure it.

I don't know so much but I learned what rules there are and made up some few on my own

That wartime crap was a lot of crap and they can still shove it, for all I care. *Now* everybody knows it was a lot of crap but they don't pay off for being a wise guy. I wasn't a

237

wise guy, as it really was. The thing was that they no sooner got me in the saddle than they tried to call off all the rules. You know, the whipping at the Mayflower Hotel was the worst I ever had. If I'd got me a Purple Heart for that I'd wear it on my jock strap...

which is all a man can do by his own lights

What the hell do they want? They want blood, is what they want. They've been sharpening their knives ever since they read my name on that first damned ballot. All I ever did was counterpunch. They push you and you push them back. What the hell?

I call them as I see them which is all I can do. Sure as hell it wasn't me that invented this hog rassle but I'll be here til they carry me out

So who gives a damn? And what am I writing it for? The newspapers write your obituary for you. Nobody, absolutely nobody, will read this. I don't know a single damned person to send a letter to, and that's a fact. One million gulley-jumpers in the JLC and not a single one I can send a letter to...

Skinny Walker sat in his Toronto hotel room and re-read the note he had so laboriously scribbled. It had the scantiest punctuation but it was surprisingly neat, with an even margin, and certain of the lines had the pathos of poetry like a swallow's wing and a roll of thunder, like this:

> I should of kept on walking but Akron looked mighty big to me in them days besides I wanted Burke Danver to run for President in the first place. It was him that put me up and is responsible if anybody is. His missus will vouch for that if she only will. I give the Union what I give and no complaint of any kind. I don't blame it because I never made myself a home what's more I owe not a damn excuse for anything that came my way. I can go back to work tomorrow and earn my wages with

238

any man. Upper Management made so damn many mistakes that all I made won't tip the scale. I made a few I suppose. I don't know so much but I learned what rules there are and made up some few on my own which is all a man can do by his own lights. I call them as I see them which is all I can do. Sure as hell it wasn't me that invented this hog rassle but I'll be here til they carry me out.

That was it. It lacked, of course, the cultivated precision of Tom Jefferson's correspondence, but Jefferson knew how to write, although he never walked a picket line. And Jefferson didn't invent this hog rassle any more than Skinny Walker did, and it is entirely possible, at Monticello or Devil's Own (whichever it may be) to wonder: *so who gives a damn?* Which is not an elegant thought, no matter how you say it.

Skinny practiced signing his signature with a flourish. He had signed a lot of documents. First he wrote *E. H. Walker*, then *Erskine Walker, President.* Finally he wrote: *Skinny Walker.* Having done this, he tore the pages up, rolled them into a tattered ball. Threw them into a waste basket below the desk. . .

He thought, any red apple can write a letter. I wonder what Canadian skinch is like on a Wednesday night?

Home is somewhere below a winking navel for Skinny Walker and his penmanship is written with tumescence and explosion.

Whether you've made out or not, you fight your machine until the shift is over. . .

When the Joint Labor Congress held its first convention (in June of 1951) 42,000 delegates thronged into the Cleveland Stadium. There were rubberworkers there, of course. There were teamsters, dock workers, farm implement workers, railroad workers, electrical workers, auto workers and steel workers. Aside from the American Rubberworkers Council, the other industrial representatives were splinters of older established unions. They were, however, angry, determined splinters. They represented one million angry, determined members.

These one million dues-payers, with their families, represented 4,162,075 American men, women and children. This was more than two and a quarter percent of the total population at the time. *They all belonged to Skinny Walker. . .*

In its aggregate the convention contained all the dissident sentiment in American labor. It required a strong, unwavering personality to express that dissidence and hold it together. Plain fakery wouldn't do the job. Goons couldn't do it either. The Joint Labor Congress needed an authority that was radical, sincere and prepared to defend itself with force.

They had it in Skinny Walker. He belonged to them.

Their conclave opened with no hokus-pokus. No visiting firemen in the papier-mache figures of mayors, congressmen or the President's Secretary of Labor. Strictly business it was—the credentials committee, the resolutions committee, the Treasurer's Report. . .At the press table, the labor reporters played around with lead sentences for their early dispatches. One already had these words on his typewriter:

"CLEVELAND—A humdrum assembly began its humdrum business today. . ."

The sun was hot by Lake Erie. There were no trumpets or bugles or fanfares to alert the press table. No warm-up stooges beating the drum to prepare the convention for the next event. All that happened was that a man in a white, open-necked shirt with the sleeves rolled up stepped in front of a battery of microphones and said, *"Brothers and Sisters. . ."*

You could study his form and visage closely from the press table. His shoulders were wide and his wrists were strong. The hips were lean. His head was aquiline with a high-contoured brow topped with brown, not-well-combed hair. The muscular face looked old, at first glance, with a Satanic cast, over-weathered like driftwood. High cheek bones, carved lines down to the jawbone, almost-black eyebrows—these may have helped give him the aged Satanic look. But the blue flash of his eyes was young. He was lithe-waisted and when he waved an arm at the crowd you could tell it was a strong ready arm.

He could have been an electrician or a bus driver (as far as looks were concerned). He wasn't white collar by any means. There was something too active, too vulgar, too dramatically vigorous about him. He wouldn't fit well at a cocktail party. You couldn't picture him at a dinner party honoring Adlai Stevenson.

241

So he said, simply—*Brothers and Sisters. . .*

That "humdrum" assembly went up in smoke. The press table whispered among itself. Some reporters didn't know who the speaker was. Others thought there must be some disturbance in the arena or a message in the sky.

It wasn't. It was only Skinny Walker talking to his own.

There was no prep-school chanting. No carefully rehearsed Indian dances down the aisles. No placards commanding LAUGH-CHEER-APPLAUD. There was a simple explosion of sentiment—a cataclysm of response. When mean, taciturn men, (and women too) get together in a huge meeting place, they rumble all the time. It is not like a PTA meeting with gabble-gabble. Nor the hissperwhisper of a concert. Nor a legion's drunken clowning. And when mean, taciturn delegates allow their rumble to erupt in a great volcanic cheer—you know that something real has happened.

Skinny took it. It was like a cannon-shock. The press table couldn't see the goose flesh on the back of his neck. He stood there in the sun while the roar of greeting and the calls of "Skinny!" "SKINNY!" "*SKIN-NYYY!*" bathed him like a drenching downpour.

Our reporter hastily rewrote his lead:

"With all the fervor of a Jehovah's Witness convention, 40,000 ragtag delegates. . ."

Skinny stood and waited. They simmered down and he began to talk. He talked plainly. He talked straightly. No Shakesperean phrasing. No fancy rhetoric at all. His voice was bell-clear with a tenor ring hiding in the West Virginia softness of it like a jackknife. What he said was so direct and bluntly said that it was often vulgar. The reporters noted the principal points he stressed, and the occasions when the applause was so tumultuous it pulsed out over the water.

Skinny said: *This thing in Korea stinks to high heaven.* (Deafening applause.)

Skinny said: *They've sucked their thumbs and scratched their butts down in Washington and they still don't know*

242

what to do about lay-offs. (Deafening applause and catcalls for Washington.)

Skinny said: *Take the C.I.O. and the N.A.M. and turn 'em upside down backwards and you can't tell 'em apart.* (Deafening applause.)

Skinny said: *If Harry Truman walked in John L. Lewis's shadow he'd freeze to death.* (Deafening applause.)

Skinny said: *They can jabber about this here inflationary spy-rall all they want, we're out for higher wages and better job conditions and we're going to damned well get them.* (Deafening applause and prolonged angry muttering.)

Jimmy Hoffa couldn't talk like that—with the honest power of Skinny Walker and his 4,162,075 Americans. Reuther stuttered by comparison. The high-flown sonority of Bryan, Debs, Darrow and Lewis would have been a different language altogether. Skinny talked the gatehouse tongue. The kind of talk you get in the locker room, around the time clocks and the picket line.

Take a look at this maverick contingent of American workingmen in the Cleveland Stadium. (You may never see it again.) Labor in this country has gone through a series of distinct stages. This is the one that needed Skinny Walker. He was there. He was not possible before and he will not be possible again. For certain, he was not the worst of the lot.

When the convention came to its end, our reporter wrote the following commentary:

"The Walker group is a one-man show standing on the side lines yelling 'Foul!' at everything the major labor movement accomplishes. It is a collection of Know-Nothings under the dictatorship of an ignorant demagogue who can't go anywhere but down..."

Which was probably pretty good news interpretation. Skinny Walker was satisfied with the work of the convention and stepped up his organizing drives. But he, too, knew that time was limited. The stronger he looked (on paper), the weaker he felt. He didn't stay awake nights worrying about it.

(He'd stay on his machine until the shift came to an end.) Inside his bones he must have known—*there was nowhere to go but down.*

His office payroll now was thirty times what it had been when he assumed the presidency of the old International Union. He had a private plane (which took him away from the company of stewardesses). An entire department of college-boy types wrote his speech drafts, researched his wage propositions and gathered statistics. He was surrounded by hirelings who didn't know a Banbury from a third-ply.

He had bright young things in the Public Relations Department, the Time and Motion Study Division, and even an Administrative Section. His office personnel were organized into their *own* union, the better to bargain with Skinny's union, their employer. The extent of his bureaucracy can be judged when you know that there were good looking women in his staff who had never even slept with Skinny Walker. Never had been asked. . .

One of these was Marsha Lentz. She was a tiny brunette with oversized, sharply pointed breasts and Skinny *had* noticed her in the course of things. (She was classified "Skilled Office, primary: 1.62 per hour.") Marsha was sloe-eyed and college-bred. She often studied Skinny as he walked through the office and her carmined mouth would work in slow, nervous shapings. . .

She intercepted him one day at the elevator.

"Mr. Walker?"

"That's what they call me. . ." he smiled politely. He was moved to wonder if her breasts were in any danger near a pencil sharpener. . .

"I'm Marsha Lentz."

"That's a good thing to know."

"I'm in the P.R. Department, Mr. Walker. We're having a little party tomorrow night. It's over at Jack Carney's apartment on Goodstone Boulevard and we'd be delighted if you would come. . .?"

244

He looked at her sweater and thought how tired he was. He also reflected on how separated he was from these people who worked around him. He patted her on the shoulder in a kindly way.

"Put the address on my desk, will you? Tell Jack I drink rye. . ."

The apartment building surprised him. It was one of the new, much-glassed buildings. He hadn't reckoned that Jack Carney or any of the researchers made enough money to live in such high style. The decor of the apartment itself was very modern, very stark. White leather and dark walls—little pieces of impressionistic sculpture. It all surprised Skinny Walker very much. As did the company at the party. . .

Jack Carney was married to a blond, boyish-looking girl named Bunny. Morris Rabin was there with a cuddly-plump girl who called herself Kuku. (Skinny couldn't place her on the payroll at all. She must have been an outsider.) There was also a tall, gaunt woman from Skinny's Radio-Research Department who shook hands aggressively, saying, "Call me Babs and I'll call you Skinny." She shaved the back of her neck.

This then was the party: Jack and Morrie. Marsha, Bunny, Kuku and Babs. And Skinny. None of the others was over twenty-five or six years old. Skinny was thirty-six. Except for Bunny, they each had one or more college degrees. Here in their own environment they spoke with great ferocity about integration, Charley Parker, Zen-Buddhism and Colette. None of which Skinny Walker understood. They all seemed well on the way (alcoholically) when he arrived. They were drinking from little amber pony glasses while a hidden console sounded "Blues In the Night". . .

Babs and Bunny danced while everyone else lounged limply on the sofa, the floor, or on absurdly ugly chairs. Skinny drank quickly to catch up. His presence had been acknowledged with greetings when he arrived; for a while after he was free to move around and drink. Practically unnoticed. . .

When suddenly Kuku and Marsha were engaged in a violent dispute. Through a gentle fog of uncaring, Skinny heard them appealing to him. The voices were sharp and strident and sincerely corrupt.

"Girls, girls!" he responded sadly, feeling the patriarch. "Remember you're among friends. . ."

"I say a woman's body is classic!" Kuku shrieked. "I spit on Vogue and its damn giraffe-necked fashions!"

"What does a man say, Skinny?" Marsha asked, sitting on his knee. "How about it, fella? Don't you agree that the female figure is changing? That men are aware of the change and *want* it that way?"

"I say you judge a tomato by its touch," Skinny laughed insipidly. "Let's see what the hell you're talkin' about."

So he was responsible at the beginning. Marsha and Kuku undressed on the spot. The decorum of the party shattered like a brittle glass bubble—all at once. The other girls abandoned their dancing to join the fun. As they stripped too (with bits of apparel flying through the air) Skinny lay back on the couch and wondered what the hell? There was a curious array of breasts and buttocks and squinting navels. (He genuinely preferred Kuku in the nude to Marsha whose shanks were on the meager side. And he was sorely tempted to tell Babs to get dressed and to stay forever dressed—for goodness sake. As a gentleman, he said nothing.) Carney kept serving drinks, spilling them and laughing with a twitch. Morrie lay on the floor, moaning in mock ecstasy.

"Unfair!" Bunny squealed. "Here we are all in the raw and these boys are still dressed!"

Jack and Morrie were easy converts. Bunny and Marsha descended on Skinny intent on removing his clothing. When he saw they were dead serious he took a deep drink and reluctantly permitted them to pull off his trousers.

It was silly. He felt cold and unnerved. Erskine Walker had never so much as necked a girl in public. He had incredibly stuffy notions about sexual exhibitionism. He pulled a willing

246

Kuku onto his lap to cover his embarrassment. It just wasn't his kind of a party. . .

In time, after much clambering around and interchanging, there were naked figures sprawled all over the floor. They found connections like big, blind, hairy, mouth-hungry infants. . . "*Let's you and me hit the bedroom*" Skinny whispered to Kuku. "*And spoil the chain? Oh Skinny!*" she protested.

He disentangled himself—strongly and irrevocably moved to get the hell out. They didn't notice his departure. "It may be something," he told himself in the cab, "but it ain't for Skinny Walker." The wriggling bodies back at Carney's apartment had quite forgotten him. He was on the sidelines again—calling '*Foul!*'

On Thursday, March 11, 1951, Skinny Walker was sitting carefully at the White Front Bar:

Whole world stinking moose with clock in its belly...Whole damn world. Clock off, too. Can't trust clocks, moose or Goodstone, either. Five after eleven isn't right. Round and round it goes but old Skinny catches the lying clock in the lying moose, holds it with one old hillbilly eye cocked like a hunter to shoot the right time down but it isn't there.

Boy, it's going round. Old bar slopes up one hill and down the other, and the sloppy beer steins hold on like flies in a commode. Moose got glass eyes. Wrong time, too. It's Thursday altogether. Not five after, not ten after. Frigging moose don't know. Bartender don't know. Whole world and Goodstone too. Don't know the right time. Wouldn't give it to you if they did.

Try to count the shots. Straight rye and beer chasers— make the old gut hotter than a clock in a moose. Tell time,

248

by God, by the shots in a man. Twenty-five shots to the fifth—twenty the way Frankie pours 'em, and we got us a fifth and a half, shy one finger. Thirty shots and maybe twenty beers...Go to hell you moose! Been here a good two-and-a-half hours, anyway you look at it. Time enough to make out, whatever the rate is.

Everything goes around, like a tire machine. Spin, spin, spin. Everything goes back to the beginning. Joke is, you don't know the beginning when you get there. Spin, you coxmen! No beginning, no ending—Skinny Walker all the way!

Barefoot when I hit this town, barefoot when I leave it. Skinny Walker coming and Skinny Walker going. No difference. If you could tell the difference you'd never make the track. Why try? Tell you why, you ignorant hillbilly: *the track is for trying.* That's why. Try anything for size. Moose, Goodstone, Marshall's wife, Case Avenue biddy—no difference. Just try the track for size, for Christ's sake. That's why. That's what a track is for...

What the hell you think Goodstone is for? To make tires? How damned stupid can you get? Goodstone is to try for size! Goodstone is the track. Goodstone is what makes the thing go around. Who cares anyway? Put you on this machine, put you on another. No difference either way. Make out, or—don't make out. Suit yourself, if you're man enough. Not a lousy red apple. Be a red apple. See if Skinny Walker cares. Laid a red apple once. Biggest ridge runner I ever seen. Did I lay her? Who cares? Nothing wrong with red apples. Just plain folks, that's all. But they're at the beginning, and can't find the track.

Who's going to show them the track? Skinny Walker—that's who!

Round and round she goes and where she stops nobody...Skinny knows. She stops at the beginning, that's where. All roads lead to the first road. There's nothing happening, that's what's happening. Old moose is fresh and going to drop a baby moose. Tell her next time she comes around.

Hallo, old moose! Your calf looks like a rotten clock! How you like that? Wrong time, every time. Tell old Daddy Moose, why don't you? Go scratch yourself, you wouldn't make a pimple on a big moose' butt. Tell you next time you make the track. Silly frigging moose.

Frankie! Hold down the damned bar! Think you're working out of classification? Look, any Stahlmater can serve a drink. Takes a man to keep the bar steady. Use both hands and slow it down. Never use one hand, fellow, when two hands will do the job. You got a bar on Case Avenue that won't sit still. Thinks it's a merrygoround. Silly damn bar.

What was today when it still was today? What was the time before that red apple moose got hold of it? What was I doing before I stopped doing it, and started telling time with rye whiskey and a stupid moose? Hold onto one damned thing—whatever happens to the bar. I'm Skinny Walker. I was Skinny Walker when I came in, and I'll be Skinny Walker when they carry me out. That was the beginning and that'll be the end.

You can't corner a man on a round track. I'll run faster than they can run. I'll run better, too. Sweat, sure, and strain a little, but not so you can tell it. They want to track me down, they have to catch me at the beginning. To hell with 'em. Know what they'll find? Round and round they go, and when old Skinny gives out they'll find him. I'll be the same damned Skinny that started. So—who's ahead? They could get me now, and they'll get me then, but not until they run the track. And they won't be what they started to be.

But I will! I started out to be one thing for sure. Not Local President, and not International President and not Congress President. Ho, you lying moose! Come around once more and call me a liar! I'll show you what a silly moose you are. That's all right, Frankie. I know, you dago son of a bitch. . .

Put it on the bill. I broke your moose. I know it. It was a

finkish moose anyway. Lied about the time. Write it down. One moose: screwed by Skinny Walker. You lie when you write it! No moose no more! Never was a moose. Dead broken moose. Ataboy, stop the bar and I'll sign it. A broken moose. . .three dollars? 'Stoo much for a stupid moose. Clock never was right. Cheap dirty bar anyway,

I been to clean bars. They're cheap dirty bars too. One's a beginning and one's an ending and I don't give a damn which end you take. Or beginning. Way I feel about it, Frankie. . .Way I feel. . .

You write this down, too, while you're at it. I didn't start out to come in and get drunk at the White Front Cafe. I started to get on the Goodstone track because it was the biggest track I could find at the time. I walked all the way, and then I started running. I won't stay at the White Front Cafe either. I'm moving too fast for that. You just keep the damned bar from moving too fast for me to see it, or I'll knock the mirror down like I did the moose. This wasn't where I started and this won't be where I end.

You know I'm Skinny Walker and the moose knew it too. Goodstone can't figure it out. They've been monkeying around with fifty thousand Skinny Walkers and never knew what it was. To be Skinny Walker. I know. You bet your bottom dollar I know. And Goodstone will know. Maybe. I can't guarantee Goodstone. They get drunk up in the tower too. They all get drunk. Drunk with being Goodstone. Like I'm drunk with being Skinny Walker. No difference. Glasses cleaner. Whiskey leaner. Bars shorter. But they all go round.

You bet your bum they all go around. Tire machine goes around, and all bars go round. Faster and faster. . .takes a real good man to hold a hand out and stop 'em. We've stopped bars before and we'll stop Goodstone. Bet your shirt. I bet mine. And it's all Walker shirt. Walker shirt at the beginning and Walker shirt when it stops. Never tried to be anything else.

Frankie, you lovable wop. Ever want to be something else?

Good bartender—right? Best bartender on Case Avenue? Right? All I ever wanted to be was Skinny Walker. Best damned Skinny Walker on Case Avenue. What's so wrong about that? All depends whether you're at the end or the beginning. I'm always there. Wherever it is. On the track. Boom! That's me! That's old Skinny Walker. I don't give a futz if you like me or not, Frankie. But I'd think more of you if you liked me. I can't help you be anything you're not. But I'll help you be more of whatever the hell you are. That's worth liking. You're damned right it is. . .

We got classifications and job protection and seniority rights. Right? And these stumpjumpers got their homes paid for and sending kids to college. Right? I never told 'em they'd be anything else. I said stick together and don't take anymore crap than you have to. All I ever told 'em. Frankie, you know that's a fact. What they want now? Wanta be steelworkers? Grocery clerks? Lawyers? Baloney! They're gum miners. What they are. All they'll ever be. Best paid. Best organized. Gum miners, for Christ sake. Whoever told 'em they were civilized?

All I ever told 'em was be yourself. I'm *myself*. Whatever I am. Whatever you are. Just a point on the track. You know? Going round and round and round. But always there. Right spanking there!

'Zept I don't know where the point is right now. I don't know for sure where right now is, either. Boyo-boyoboy. .,.she's really rollin'! Ooo, look at her go! Christamighty, where's the moose? Ol' moose gave out on us. Ol' Frankie's gone. . .White Front smashed and gone away. Round and round she goes. . .

No? *Yes*! Goodstone's melted in the twister, too! Never could count on· 'at Goodstone. Not in a clinch. Red apples, through and through. So, don't stop! Don't you give a poop how dizzy Skinny Walker gets. .,.He'll get over and over and over. . .

Ol' Devilshown be there. You ol' twister goin' 'round and round. . .makin' ol' Skinny dizzy. . .grindin' all of 'em up 'n'

252

Gooshstone too. . .go ram y'rself. . .goin' shlow down sometime, stansta reason. . .shlow down some time 'n ol' Skinny get off Devilshown. . .

Still be there. ..

It wasn't long before there was very little that Skinny Walker found appealing. There was in point of fact, damned little he could put up with. . .

By 1952 (which was some kind of a pivotal year) he found himself in flagrant dissension with just about everything that was happening. There was a police-action war going on in Korea, an undeclared war where United States strategy seemed committed to defeat by invitation. Skinny hated the Korean War and it weighed on him more than the entirety of the Second World War.

Harry Truman was President and a great many people admired him because they wanted so badly to feel superior to somebody. He was easy to feel superior to. Skinny thought Harry Truman looked and smelled like a county judge. County judges, in his eyes, were necessary but insignificant evils, like constables, sewer inspectors, and marriage license clerks. You might have 'em around, but you surely don't give 'em an H-Bomb pushbutton to play with?

254

Senator Joe McCarthy was making big noises about Communists. From time to time, he sounded like a man to Skinny's ears, but it never lasted. He was a low-born Mick, Skinny decided, nothing but a loud slob, and he'll never make it. You can't get rid of Commies by yelling at them...

They'd straightened General Eisenhower up by 1952 (after a long hard war in Paris) and were parading him like Daddy Warbucks through the streets, intent on making *him* the President. He looked like a retired bond salesman to Skinny Walker, but if he wanted to be President badly enough he could have it. He'd find out later that it wasn't much different from SHAEF, except that he'd have to watch his health and sobriety a little more.

Nothing in the public eye looked good to the baleful Skinny Walker. He held his Joint Labor Congress back from giving an endorsement to Adlai Stevenson because Adlai struck him as a queer duck, nothing more.

The AFL and CIO joined forces in a new "united" organization, their fusion sparked by the aggressions of Walker's JLC. To Skinny the "new" movement was now twice as phoney as it had been. He gave it scant recognition.

There were several things he didn't recognize at all—having done battle with them and coming to a stand-off. One was the Taft-Hartley legislation which the JLC went around, using a "no-union" choice in NLRB elections to designate their jurisdiction. Another was the new media of television, called "video" or "Tee-Vee" (the semantics not yet having congealed).

Skinny participated in a session of "Meet the Press", originating in Washington, D.C. He wasn't designed for polite palavers, and when an undersized, rodenty little jerk sought to needle him in front of the camera, Skinny had leaned toward him confidentially.

"Come up to Akron," he told the interrogator, "and talk smarty like that and I'll run your raunchy little butt right out of town."

255

The networks and newspapers rebuked him sharply for this impropriety. He didn't like television.

He was almost thirty-seven years old, a very important fellow in his field, and there wasn't much he cared for, no matter where he turned.

It was a hot summer. All of the things he didn't like were on people's minds and in the news. He took a vacation, the first of his life—with a compulsion to "get away from it all" stronger than the average tourist's.

The "Dog Days" were on; Union business was at a standstill, and the world was concerned with a variety of issues—none of them to Skinny Walker's taste. . .

He traveled light, driving a leased car, his bag in the back seat and a pint of whiskey in the glove compartment. It was late morning on a weekday as he drove West from Akron, not knowing, not caring where he was headed.

There had been a time (thought Skinny as he steered his way along the highway) when he had liked many things. He saw the farmlands, groves of trees, meadows and winding streams as he drove. He had liked the outdoors.

By God! Nobody knew how much he liked the outdoors! The smell of morning when the white April sun burns off the dew. . .The crackle of a dry, red leaf as it floats to the forest floor. . .The mist on a hilltop, the whistle of the wind in winter, the silver sheets of rain that come at the season's turn. . .

He'd always had himself a gun, and it was boots in snowtime, barefoot all the rest, because he'd been an outdoors kid.

School had been a painful chore, not because of learning but because of walls. Because young Erskine couldn't breathe freely encamped in the schoolhouse, with all outdoors in palpitation just beyond his lungs.

He hadn't seen a gun since the 1938 riot. He had taken himself into a worse school, the chest-panging dust of the factory. He hadn't laid a bare foot in the rich earth for

256

fourteen years or more.

Driving toward the Indiana line, he felt he had turned his back on every good thing he'd ever liked. All the things he'd treasured, admired, respected and desired. . .

Granddad Bates Walker was dead two years when Skinny walked away from Devil's Own. Eighty-eight years old at the time he went, a man with a rumble still in his throat, and a grip in his long blue-veined hands. The old man had taught Skinny a lot, some of which he worked at, and some of which was learned without the telling of it.

How to be your own man, yet abide by your neighbor's law. How to love a woman without becoming her chattel. How to command action and know the command will be obeyed. How to act when it is not. . .

The grandson grew up at the old man's knee (with his mother dead there was only the old man to tend the cabin). Of all his kin, the boy Erskine loved the patriarch, with his tales of Grant and Appomattox, his tobacco-chewing homilies, his lean, hawkeyed visage, and especially the way he died. . .

"I ain't getting up today, Buster," he had called to Erskine from his room. "You'd best to fotch me a bucket of water. I ain't fixin' to get up at all. . .''

The boy had "fotched" the bucket and sat beside the dying man's bed all day. There was no fuss, no commotion. Granddad lay like wax, giving Skinny reports as death moved in.

"I won't make it to sundown. You tell your Paw I'm much obliged for my long stay."

He lay like a victim on an altar, without complaint. Skinny watched with compassion. It was like a sunset in itself.

"I'd just as soon go in the daylight, Erskine. It's cold beyond the hills. It's getting colder all the time."

When the old man started to shake, it was his first animation. It made his speech more difficult.

"I-I'm going on ahead to meet all our folk. I'll s-s-say Howdy for you and your P-P-Paw. There won't be m-m-many of you left. There warn't a lot to b-begin with. . ."

They laid him to rest that evening. He was one of the men Skinny Walker most liked, and he thought (as he drove toward South Bend) "I've never even been back to the old man's grave." (Which was beside Goldy Walker's grave, but we won't talk about that. . .)

How can you compare a man like that with the little men around, the Trumans, Reuthers, McCarthys and Eisenhowers?· His voice rolled out of the West Virginia hills, mixed with the outdoors in its vastness and its void, *"There won't be many of y' left. . ."*

He drank a quick toast to Granddad Walker. Skinny liked whiskey, and he kept on liking it. The pint in the compartment was dry before he reached the outskirts of Gary, and he'd only used it to "wet his whistle."

Whiskey was like spring water. It had its own way to go like a fire through dry grass, and you had to move ahead of it, or be burned along the way. All the Lenox Cafes in the world couldn't match the pleasure of sitting on a stump in a hollow with a jug over your elbow, and the diamond-cut of homemade whiskey burning in your gullet.

He'd tried fancy drinking, with candied confections called Martinis and Daiquiris and "cocktails". They had whiskey in them, which was some excuse, but they really couldn't compete with plain whiskey-drinking for pure pleasure. They really couldn't.

It was impossible for him to recall his first taste of whiskey; he'd been a boy in short britches at the time. But his first real drunk could be remembered well enough. It coincided with his first experience with a woman.

There'd been a church social in Devil's Own and Matt Owens, Parren Pike and Skinny had put together enough money for a two-dollar jug of corn liquor. *Damn but that was the best jug ever invented!*

It helped lure some girls down the road, giggling and whispering—each taking turns in furtive swallows. Skinny could recall it well, and the final scene in the scrubby orchard with only himself and a girl remaining. With over half the jug undrunk. . .

"Where'd they all run off to?" she asked him with a show of embarrassment.

"They're in the bushes somewhere," Skinny grunted. "You a Braddock girl?"

"I'm Lila Braddock. You the Walker boy?"

With the jug in one hand, he used the other to reach for her hips. His first bodily contact with his very first girl, Lila Braddock, had been right between the legs. He'd not been the first one there, but he made his own good impression.

And they drained the jug between them, lying on the ground, drinking while joined, with corn whiskey spilled on their chins and its fumes adding music to the night. Lila was loud in her cries and Skinny would pause because, in his illiterate way, he feared she was hurt.

She held his face cupped in her hands and moaned "*No!*", meaning not to stop, and when he sensed her meaning he knew enough to keep on going.

The moon through the apple trees was like whitewash and he lay afterwards in baffled study of Lila Braddock's beauty. She held her eyes open to the sky and she told him her feelings.

"A thing so good can't be bad, can it, Skinny?"

He didn't respond. The idea that womanflesh could be had in any way hadn't even entered his mind.

"I just felt like I was bleeding all over. I never felt like that before."

His first woman (who was all of sixteen to his fifteen-year-old manhood) didn't confuse him with talk of love or apologies for being drunk or any such discussions.

She was young enough and candid and she told him what any man would love to hear, how he had satisfied her and she could ask no more.

"I thought I was dying, Skinny, really dying! And I

259

wanted to keep on living—just so's I could keep on dying!"

These were the things and the acts and the sensations he liked. Plain whiskey and a willing woman, the prettier the better. Politics and government, factories and unions, factions and elections could all go to hell.

In a second-rate Chicago hotel, he had the bellhop bring him a fifth of whiskey but no woman. He sat in the muggy room looking out at the bleak anonymous back-sided fire-escaped buildings until morning came in over Lake Michigan. He sat in an uncomfortable chair with his feet on the window sill, thinking of all the things he hated, and how he had not a damned bit of what he liked.

She wasn't any prize winner, to look at her. But she was smarter than hell and she had been Senator Fisher's secretary for as long as he'd been in Washington. Her face, like her body, was lean and angular, interesting in its angularity, provocative in its athletic leanness. Behind her glasses were surprisingly large, quick-moving, intelligent hazel eyes. Beneath her tailored jacket were surprisingly large, highly-placed globular breasts.

She was wearing neither her glasses nor her jacket as she watched Skinny across the bed. He smoked a cigarette and stared at the ceiling, thinking, "It sure takes a lean horse for a long race. . ." He let her talk because he needed the rest and, while talking, she'd let him alone. It was 1954, and he was getting more careful about "pacing" himself. What she was saying was not so offensive, and the bare, coiled litheness of her figure was a symbol of pleasure and danger too. The pleasure was in knowing that she was obedient, responsive and ready; the danger was that she might kill him with the vigor and readiness of her response. So she talked and he listened, and her sharp voice was the only sound in the bedroom.

Her name was Martha Hedrick. She hailed from Minnesota, had a Physical Education degree (plus Secretarial Science), was unmarried, earned a lot of money by Washington girl standards and paid none of her own bills. She sent four hundred dollars a month back home to Hubbel, Minnesota to support her aging parents, a crippled sister and a five-year-old son who had Martha's mobile eyes and the ruddy coloring of a Congressman who had since lost his seat. She was almost as old as Skinny.

"So I'm leaving Senator Fisher's office," she said, "when the next session begins. I'll really miss the old goat. He takes it as a personal blow but the fact is I'm leaving him a very well-trained office staff and he'll never know I'm gone. Oh, he'll look around every morning and grunt, 'Where's Marty today?' but they'll tell him I'm not coming in today, and that's the way it'll be. . ."

"You been with the old boy a long time?"

"Almost sixteen years. He brought me into town when he was elected. I love Sam Fisher, y' understand? It's not that I'm disloyal in any way. It's just, well—he's not *going* anywhere, y' see? He's old and our people love him, but he's not *doing* anything. The Senate is sort of a retirement program, and he muddles along, day in and day out. I suppose he'll keep on until he dies. There's nothing wrong with it, really. It's just that for *me*—well, I know too much now to waste it all, this way—do y' see?"

He looked at the spring-taut restlessness of her body and wondered, appraisingly, if he could be ready shortly to match its needs with his strength. He decided: not quite yet. Let her talk.

"I hate to see you waste anything, gal. So where are you going when you leave Fisher?"

She laughed tartly and leaned over to light her fresh cigarette on the shortened stub of his.

262

"I'm already working with my new boss. You aren't going to like it, I know. I'm going with John Hobhouse. . ."

"The fink from Kansas?"

"The fink from Kansas. He *is* a fink, I know. I couldn't agree with you more. But he's a red-hot fink, y' see? He's on the move and he knows where he's going. He knows what he needs and he wants me. It's a big opportunity for a small town gal. Hobby is going to make a big name for himself. He wants me and he knows how to use me."

Skinny was much aware of Senator Hobhouse and his noisy ride to eminence as the investigation chief involving something called Labor Rackets. He knew a fink when he saw one. But he didn't care where the girl went to work. He had no direct personal relationship with the Hobhouse Committee. It alleged to be interested in hoodlums, Syndicates, sweetheart contracts and that sort of thing. It was all outside Skinny Walker's orbit. So he said nothing, although her voice appealed for his condonement.

"He wants *you* too, Skinny."

This announcement made him sit up, eyes widened as if he had been assaulted. *Damn*! he thought. You'd think this smart skinny gal was a machine for fornicating. You'd just about feel apologetic for not servicing her better. And then, you see she's in bed with you for something else altogether! He winked, compulsively, at the ceiling.

For its own reason this Fall of 1954 was Skinny Walker's time for critical encounters with women he had known. He lay in bed with Martha Hedrick and felt inertia in his loins, astonishment around his heart and over all of him fatalism like a cold, melancholy sheet. He had the notion he was in his coffin, disrobed and on display. Old lovers were gathered around clucking, chattering. Things were happening, being said, planned and plotted—as if he were the center of the party. Which he was—but dead, cold and uncaring.

He felt as he had felt when he heard the news of Helen MacDougal.

Helen had grown puffy with excessive drinking. Still on piece work in Hollywood, she had gained a wide reputation for "making out" with any horny tirebuilder who caught her when she was drunk enough. It had been a long time since she and Skinny had shared any intimacy. Some oldtimer remembered their association, and thought enough to bring the word to Skinny before he read it in the paper.

"Helen MacDougal?" the man informed Skinny in his office.

"Helen MacDougal *what*?" Skinny had retorted, with some irritation.

"Helen's dead."

"Helen's dead?"

"She's dead all right. Found her this morning. Cut her own throat."

"Cut her own throat?"

"Cut her own throat."

He had no epitaph for Helen. It was a hell of a thing to do. He had kissed that throat, and now the gushing blood choked him, blinded him, made him nauseous.

He lay in the crude coffin of being dead, all by himself, ahead of time and he felt *out* of it. Just *out* of it. He'd been that way when Betty Marshall called him, a week after Helen's death.

"Of course I remember you," he told her on the phone. "Why shouldn't I?"

"It's been such a long while, Skinny, that's all. Such a damned long while. I'd like to talk. . ."

So they talked, in the dark corner of a plush roadhouse on the Cleveland Road. She was exactly the same and he remembered her very well—the Chivas, the apron and belting her once or twice. She told him she was divorcing Bennett Marshall.

"He's not a bad guy, Skinny. It's just that I've *had* it. The petition's filed, and I have a marvelous attorney. The point is that Bennett can't risk a battle. He'll settle. He'll settle very handsomely."

264

"Bennett does things in high style."

"Most things—if money is involved. Skinny, you say you remember? Well so do I. I couldn't stand Bennett a minute after you and I—. I've had it. That's what's wrong!"

What the hell could you tell her? Go talk to Helen MacDougal? Find out how to cut your throat in one easy lesson? Skinny's coffin of non-involvement was cramped and uncomfortable.

"You wonder why I'm telling *you*?" Her light voice was girlish and lacking the vanity of contrived phrases. She was selling strong, Skinny thought. "I'm telling you because there's only one thing I want now. *I want to become Mrs. Erskine Walker!*"

It was enough to make a cold corpse gallop off in the night of bewildered cries. She was a fancy lady, all right, with a fur and a veil and false eyelashes trained to flutter pertly. It had been twelve years since he had broken her teeth for her.

He was getting old. The problem was that he couldn't laugh at her, lay her or hit her again. He sat mutely.

"I can help a lot, Skinny. We *were* good together! I've got money, and Bennett will give me a lot more! I'll have children if *you* want them! I won't hold you down, either. I know you're accustomed to a bachelor's pace. I know that. But we can have loads of fun—."

Skinny Walker did what a gentleman would do if a gentleman were Skinny Walker. He got the hell out of there. He rose, walked to the door and left her, without a word. She had a very small check to pay...

But it made him think of having children—wondering if his broken testicle robbed him of fatherhood forever? As well as slowing him down?

He learned at the rubberworkers picnic in the heat of summer that Pauline Danver had remarried. This was at Summit Beach Park, near the softball park, and Skinny was hailed by Charlie Morrison. Charlie was a plain, paunchy little foreman at Plant One—an undistinguished company man, grey and mediocre.

"Skinny! Whyn'tcha congratulate me? Whyn'tcha wish us luck?" He was well on his way, apparently, with the free beer provided by the Union Commissary. "Why in hell don'tcha say Howdy to the new Mrs. Morrison?"

He looked at Pauline Danver Morrison who was wearing a flouncey straw hat and munching on cotton candy, as handsome and radiant as ever.

"Howdy," he said to her, his eyes narrow in the sun.

A potbellied foreman! Behind her he saw the monumental shadow of Burke Danver, chiseled in the sky. *Burke!* Skinny beat at his coffin walls and tried to call his old comrade. *Burke, she's betrayed us both!* Heat waves rose from the picnic grounds in a wraith-like rhythm. The foreman and his bride walked down to the Dodgem hand in hand, and Skinny died some more.

Which was why he could lie beside Martha Hedrick in a Maryland bedroom and listen as she told him, "Hobhouse wants *you*, too"—and why he listened only. Did not strike her, cut her throat, throw her from the window. He was a line commander, tired from battles without number, numb in his inability to react. Besides all this, his scrotum ached.

Only a week ago the police had called him because Ruthie Rastek was in jail. Yes, he admitted, he knew Ruth Rastek, a Case Avenue whore.

He couldn't recall *her* in bed, but Doc Milliron often reminded him of a bad dose she had given him. But why, he asked the sergeant, does she want to reach him?

"She needs a lawyer, Skinny. She needs one bad."

"What have you booked her for?"

"First degree homicide, Skinny. She's booked tighter than hell."

"Who'd she get?"

"She shot a customer's head off last night. Some Greek from Youngstown."

"Why'd she do it?"

266

"Says she never did like Greeks. That's all she says."

"Sounds reasonable. Who the hell likes Greeks, anyway?"

He sent an attorney down to bail Ruthie out. It would take all winter to get her sentenced to the prison hospital at Lima, for the criminal insane.

They lined up around his casket, Ruthie, Pauly, Betty and Helen, and their voices melted into Martha's brisk tones.

"He's ready to buy, Skinny. He'll pay real-life money, not green stamps. He wants you *very* badly."

"Why should Hobhouse want me?"

"Because he wants a scalp, and yours is a big one, baby. He needs you for his career."

"He wants to bust up the JLC!"

"Hobhouse couldn't care less about the JLC. He's not out to bust unions, Skinny, he wants *you.* He needs a name to crucify. He wants all the credit for putting you out of business. You can be *his* Alger Hiss. Y' see?"

Skinny saw. The fink wanted a stepping stone. It wasn't hard to see.

It was ridiculous to sit in bed with a naked woman and get a message from U.S. Senator John Hobhouse. The impropriety caused Skinny to seethe.

"To get me, he's *got* to get the JLC! He can't get through to me unless he goes after the whole kit and caboodle! I'm clean and he knows it. Let the bastard know he's got a fight on his hands."

"Hobhouse doesn't want to fight. He wants to buy. He's ready to buy you."

"What the hell's wrong with him, anyway? Since when does he do all this *buying?*"

"You just don't fight when you can buy. Not these days. Not in Washington. Fighting costs money, too, y'know."

"It's the damned taxpayers' money!"

"Of course it is. That makes it easier to spend, after all. Hobhouse wants to save the taxpayers' money. He's a very conscientious public servant. A veritable watchdog of the treasury. If he tried to take you the hard way, by fighting, it would cost millions. Just *millions*. That's why he wants to buy. It's the economical thing to do. Aren't you curious about the price tag he's put on you?"

"How much?"

"What's the current membership of the Rubberworkers?"

"About 200,000, maybe more, maybe less."

"He'll pay you two dollars a head."

"What's that?"

"Two dollars a head."

"Two dollars to *me* for every member in the ARC?"

"Two dollars each—cash."

"To me?"

"To you."

"That's a lot of money."

"It's worth a lot."

"That's four hundred thousand dollars."

If you've never been offered four hundred thousand dollars for anything, it will be difficult for you to grasp Skinny Walker's reaction. Consider this: he was practically a barefoot boy, all but illiterate, with no friends and no skills. Now he was worth $2,000.00 a pound just as he was standing, in Martha Hedrick's bedroom. . .Consider this, too: He was being offered a king's ransom not for any betrayal of his cause or his kind—but just for the yielding up of his person. His own person. There's one more thing to consider (if you had been in Martha's bed): Skinny Walker's person (in terms of his active manhood) was worth, in his own eyes, at that moment, *one plugged nickel.*

"Skinny, that will buy a lot of anything."

Martha lay sprawled across the bed, her arms akimbo, her big eyes wanton with earnestness. She looked wicked and desirable, sweet and satanic.

"If you'd take me, Skinny, I go with the deal."

This was her greatest offering, all to further Senator Hobhouse's career. In her own vanity, her person was worth

268

more than four hundred thousand dollars. It signified, in passing, that she was prepared to renounce the Hobhouse banner, once her commission to purchase Skinny Walker was fulfilled. But this was womanly, on her part. Love must conquer all—Walker and a new fortune would keep her more from lusting than all the other impulses and compulsions of her time and place.

"I'm with the deal, too, Skinny," she repeated softly, "if you want me. . ."

He was in his coffin, paralyzed with eternity. He was stricken dumb with the awful eloquence of useless speech. He stared at the mourners who paraded by.

"It sure is a lot of money," his voice was dry and expressionless.

This offended her; it dramatized gold over the treasury of her person.

"Yes and I sure am a lot of woman! And if Hobhouse can't get you the easy way, he'll do it the hard way. He'll spend a million or more if you won't let him buy you out now. How about it, doll? Why don't you save the taxpayers some money?"

He dressed slowly, as if he were alone in the room. Martha Hedrick knew she had said all her lines. She watched him fearfully. It was hard to breathe in the room. She wanted him so badly to say "Yes." She wanted a triumph. She wanted Skinny Walker to live. . .

Hat in hand, he stood by the door.

"You got this all from Hobhouse personally?"

She assented with a nod.

"You going to take my answer back to Hobhouse personally?"

Again she nodded "Yes."

"You tell him some things he's got to fight for. Tell him he's got a bitch of a fight on his hands."

He opened the door. She lay there nudely, quietly.

"Tell him to get you another stud."

Which is how Skinny Walker rejected his grand opportunity to sell out. It's true that he was already dead. But this had never stopped anyone else from selling out. It's true that it wasn't nobility that stood in his way. Unless nobility reduces to the absurd terms of vulgar honesty.

He'd been offered four hundred thousand dollars and the price alone warned him that the deal was corrupt. He just wasn't worth that much.

270

The sociology instructor recognized him when he entered the club car. It was the Pennsylvania line's "The General" and it was roaring through the night-filled Alleghenies, due in Washington by morning. It was Fall, 1957.

"Aren't you Skinny Walker?"

Skinny acknowledged the plump, young-balding man. He'd learned long ago not to respond with his natural zeal, "You're damned betcha I'm Skinny Walker." When people came up to him tentatively, as little bunny-boy was now doing, it was not to question his right to his own name, as if he might be an imposter. It was only to acquire the privilege of addressing him. So he restrained himself and nodded politely when they inquired. He used the time to look around for knives and secret weapons.

"Mr. Walker, my name is Malcolm Scott and I'm on the faculty at Bryn Mawr, in the Sociology Department. . ."

Skinny hadn't the slightest idea what or who was "Bryn Mawr". It might have been an institution, place or a condition, as far as he was concerned. But he got the college odor and the aggressive look of congenital failure that goes with it. He'd surveyed the car and there was no woman within range, so he made his offer.

"Let's have a drink, fellow, and you tell me what your trouble is."

The porter had taken their order before Scott could get the interview on the proper plane.

"It's no trouble. I mean I'm working on my paper. . ."

Skinny grunted at the thought of another reporter and said something to the effect that newspapers were a *lot* of trouble. . .

"Not a newspaper, sir. It's my thesis for my doctorate. I call my paper, just a working title, y'understand, 'The Hero on the American Scene'."

Skinny thought, "My luck, and five'll get you ten he's a queer," but he tossed his first drink and got another one on its way.

"You've got your troubles, fellow. I've got mine."

"It's a real break, Mr. Walker, stumbling into you, if you have a few minutes. I'd like to explain my premises. I'm really trying to steer a clear course between the Marxist-determinism of the 'Crowd Man' on the one hand, and the Jesuit-mysticism of the Western Yogi, on the other. Obviously, I've begun with the fixed notion that a hero comes from somewhere in order to be recognized, but the implicit fallacy. . ."

He droned on with an anxious intensity to his story, and Skinny felt a kind of nausea that came not from the drinks nor from the roll of the train but from being directly confronted with a whole complex of unwholesome (to him) affectations, all bearing the name Malcolm Scott. He let him talk.

"The pioneer strain has run out, although the myth of the cowboy still pursues us. The contemporary hero, to qualify for *my* premise, has to come athwart established order. If he doesn't express dissidence, then he'll never make it. But since the status quo is so solid and unrelenting, y'see, the hero must eventually come to no good end. I know it's objectionable on several grounds—the Arthurian legend for one thing—but I've set my sights on documenting the thesis."

"What's your point? What are you trying to prove?"

"*That all heroes are failures*! The characteristics of a hero—from Robin Hood to Billy the Kid—all demand an end-in-view which simply cannot be vindicated. The hero gets recognition from a certain social fragment on the basis of his against-the-stream expression. But the stream—that's the status quo, of course—sooner or later engulfs him. He has picked up some thread of oppositionism, and been picked up in turn, by the crowd, only to be smashed to pieces. He's a sacrifice, in other words, for aspirations the Crowd couldn't collectively express, and if they had, *they* would have all been destroyed for it. He's neither inner-director nor. . ."

"Scott—what do you want from me?"

It was an honest question, gruffly put. Skinny couldn't, for the life of him, make sense of the fellow's garbage. He had tried, not very energetically, to orient himself in relation to it. Did the egghead want somebody knocked, or was he just in search of a listener?

"It's just that I am using you as an example, Mr. Walker. . ."

"Call me Skinny. Makes me feel easy if you do."

"Of course. But I have you illustrating my case, y' see? Your name is heroic, in our limited context. You have followers. You are defying the Elders. I don't mean that I, personally, by no means, can be counted as an idolator of yours. That's not the question. Within my standards, you qualify as a hero. . ."

"What's the difference, Scott, between a hero and the bad guy?"

The sociologist shivered. He'd drunk one-half of a whiskey sour while Skinny had put away three shots. He was excited

273

by the encounter and by his chance to use a footnote based on direct research.

"That's the academic question! It has always been assumed that bad guys, as you say, lose out, and the good guys triumph. My thesis is that victory or defeat is *entirely* ir-revelant! To be a hero, the hero only has to act out his role. . .*heroically*. Does that make sense to you?"

"No."

This saddened Scott. He clutched his glass nervously, fearful that he would lose his butterfly before the pin was secured.

"Well, perhaps not. You must believe, by virtue of your position, that the Crowd is right in its selection. . ."

"You mean election'? I seen more crooked elections than you can shake a stick at."

"I suppose. I really meant 'selection', but elections some-times serve as the choosing-mechanism. In any case, there's no hero unless the Crowd makes its choice known. . ."

"Bull. There's no hero or whatever unless the guy stands up. I figure he's something if he stands up. Everybody that was counting on him *not* standing up, is going to label him a son of a bitch. But I tell you, buster, there's something in a man makes him stand up or not. You take it from there."

"O, I do, too! That's the destiny-factor. He's *compelled* to stand up, as you say. I'll be glad to work with your terms, Mr. Walker. What I'm trying to probe is whether the syndrome that makes him stand makes him an instrument for good or for evil?"

"You ever figured out what side *you're* on?"

"No side, really. I'm simply trying to correlate the data. Where do heroes come from; why? What happens to them and why?"

"You can't tell which player's which, buster, unless you got yourself a program."

"It doesn't matter, Mr. Walker. I mean, Skinny. I can hear the crowd roaring in the stadium. That's all I need. But

274

there's one thing you can tell me, if you will. Does the hero know where he's going? Is he out to do *good*? Is he carrying a spear for immortal ends, or is he merely self-serving? From your point of view—what's the answer?"

"From my point of view, I'm on my way to Washington. That's all the ticket I bought."

"But you've stirred up an entire nation. You have hundreds of thousands of devoted followers. *Why*? What possessed you? What made you a candidate for heroism? Do you *know*—or are you an instrument of forces beyond your consciousness?"

"Professor, I've been asked that question for twenty years. If I gave you a pat answer, I'd be lying to you. You ask me why I get up in the morning and I'll sure enough tell you. I had me enough sleep and I've got work to do. You ask me why I take a crap and I'll tell you. I got a bellyfull, and a cramp just hit me. You ask me why I'm going to Washington and it's because I got me some business there and I could afford the train ticket. . ."

"But *why* did you stand up? Those are your words, now. Are you only a puppet for your particular crowd, or is your notoriety, I mean your fame, a thing you contrived out of your own ambition?"

Skinny heard the words and he understood the question (which he thought was silly enough). Scott was a queer, no doubt of that. And the ride to Washington was getting longer and longer. He thought: I'll get a bottle and go back to my compartment. There's no action here tonight.

"I'm not one hundred percent my own man," he said, "but this hero crap is for the kids. The newspapers make the heroes and they're good for ninety days. You got a team and there's room for a pitcher. Somebody says 'Hey, pitch a few, will you?' and the next thing you know you're a pitcher. Your team wins a few and you get a write-up in the papers. Get knocked out of the box and you can forget it. . .That's your hero for you."

"Mr. Walker, thanks an awfully lot for your time. I know you have things to do," Scott said. "I can't tell you how much your comments have helped me. Really fine stuff. . ."

The instructor from Bryn Mawr made his way out of the car. Skinny Walker, hummph! A damned alcoholic, to begin with. A perfect ignoramus. And the simplicity of his self-diagnosis! Perhaps, though, the poor fool just can't comprehend what he's up against. Scott passed a platinum blonde between cars—a flamboyant creature headed for the club car.

"Dreadful," he thought. "I should write the president of the Road about the prostitutes on this train. . ."

She wasn't a prostitute, or if she was, a new term should be invented. She collided with Skinny halfway to the bar and they were together, drinking, before there was time for words. Words like:

"You *are* Skinny Walker, aren't you?"

"You damned betcha I'm Skinny Walker."

"Oh God, have I wanted to run into *you*! I'm Wanda Dillon."

In his compartment, with the bottle and the blonde, he found time for a few more words.

"Baby, you know what a hero is?"

"Hero! Come here, doll, and I'll show you I know. . ."

"What's a hero, for Chrissake?"

"You're my hero, lover! God, are you my hero!"

They tossed and turned as the train chewed its way through Pennsylvania hills. Skinny felt the tracks zipping below and the hoot of the engine warning him that Washington and Hobhouse were waiting in the morning. He felt the pelvic clutch of the Crowd goading him to heroic acts. With appropriate adulation, he could still make out, from time to time. He winked to himself and thought, "They ask you to pitch a few, and the next thing you know, you're a pitcher."

276

I'll tell you exactly how it was, when he was gone. This is what happened...

Nothing happened.

Akron died. It went on being Akron, only less so. But the death of the Akron-that-was, and the conversion to the less-than-Akron-that-was-to-be wasn't marked by even a spasm. For two decades it had been convulsed with petulant management, dumb cops, illiterate politicians and Skinny Walker's ilk. With the Hobhouse era, it was very glad, as a city, to be done with all *that*.

Akron was never very much. A town that size can only be an album for the rogues who frequent it. Once Skinny Walker left as inconspicuously as he had come, Akron settled down to a civic stupor, pretending it was a normal Chamber of Commerce-Kiwanis town (which it never was), ignoring the fact that it had dozed off into death (which it really had).

During the days of the hearings and the court action, the people of Akron, Skinny's kind, were not much with it. There were lots of reasons. A lot of the hullabaloo was in Washington, for one thing. In Akron, it took place in the judge's chamber, and judicial events (over the bench or under it) are never much for mass action.

For another thing, Skinny didn't fight. He rallied no defense and appealed for no support. Which was a very wise thing. He couldn't have raised a penny or a token picket, if he had tried. He was numb, nonmilitant, very un-Skinny like. He'd "pitched a few" and he was leaving the game. His mood of resignation communicated itself to everyone, especially those who might have joined a picket line of some sort, if the call had come.

For years, Skinny had been busy cauterizing whatever sensitive points of contact still existed between himself and the echelons which had originally raised him to prominence. Who knows? Did they not respond because he made no call? Did he not call because he knew it was too late for their responding?

An idle question, because no new pitcher was going in. The game—at least this wild, bizarre version of it—was over. Akron was dying. The last bright speck of the thirties, the hillbilly hellion "slab-faced Walker," was going out. The act of his extinction was not even loud enough for a dismal sputter. The conflagration that had been Akron twenty years before was now a grey and undistinguished cinder.

It died, that's all.

Its album pages had hosted mighty men before—the John Browns, Wendell Willkies, and the Whisky Dicks. It had died before—from epoch to epoch, just as, with great good luck, it may die again.

The burial mounds of Akron, Ohio have played the circus for marching men and unbelievably gross tycoons; for harlots and harlequins; and for cultural spores spotted with the taint of genius which gave them the good sense to move out and away. Now, with *his* departure, the demographic landscape grew cold and dark. Akron died, just as the moon dies when

278

it leaves the sun's cast.

Not because Skinny Walker killed it. This was not in his power nor his wish. Akron died the way a stadium dies, with empty bottles, ticket remnants and the filth of crowds, because the game is over.

Lots of little living went on. The expressways connected all the shopping centers, with blatant exit signs for Market Street, Arlington, and Sam's Court. The University expanded into Niggertown (the most unlikely spot for it), having expunged the most flagrant homosexuals from its faculty list, and carrying on, artlessly, the pretense that it was *not* Goodstone's industrial extension. The police became more civilized (many could read and write and didn't pull wings off flies).

The rubberworkers' union settled down to the humdrum of "business unionism" with a bittersweet sense of complacency. The smarter committeemen became foremen for the company; the lesser lights retired on the staff of the International Union. The presidents of Goodstone Local, in rapid succession, took on the luster and multiplicity of Presidents of Mexiço (as Dr. Shrank had predicted.)

Arbitration and automation, hand in hand, changed the guerilla character of class war in Akron. Frank Lloyd Wright came to town and recommended an A-Bomb to provide basic architectural solutions. He was not well-received.

Akron moved into the Eisenhower years like an Egyptian funeral bark, loaded with mementoes and grisly reminders— somberly floating, not down the Nile, but down Summit Canal; crisply cutting its morbid path through yellowed scum and the swollen bodies of dead dogs. . .

For a while there were subpoenas and depositions, hearings, suits and threats of suits. There were some nasty indictments handed down, but they were designed more for punitive negotiation than for "keeps." What, in fact, were Skinny Walker's crimes?

He wasn't in league with the hoods, or the Communist

279

conspiracy. He was a bureaucrat, but not a lavish one. He had, admittedly, impeded the war effort, but the war was long over. No—when Hobhouse moved in on Walker, he couldn't snare him for any superficial crimes. He got him for the big ones. These were: Skinny was alone. Skinny was not a family man. Skinny was tired.

And, over all else, Akron was dying.

Skinny Walker didn't kill Akron, any more than Senator Hobhouse did. A city lives, if it lives at all, in occasional cramps of glory. Akron, for example, has come to life in a variety of vivid convulsive moments—as a canal town, a burgher town, a hillbilly capitol, and Rubber City. The glory of each moment comes from the agony of men caught in a need that is less than bearable; using the theater of the city for expression that is commonly violent. Then the moment passes and the city dies. The need is gone and the wicks of its lamps are shortened. I'll tell you exactly how it was. . .

At the Sons of Herman clubroom on a Saturday night in 1958, there was a bit of conversation which might pass for an expression of Akron-type feeling. Or *not*. Let it enter the record as a slight postscript, illustrative but not necessarily indicative. . .

This Sons of Herman is a big saloon surrounded with the amiable fabric of a fraternal insurance and welfare plan (a formula which applies to the Moose and the Elks, as opposed to the Legion or the VFW which are only big saloons). The decor is common, not quite dingy; the prices are right; the waitresses are older and more churlish than, say, at the Lenox Cafe (which is a penalty you pay for getting fancy). The habitues are from Goodstone's payroll, in their go-to-meeting clothes, glowing with that muddled awkwardness of moderate inebriation which characterizes husbands and wives, together, on an evening out. . .

Mr. and Mrs. Henry Gibbs were at a table with Mr. and Mrs. Jason Cameron when Mr. and Mrs. Marvin Wheeler left the dance floor to say hello.

Wheeler was garbed in a hand-tailored suit with the new look of narrow lapels, and two recent events combined to make him feel extraordinarily man-of-the-worldish. A month ago he had married a pretty little girl from accounting, some twenty-one years younger than he; a week ago he had undergone surgery for hemorrhoids.

"Alabama! Florabella! Red! Juney!" he beamed to all of them.

"Hello, *Bull!*" they acknowledged.

"May I present the new Missus Wheeler? Honey, meet the Gibbses and the Camerons—you folks just call her Rhonda, will y'?"

So there they were assembled, on a weekend when their old mate and leader was being shorn of everything. It was several rounds of beer before the subject arose—

"Papers seem to be lettin' up?" Alabama mentioned to Red, tentatively.

"Yeah. Should all be cut and dried by now."

"Skinny won't actually be going to jail, or fined, will he?" Florabella asked.

The men looked at each other and "Hummphed!" in concert.

"Ol' Skinny'll feather *his* nest before this is all over," Wheeler avowed.

"He sure won't be asking any help from the likes of *us*," Alabama said.

"What makes you think he *needs* any help a'tall?" asked Juney Cameron.

"I never said he's in need of help. Christ, I just said he wasn't *askin'* for none!"

"Skinny's weathered a lot bigger things—startin' with Goodstone itself and the whole world war."

"Not to mention the Commies and Reuther—"

One wife at the table looked at her husband's sightless eye, "Not to mention weatherin' *you—*"

Red and Alabama looked into their beers, recalling the

time they wrecked Skinny's office, and he had wrecked them. . .

"I'll tell you the trouble with Skinny Walker," Bull Wheeler announced.

He summoned the waitress to order another round, establishing his right to tell this group the trouble with Skinny Walker. He wiped froth from his mouth with the back of his hand and set his mug down authoritatively.

"Skinny Walker's dumb! He's a dumb, ignorant hillbilly! He just don't know what's what, and which end is up. I mean it! Nobody said he couldn't stand up and fight." (Which was a healthy admission, for all three men at the table had been whipped by dumb Skinny Walker.)

"Hell, Skinny could agitate, all right, and he could *do* lots of things—" Wheeler continued.

"I'll say this much," Alabama intruded, "he was a good tirebuilder in his time—"

"But he couldn't think. D' y' see what I mean?" Wheeler appealed for understanding. "He couldn't figure things out. Dammit, you just couldn't reason with the man!"

"I don't know about that," Florabella said rebukingly, "I always took Skinny to be a very *bright* man—"

"But you never had to reason with him," Alabama reminded her. "*Bright* he was, but Bull's right. It was next to impossible to reason with him."

"If I can say something," the new Mrs. Wheeler proposed, "*I* never thought he was bright. How can you say he's bright when he's in the mess he's in now? The Hobhouse Committee has really—"

"The Hobhouse Committee is a red apple deal all the way!" Cameron snorted.

"Why didn't Skinny *see* that?" Bull argued triumphantly. "Why couldn't he figure ahead, how the wind was blowing? Any way you cut it, he dug his own grave, and I say the kid just didn't have the brain power. His trouble was dumbness— just plain *dumbness*."

282

Nobody, except Bull Wheeler's bride, believed his theory. But they sat silently at the Sons of Herman and heard him expound it. The trouble with Bull Wheeler was that Skinny Walker was smarter than all of them put together, and they knew it.

The smartest thing he did was *not* to try to revive them. They'd all been betrayed by Skinny, each in his own way, but the level of betrayal *now* was that Skinny Walker was far beyond any need of help they might have given, if he had called—and *if* they had chosen to answer.

Just three tirebuilders, accompanied by their wives, sitting around a table on a Saturday night. They were strong, intelligent, perspicacious men. They were not very "bright", however, and the dullness of the Eisenhower years was upon them. Their homes were paid for, and their seniority status in the shop was secure. Along with others, they had been asked for depositions on the Walker case, and, without advice from counsel, each had tried to make an "honest" statement. Each had helped lift Skinny to the gallows. They hurt with the experience of it.

Tirebuilders always hurt, on their own time. Hands especially. Big, deformed hands, welted from making out, the heel of the palm and the spatulate thumb throbbing and cramping from working the piles and pulling the treads. Well-muscled backs hurt, too. The bands and cords and tendons knot and jerk in little spasms on a Saturday night. Beer alone cannot lacquer this kind of hurt.

Alabama feels pain from old fights and Red's damaged eye socket throbs with bitter memories. Bull's own private hurt is in his tail, and he hopes Rhonda will drink much and get sleepy early.

The biggest hurt is to be nonessential. There are automatic tire machines all over now, and they can outbuild these giants, and outlive them. (But you'll never see an automatic machine in the picket line at the Willard Street gate, nor playing a little grab tail at the Lenox Cafe.)

They are no longer essential to Skinny Walker. He needed them to win, but he doesn't need any help at all to lose.

From the Akron Beacon Journal, Sept. 17, 1960:

WHATEVER BECAME OF –
Skinny Walker?

Erskine ("Skinny") Walker, firebrand chieftain of the independent Joint Labor Congress 1950-57 first gained prominence in 1942 when he was elected president of the Rubberworkers International at the age of 27. Through the war years he led his mavericks against the no-strike pledge, labor-management collaboration and broke into national news in 1944 when he openly defied the War Labor Board. Walker's regime was broken in 1957 by the Hobhouse Investigating Committee which placed him under indictment, turned his General Board against him and smashed his almost mythical standing with the rank and file. At the height of the scandal Walker was badly injured in an elevator accident, losing one leg as a result. The charges against him were quashed and he retired completely from the labor scene. He is currently reported to be running a hotel in Miami with capital allegedly provided by New York City mobsters.

So you see he didn't die... The above dispatch is as close to accuracy as most obituaries. From his bed in Akron's City Hospital, Skinny signed the necessary affidavits and escaped prison at the price of complete withdrawal from union affairs. All the charges weren't quashed, however. Several convictions were eventually handed down. Sentence was suspended in each case and in these cases Skinny Walker lives on extended probation.

He lives alone. It is not much of a life. Because he was not a veteran and because his slim bank holdings were impounded, he was never fitted with a workable prosthetic limb. He uses a forked stick, shoulder-high, and he hobbles about on it. It is fashionable enough transportation for where he now resides.

It is not Miami. Nor is it a hotel. It is on his father's farm, three miles out of Devil's Own, West Virginia. They call it a farm. It is rocky, hilly land and scrub trees grow there—not much else. J. B. Walker is an inspector in a coal mine not far away and his wages pay the taxes and the feed bill. Skinny's mother has been dead a long, long time.

He's well into his forties now, getting on toward fifty. His face has gone leathery and his hair remains brown. Although his beard (which is usually evident) comes out in greyed whiskers.

His eyes are squintier. Not much blue shows through anymore, and when it does it shows pallidly. There is always a pint bottle of green liquor in his pocket. He tells the old man his leg hurts and the old man tries to ration him to a pint a day but it is usually more than that.

In good weather he sits on the stoop of the old one-story farmhouse and suns himself. Looking over the hills that stretch so far and wide you can't imagine that Akron, Ohio is only three hundred miles to the north and west of here.

There is not much talk in him and he seldom reads.

286

Sometimes the old man turns on the radio at breakfast time and it will make noises all day but Skinny seldom hears it. He will make himself moderately useful by sweeping out the linoleumed kitchen floor. Soaking the tin dishes in the sink. Hobble back and forth to feed the cow, the pig sty, and the chickens who are long-winged and fly around the Walker hill. Sometimes he looks for eggs.

The way he dresses and all, you'd take him (anyway) for a man who's close to sixty. Unshaven. Not well washed. Half-drunk. Sleepy on the warped front stoop or on the floor beside the stove—*this is what became of Skinny Walker.*

This is no Napoleon on Elba. In him there are no dreams of recouping, plotting vengeance, being swept again to power. (With a private shower in his office and a private "secretary" in his shower.) In his ears there is no echo of the mass assemblies roaring *"SKINNY"*. No active memory of picket lines or caucus meetings, riots, or the sentimental violence of Case Avenue on Saturday nights. . .

This is no U.S. Grant, drunkenly disheveled before a country store—humiliated by the powers-that-be; waiting for the Civil War to come, and with it fame and glory and the Presidency of these United States. This is a U.S. Grant of sorts—for whom no Civil War will ever come. And no more fame. No glory. Nothing anymore at all.

Skinny Walker's lusty conquering has spent itself. *He harbors no more fear.* He is afraid of absolutely nothing. There are no deputies from trouble spots to bring him hot reports of battle ("What would you do, Skinny? Skinny, what's the word?") His old cohorts read the Beacon Journal and they think he's down in fat Miami if they think of him at all. There is no mail for him. He waits for no more messages.

His leg does hurt. His throat is always dry. Now and then he shaves because he doesn't like how grey the whiskers get when they are five or six weeks old. This much of vanity he still retains.

His liver is quite bad—with spots and palpitations. Things

are not right inside him. The whites of his eyes have yellowed and they droop along the outer edges. Skinny Walker is a sick man but he has no pension, no insurance, no rights to hospitals and surgery, none of the things he fought for—which his "boys" enjoy.

Sometimes he misses women. He doesn't particularly miss particular women (Pauline or Helen or Shirley or Kuku). His glands are slack and there is little memory there. But he will have a sharp cramp of nostalgia, now and then, for *women*, their kind and their appeasement. When he does, he looks across the wild lean sky above the bony hills and the sad feeling goes away. On the rare occasions when his fingers itch for womanflesh he smiles a horrible cracked-leather smile. And winks at Fate as if it were a bird above the West Virignia hills. . .

He'll sit there on the step and pick a dry leaf from the ground. He'll whirl its stem between his spatulate fingers, trace the veins in its parchment. Hold it high to see which way the wind is blowing. It is not strange for him to pass an hour on his father's porch just playing with a leaf.

Or he will hear a bird cry in the trees. He stops his breath to listen most acutely for the cry to come again. It comes—and then he slowly turns his head (as if he were a hunter) searching all the countryside for quarry. He does not see so well. Often he will never find the bird unless it shakes a flash of color out for him to spy. And is not far away.

Of course he sleeps a great deal. The old man cooks an early supper for the two of them and calls out "Er-*skine!*" with a note of irritation in his voice. Then Skinny reaches for his stick and hobbles in to keep his father company at the table. He tries to keep a little in the bottle for an after-dinner drink. If not, and if he's eaten fairly well, J. B. may give him a fresh pint. It helps him sleep. When the sundown chill comes through the house, Skinny finds his bed and stretches his one leg out long. He holds the other's stump with two big hands until it stops twitching. When it finally does, he falls asleep.

288

His life is like this. Not so bad. Once or twice a year some chemistry of rage and disillusionment seizes him and he will curse the pigs or slam the doors or shout against the lonely hills. (It can't be heard in Akron.) Several times, when this happened, J. B. had been at home. Skinny had struck out at J. B. with his stick—intending to demolish him. Each time the old man clobbered him. Left him where he had been felled, without the stick. This meant he had to crawl and hop. When he crawled and hopped enough, J. B. returned his stick without a word.

There are still troops poised somewhere. There are still whores on Case Avenue. Tires are still being made. The Greyhound Bus Company still unloads in Akron and there are young, strong hillbilly boys coming into town to seek their fortunes. But Goodstone now has automatic tirebuilding machines (which can turn out ten times the tires to a shift that a good man can do). There are no more Skinny Walkers measuring the brick-red walls. No Henry MacDougal, no Burke Danver. No Red Cameron and no Alabama Gibbs to greet him. There may never be another riot. . .

The names of Hoffa and Reuther and MacDonald no longer appear in the newspapers. Union treasuries are immense these days; millions upon millions are paying in their dues. Gloria Morrow and other Hollywood stars have been on strike (". . .*Terribly* exciting, dear!"). Alex Scheiderman has been deported. This wasn't much of a loss because Nikita Kruschev is being imported from time to time. (Nikita is a little hammer-headed beer-bellied fellow with all the amiable foul attributes of a retired executioner.)

Akron is still there. It now has many splendid acquisitions—an expressway system, for example, which turns the whole town into a back street. It has built itself a "suburbia," an outer periphery of lower middle class developments, just like other cities. Which is the most ridiculous thing about it—like a shabby fur coat on a woman whose underthings are soiled and nasty.

289

Akron has had good riddance of the likes of Skinny Walker and it is ready now for an atomic bombing.

If enemy bombers are as inept as ours are, the bomb will miss Akron by three hundred miles and blow the living hell out of Devil's Own, West Virginia. It won't bother Skinny Walker much. . .

Today he sits as usual and puts his mind to Suzie. She is the bitch hound who lives around the Walker place and calls herself the Walker dog. She is a black one, gaunt with sagging dugs and a limp tail. Her ears are big and lifeless. Her mouth curls back from ambered teeth. There was a time when she would lead a hunt for old J. B. but that was years ago. Now she lopes sluggishly around the hill and nags at flies along her bony back in a degenerate way.

On days like this (like some small boy) Skinny tries to practice mentalism on the dog. He wills an imaginary order—"Turn around," or "Lay down," or "Go to the barn." He pushes hard, all with his mind, to see if this old dog will yield to a command not spoken—only thought.

She never does. (You've done the same thing. "When I count to ten the phone will ring or the rain will stop or love will touch me with its magic." Things like that. *It never does.*)

Now Skinny Walker is sick at the sight of of her as she lies in the dry-caked mud refusing his mental impulses. So he shouts at her,

"You *Suze*! C'mere! Come here y' misbegotten bitch! *I SAY COME HERE!*".

It is an old man's voice, the shrunken corn cob with all the golden kernels gone. It has nothing to do with the radio voice of the old days which stirred so many listeners. It is no kin to the young man's voice which one time cursed in the tire room, rang in union halls, echoed in the streets and whispered hot obscenities in Bennett Marshall's bedroom. It is not even a poor parody.

If you take Skinny Walker and drain his groin. Cut off a leg. Slacken his muscle. Dilute the blue of his eyes. Grey his whiskers and send him back to Devil's Own. Then his voice will sound like this. . .

"C'mere Suzie! Ol' gal, olgal-olgal-olgal!"

Suzie hears the noise and leg by leg she lazily rises. Once on her feet, without lifting a leg but only leaning forward as if against the wind and bending her legs slightly, she lets go a sloppy stream of urine.

"Come here!" Skinny shouts at her in fury. He waves his stick in hot futility, but Suzie doesn't come. She walks away, her long tail drooped in arrogance.